About the Author

John Steinberg spent many years in business before becoming a writer in 2007. Since then, he has co-written and produced comedies for the stage and created a series of books for children. *Three Days in Vienna* is his fifth novel.

By the same author

Shimon
Nadine
The Temple of Fortune
Blue Skies Over Berlin
Three Days in Vienna

THREE DAYS IN VIENNA

John Steinberg

2QT Limited (Publishing)

First published in 2021 by 2QT Limited (Publishing)
Settle, North Yorkshire BD24 9BZ www.2qt.co.uk
Copyright © 2021 John Steinberg

The right of John Steinberg to be identified as the author of the work has been asserted by him in accordance with the Copyright, Designs and Patents Act 1988.

All rights reserved. This book is sold subject to the condition that no part of this book is to be reproduced, in any shape or form, or by way of trade, stored in a retrieval system or transmitted in any form or by any means, electronic, mechanical, photocopying, recording, be lent, re-sold, hired out or otherwise circulated in any form of binding or cover other than that in which it is published and without a similar condition, including this condition, being imposed on the subsequent purchaser, without prior permission of the copyright holder.

Cover concept & Illustration by Fiona Wilson

Printed in Great Britain by IngramSparks UK

All characters in this book other than those clearly in the public domain are fictitious, and any resemblance to real persons, living or dead, is purely coincidental.

A CIP catalogue record for this book is available
from the British Library

ISBN 978-1-914083-34-1 (Paperback)

ISBN 978-1-914083-35-8 (eBook)

Acknowledgements

My thanks to 2QT for agreeing to publish the book. To Fiona Wilson for the cover design and original illustration. To my editor, Joan Deitch, for her continued support and for being my sounding board. And a special note of thanks to Alexa Brauner for her guidance on the finer points of Vienna.

*In memory of Traute Morgenstern.
A special lady from Vienna.*

1

Central London, February 2000

The graceful Nash terraces of Regent's Park shimmered in the winter sunshine like bands of iced sugar on a wedding cake. It was a stunning sight, and one that never failed to lift her spirits, Elizabeth McCreary found, as she drove around the Outer Circle before parking her brand-new Range Rover in front of an exclusive block of flats.

Elizabeth had a ton of things she'd much rather be doing on that Saturday afternoon, but as sole beneficiary of Charlotte Brown's will, it was her responsibility to clear out the small flat that had been the woman's home for the last thirty years. Not, she knew, that the contents would add up to much. 'Aunt Charlotte' had been a woman of modest means, so the job shouldn't take too long. The one item of potential worth that Elizabeth knew about was the Monet painting, one of the Water Lilies series, that Charlotte had always cherished, despite it being no more than a very accomplished copy.

'Good morning, Dennis, how are you today?' Elizabeth enquired of the concierge on duty, who'd been around for as long as she could remember.

'Apart from me arthritis playing up, can't complain,' the

small man answered without looking up from his copy of the *Sun*. 'More o' them asylum seekers washed up on the beaches yesterday,' he mumbled, focusing on the double-page image. 'Not that they've got a hope in hell of finding work here, poor bastards.'

Tearing his eyes away, he looked up and said, 'Good Lord! For a minute there, I'd swear it was Rita Hayworth herself standing in front of me. It's the red hair and the way you hold yourself, love. Class, that's what does it.' He nodded to himself. Then: 'Haven't seen you in a while, young Elizabeth. Expect those kiddies are keeping you busy, eh?'

'They certainly are,' Elizabeth answered politely.

'Your mum is still away with her husband if that's who you've come to see,' Dennis said helpfully.

'Yes, I know,' Elizabeth replied, relieved that she would not have to call in at her mother Lillian's apartment, which was just along the corridor from Charlotte's. Elizabeth had never taken to Allen Paul, the brash American antiques shop owner who'd eventually won her mother over after a long courtship.

'Could I possibly have the keys to flat twenty-five?' she asked.

'That's the late Miss Brown's place if I'm not mistaken?' the concierge said nosily.

'Yes, but the property is in my name, if you recall,' Elizabeth reminded him.

'Course it is. Totally slipped my mind. Must be me age catching up on me. It only seems like yesterday that she moved in,' he sighed, retreating into the back office to unlock the key cupboard. 'That Miss Brown, nice lady, never any trouble – unlike some of the other residents I could name,' he grumbled, returning with a small bunch of keys.

'I get a lot of enquiries for flats, you know,' he went on. 'I might be able to point you in the right direction if you're interested in selling it?' A sly look on his face indicated that he would expect to be compensated for his trouble.

'Yes, of course,' Elizabeth said, impatient to get started. 'Thank you.'

Taking the lift to the first floor, she regretted that she hadn't made more of an effort to spend time with Charlotte during her final weeks in the hospital. The truth was, the younger woman couldn't bear to see someone she loved waste away from the cancer that had ravaged her so cruelly. She could still picture the willowy woman, dressed in black, cigarette-holder in her hand like someone out of a 1930s film, giving art lessons to her beloved students from her cramped second bedroom. 'You hold the brush in this vay,' she would say in that deep voice with the trace of an accent she had never quite managed to lose despite her many years in London. The fact that she had never found happiness in her personal life but had remained alone, always seemed so unfair.

When the inevitable happened, Elizabeth stepped in to make all the arrangements, for which her mother was grateful. Elizabeth's lasting impression was not of the funeral itself, a quiet affair attended just by Charlotte's adopted family and a few of her mature students, but of the sight of her own mother, stooped at the graveside saying goodbye to her dearest, closest friend. Lillian Paul had suddenly become a little old lady.

*

Without further delay, Elizabeth set about her task of sorting and packing, putting Post-it notes on the furniture and other items to be collected by the British Heart Foundation, and bagging up all the clothes and bedlinen to be disposed of elsewhere. By the end of the afternoon, she'd accomplished a lot, but there was still a great deal to do as she hadn't finished in the sitting room yet, let alone the bedroom or kitchen, and there were so many other jobs such as taking down the curtains. One trip simply wouldn't be enough.

Consumed with tiredness, she was just about to call it a day, when she noticed a small mahogany writing bureau that had so far escaped her attention. The key stood in the lock, so Elizabeth carefully opened it and started to sort through a pile of the deceased's personal correspondence.

A few minutes later, she was sitting in an armchair, clutching a small bundle of her aunt's intimate letters to a German doctor, her expression shocked. She was devastated. It was just so hard to believe that there could have been another side to the woman she thought she had known so well. If the contents of these letters were true, the affair with Dr Johann Weber had remained hidden for many years.

She must have lost all sense of time because it was almost 6 p.m. and already starting to get dark. Her teenage son Freddie would be back from football practice by now and Anthony's parents, who had come up from the country for the weekend, would be wondering where she was. Thoughts of her family and the prospect of a few glasses of burgundy over the dinner she had prepared this morning and had yet to cook was just what she needed to make her pull herself together.

Elizabeth replaced the letters where she had found them and left the premises, determined to put the past few hours' experience out of her mind for the time being.

Arriving back at the house in Chalcot Square a mile away in Primrose Hill, the musty aroma of the vacant apartment still clinging to her, she felt something in the pocket of her sheepskin coat. It was Charlotte's bunch of keys which she had inadvertently kept, subconsciously knowing that she would have to return to the flat, and to the letters.

*

That evening, Elizabeth sat on the edge of the bed, her head full of contradictory thoughts. The evening had been a complete disaster. Until now, she had usually got on reasonably well with her in-laws, so her uncharacteristic outburst was something she ascribed to having drunk too much.

'What was all that about?' her husband's well-spoken voice enquired from behind the crime novel he'd been pretending to read.

'I never realised how narrow-minded they were until now,' Elizabeth said moodily.

'What, just because of my father's few disparaging remarks about that Pakistani chap, Mustafa? A bit of an overreaction on your part, wouldn't you say?'

'You always told me how good Mustafa was at his job,' Elizabeth retorted, turning to face the lean figure sprawled out on the king-size bed.

'True, but let's face it, he's hardly partner material.'

'Because he doesn't quite fit the mould, you mean?'

'An established practice like McCreary's does have to think of its reputation, you know,' Anthony asserted, putting his book down to make his point.

'One which doesn't include anybody other than white Anglo-Saxon public-school boys, I suppose.'

'And a few upper-class lasses besides,' Anthony said straight-faced.

'I'm surprised your family ever accepted me, a second-generation Austrian refugee!' Elizabeth retaliated.

'Nonsense. You're practically as British as I am! And in any case, they adore you.'

'Only because of the children,' Elizabeth answered back.

'So, what's brought all this on? You've been acting really strangely since you got back this evening – cutting it very fine, I might add.'

'I'm sorry, it's just that I found going to Charlotte's flat really traumatic.' Elizabeth would have liked to share the experience with her husband of twenty years but knew she couldn't. Even after all this time, there was still so much they were unable to communicate to each other.

'I understand,' Anthony said, reaching out to his wife.

Accepting the invitation, Elizabeth moved over to lie beside him.

'Perhaps I didn't behave particularly well,' she sighed. 'I'll ring your mother when they get back from France and apologise, otherwise they'd have every right to reconsider letting us use the villa in Antibes again this summer.'

'I shouldn't worry. They'll have forgotten all about it by then – and anyway, they'll probably end up cancelling the trip. Dad's political commitments are taking up most of his time; he hardly comes into the office at all these days. And why they bother going to France in the first place is beyond me, as there's zero chance of my sister coming back to London. By the way, I forgot to mention that she phoned the other day.'

'That was a bit out of the blue. What was it about?' Elisabeth asked.

'Just to see how we all were, as well as the usual stuff about how she can't fathom how I could carry on working with our father.'

'I know that he and Jess have never got on.'

'That's an understatement. They've always fought like cat and dog – and sure enough, during the call she came up with that same old cock and bull story that she was sure Dad was up to no good.'

'You never told me that,' Elizabeth said.

'That's because it was hardly worth repeating.'

'It's a shame. She and I always got on really well.' Elizabeth jumped off the bed and stepped out of the black Armani dress that accentuated her shapely figure.

'I see – so you can relate to that alternative lifestyle and those funny vegan friends of hers, can you?' Anthony said, eyeing up his wife.

'I just think it's brilliant that she doesn't wish to conform,' Elizabeth said, getting into her side of the bed.

'She's lucky she can afford not to!' Anthony quipped.

'Jess will make a go of it; just you wait and see.'

'Do I detect a hint of envy?' he teased his wife.

'Don't be silly. You know I wouldn't change places with her – or anyone else for that matter,' Elizabeth protested a little too vehemently. Of course there were times when she missed the adrenalin rush of her music publishing business, but when she eventually recovered and conceived again after going through a traumatic miscarriage, the decision to give up work became a lot easier.

She had actually met Jess McCreary first when Jess was a personal trainer at a gym Elizabeth frequented and living in a flat around the corner with Aisha, her Pakistani female partner.

Apart from helping her get into shape, the three of them quickly became friends. And then Jess introduced Elizabeth to her older brother Anthony. Jess had actually sold him to her friend, saying that behind his snobbish exterior lay an incredibly kind individual – and the fact that he was handsome, in a typically British, clean-cut sort of way, was an added bonus. Being the self-confessed black sheep, Jess had never fitted in to the McCreary family. It still seemed peculiar though, the way she had upped and left with Aisha for Paris without any warning, six months ago. Although they kept in contact, Elizabeth felt that she had lost a much-needed ally.

'With all the money Dad's happy to keep throwing at her, I do hope you're right,' Anthony said.

'Strange, because I thought he had an aversion to strong-minded women,' Elizabeth said.

'That's only the impression he likes to give.'

'You mean he really likes to be challenged?'

'Only by volatile females who always want – and get – their own way!'

'Like your daughter, for instance?' Elizabeth laughed.

'Well, she *is* just like you,' he said.

'Emily's more confident than I was at that age. Poor

Freddie hasn't got much of a chance, has he? She can't help it – she overshadows him.' Elizabeth paused before saying, 'It worries me that he keeps things inside. My mother's the same, you'd never know what she's thinking.'

'Perhaps it was wrong not to have considered boarding school; it would certainly have brought him out of his shell. Public school didn't do my family any harm.'

'Well, it did to me!' Elizabeth said forcefully. 'I wasn't going to subject the children to what I went through.'

'Ah yes, your misspent youth, sex, drugs and rock and roll. Must have been a lot more fun than serving in the Army Cadets. I can't tell you the mock salutes I got, walking down the street in that ridiculous khaki uniform that they forced us to wear at City of London junior school.'

'So much fun I nearly died,' Elizabeth snapped.

'Sorry, I didn't know anything about that,' Anthony replied sheepishly.

'You never did show any interest in the person I was before I met you,' Elizabeth griped, unsure why she had suddenly brought that subject up.

'OK, point taken, now come here and I'll show you that Dad's not the only one who finds strong-willed women a turn-on,' Anthony said with the smirk of an overgrown schoolboy who had come across a pornographic magazine for the first time.

Elizabeth knew then that he hadn't listened to a word she had said.

2

Two weeks later

Feeling harassed from the school run that had taken longer than usual, Elizabeth hurried into the disused community centre, a ramshackle building sandwiched between stalls in Camden Market where the cobbles emitted an odour of urine and stale beer. Collecting a quick coffee at the kiosk that offered free food and hot drinks to many of the area's homeless, she took the back stairs to an unheated space on the floor above. This was where her monthly group-therapy session took place at the modest cost of £30.

The facilitator of the predominantly female class was Marlene Katz, a South African hippy, straight out of 1960s Kings Road, Chelsea. Elizabeth had been introduced to the laid-back septuagenarian ten years ago by her best friend Lorraine; in those days they'd both been working at the Camden-based EMI music company, and Elizabeth had been a regular here ever since.

Despite their hugely diverse backgrounds, for those forty-five minutes the group consisted of a bunch of ordinary women who shared many of the same issues. There, Elizabeth could be herself. Not that she was a stranger to therapy, having been dumped on a number of psychologists specialising in *difficult children* by a mother who couldn't cope. No one seemed to have considered that the girl was grieving for her late father Donald, and missing the mother love that should have come her way from Lillian, who for some reason was unable to give it to her.

Elizabeth often wondered how Anthony would react if he knew how his life was dissected, like the other partners and husbands of the women here. Knowing him, it would have gone right over his head. So long as he had the prestige of a law firm bearing his name, golf at the weekends with his small clique of old school friends, and an attractive wife at home to run the house and look after the children, as far as he was concerned he had the perfect marriage. She, on the other hand, was seeking something more – maybe to try and recapture something from the past?

'Sorry to be late,' she said, swiftly joining the class of six who sat in a semi-circle and were listening to a woman named Stephanie, who had blonde corkscrew hair and who was describing another acrimonious argument over money with her delinquent son Joe.

'What images do you see when you shut your eyes?' the therapist asked, passing to Elizabeth next when Stephanie had said her piece.

Elizabeth pondered for a moment then impulsively began to recount the experience at Charlotte's flat, which had continued to play on her mind.

'Surely they were just letters between two young lovers? And it was such a long time ago,' remarked Vicky, a single mother from South London.

'I tried telling myself that they probably didn't mean anything,' Elizabeth agreed, 'but it didn't make any difference.'

'Naturally, it raised a doubt about someone you thought you knew so well,' Lorraine butted in, having met Charlotte herself on a few previous occasions.

'So she didn't ever mention the fling she'd had with that bloke Johann when he came to London?' someone else asked.

'Or that he was married?' Stephanie added.

'Not to me. But that's not really surprising since I was so much younger than her,' Elizabeth responded, bemused that they had chosen to home in on the least controversial aspects of the correspondence.

'What I find interesting is that it should have affected you to this extent,' Marlene put in, and Elizabeth saw that she too had clearly missed the point.

'It brought other family relationships into doubt, ones that I had never questioned before,' she tried to explain.

'Like with your other half, for example?' Stephanie probed, happy to be party to someone else's unfortunate experiences for a change.

'Anthony was always suspicious of Charlotte,' Elizabeth divulged.

'That's because he felt threatened by her!' Stephanie said, quick as a flash, causing an outbreak of laughter.

'Maybe. She could be quite formidable at times.' Elizabeth didn't mention that Charlotte had strongly opposed her marrying Anthony. The older woman said she had seen immediately that he wasn't the type of man who wanted a career-woman as a wife but rather one he could shape to his own, conservative image. She didn't want to see the young woman she had loved since Elizabeth was twelve years old being drained of her individuality, Charlotte had said. At the time, Elizabeth hadn't been aware just how much she was prepared to forfeit in return for a settled family life. After her own lonely upbringing, missing the kindly father she had loved and being neglected by her mother, that family life was very, very important to her.

'I'd love to hear how you got to know Charlotte,' Vicky said, totally immersed in the exercise.

Elizabeth glanced in Marlene's direction to get her approval, as she didn't wish to monopolise the meeting. The woman responded with a theatrical wave of her hand.

Elizabeth described how she and Charlotte Brown had clicked, that first time Charlotte turned up at the house, shortly after making Lillian Saunders's acquaintance on a Mediterranean cruise. 'Aunt Charlotte', as she became known to the girl, was the only one who could relate to her feelings of loss. By the time Elizabeth had finished speaking, the whole class had tears in their eyes.

'And how did your mother react to your discovery of those letters?' Lorraine asked, after blowing her nose. 'She and Charlotte were very close – best friends, weren't they?'

'I haven't had a chance to discuss it with her yet,' Elizabeth hedged. In reality, she was in two minds whether to say anything at all. What would it do to Lillian if she shared with her mother the awful truth she had uncovered?

'I reckon she does have a right to know,' one of the women said shyly.

'If it was my mum, I'd tell her,' another nodded.

'And how about you, Elizabeth? Has the experience

caused you to delve into yourself?' Marlene asked.

Elizabeth searched for an answer but wasn't able to find one.

*

As the women dispersed and came out into the mass of people in Camden Market, over in the pretty rural setting of Bourton-on-the-Water in the Cotswolds, a meeting of the British Independence Party was about to commence.

A robust man in his early sixties got to his feet, called for silence and began to address the select group, which consisted in the main of thirty or so like-minded politicians and captains of industry.

'Good morning, gentlemen. I'm sure some of you need to get to London for the afternoon's vote in the Commons so I'll keep it brief. Though if it were up to me I'd lock them all up and throw away the key! Cutting the age of consent for homosexuals – whatever next?' he bellowed. The comment brought subdued mutterings of approval.

'As your treasurer,' William McCreary continued, 'I can confirm that, as of last night, contributions pledged have passed the three million pound mark. That is correct, isn't it, Rupert?' He addressed the obese financier with a black eye-patch who sat to his right. The relationship with Meredith's Bank went back over forty years. Of course, he was aware of the controversy surrounding the bank's dealings with so-called German war criminals, fugitives living in South America, but that had proved no more than a temporary blot on their reputation and they were soon able to resume their rightful position amongst the City's elite institutions. More importantly, Meredith's remained resolutely supportive of the BIP's cause and shared its nationalistic aspirations.

'Quite so, and we are happy to match that sum – with certain provisos, of course,' the old banker croaked, appearing to have great difficulty in staying awake.

'So we are now more than able to field sufficient candidates to fight next year's general election,' McCreary resumed. 'I'm also delighted to announce, as of this morning, the signing of the lease of our offices at 18 St James's Street.'

Spontaneous applause broke out around the original Tudor drawing room. He didn't mention that the prestigious Crediton Trust, of which he was a non-executive director, had provided the vast majority of the funding. William had acted for the company, which specialised in industrial patents, as a young lawyer since the early 1950s. One day at the beginning of 1955, he was approached by a senior member of the company to establish worldwide roll-out of vaccines against polio, measles and rubella that were currently being developed. His discovery that these drugs were being made by what had once been one of the largest pharmaceutical companies in Germany had alerted William's suspicions, especially as the company had reinvented itself after the Second World War by moving to England and acquiring a suitable name to match its Devon location. To William it appeared that the company had a great deal to hide – not that it was any concern of his what they had got up to in the past. More important was how, in the disenchantment with Germany for abandoning its former nationalistic identity, he'd found the financial backer to secure his own political ambitions of turning his beloved country into a Nation State for the English.

'We'd better start working on our manifesto then,' declared Nigel Robbins, the thin-lipped chairman of Stonebrook Industries, the vast manufacturer of agricultural machinery that had just won the Queen's Award for export.

'That's simple enough! The main platform should be getting our country back from those parasites in Europe,' Piers Landsman said loudly. He had recently resigned his Shadow Home Office position after backing a failed leadership challenge.

'Blair and his socialist cronies were the ones responsible for opening the floodgates, allowing in all those immigrants,' another man bleated. 'Before long, England won't be recognisable. And you tell me we haven't got a problem?'

'We should tear up that wretched Maastricht Treaty for a start,' a flushed-faced individual called out from the other end of the table.

'Leaving the EU would require a referendum,' Landsman made clear. 'Then if it went our way, Article 50 would be triggered, bringing an end to our membership and marking the beginning of the end of that god-forsaken club.'

'At least then we'd be free to make our own trade deals. Can't come soon enough as far as I'm concerned,' Robbins declared enthusiastically.

'I can't seeing Germany going along with that. Once they get a sniff of what we have in mind, they'll fight tooth and nail to stop us from leaving,' Landsman pointed out.

'What, even now they're under the thumb of that chappie in Austria?' Rupert Meredith had woken up.

'A passing fancy. No one outside Vienna even knows his name,' another quipped, bringing howls of derision at the snub to that nonentity Oscar Gruber.

William McCreary smiled with satisfaction, knowing he was one step nearer to achieving his objective of holding the balance of power at next year's general election. Naturally, the BNP would side with the Conservatives, many of whom shared their policies – but their allegiance wouldn't come cheap. Glancing at the bust in the corner of his hero Oswald Mosley, William liked it when things went according to plan. He knew he was taking a chance, putting his son Anthony in charge of the firm that he'd run single-handedly all these years, but this would leave him free to pursue his secret ambition: to change the face of British politics.

At least with that shitty Jewess of a daughter-in-law, no suspicion could ever be attached to him of racist intolerance. Even his own dull wife Margaret – prompted by him – now took an active part in a Unesco programme to promote cultural diversity. It had all been meticulously planned. He scowled. The one fly in the ointment was his daughter, Jess. Such a pity, when she was the only one in the family with brains. One act of carelessness, leaving those secret papers where she could find them, had nearly cost him everything he had built up. And whether he could rely on her silence for much longer was another matter entirely.

3

The heavy rain that had persisted all day made the short hop from Primrose Hill to Lillian's apartment in Regent's Park more of an endurance course than the intended lazy Sunday afternoon out.

Settled in her mother's spacious sitting room, Elizabeth helped herself to another of the homemade scones. To hell with the extra calories. Just when she was beginning to feel happier, having been accepted by Goldsmiths College for a part-time degree in Music that she'd applied for on the off-chance, Elizabeth could now see it all disappearing. Charlotte was again at the forefront of her thoughts and Elizabeth knew that she had to confront her mother. She wished now that she hadn't accepted the tea invitation.

'I really don't know why you insisted on us coming. It's always so bloody hot in your mother's flat,' Anthony muttered when Lillian had gone off to make a fresh pot of tea. He rolled up the sleeves of his check shirt and was fanning himself with a napkin.

'It's the only opportunity for the children to see their grandmother during half-term,' Elizabeth murmured. 'Anyway, just think – you'll be on the ski slopes this time next week.'

'I can't wait. I suppose you won't change your mind about coming with us?'

'Anthony, I've got a lot to catch up on and it'll give you a rare chance to bond with your son and daughter.'

The truth was that she detested the snow and only ever went on those skiing holidays so they could spend time together as a family. With Francesca, the McCrearys' mother's help, gone back to Italy to visit her parents, the prospect of having the house to herself for a week was really quite appealing.

'Talking of the children, have you any idea where Freddie has got to?' she asked now, and when Anthony shrugged, she went on, 'Instead of standing around looking awkward, why don't you go and be sociable with Allen while I look for our son?' She glanced at the sun-tanned man relaxing on the sofa, while eleven-year-old Emily happily worked on a puzzle on the coffee table in front of him.

As Elizabeth trod noiselessly down the hallway, she heard voices and there, standing a few feet away in the box room, she caught side of the lanky teenager and his grandmother. They were focused on a dusty painting that her son had uncovered. Elizabeth deduced by the platform sign in German that it was a railway station. In the background was a large crowd of people, intermingled with soldiers with guns looking tensely ahead, while the train was drawing up steam, preparing to depart.

'Who is that old man in a long coat and the woman with that strange hat, Grandma?' the boy enquired.

'My mummy and daddy,' Lillian answered in a voice so quiet that she could barely be heard.

'And who is that young girl they are waving to on the train?'

'That was me,' Lillian replied.

'But why are they crying?' Freddie wanted to know, clearly affected by the scene.

'It was during the war and I was going to live with a family just outside of London.'

'But why didn't they go with you? Surely there was enough room on the train?'

'No, Freddie dear, it wasn't quite as simple as that. You see, it was difficult for Jewish people at that time,' Lillian explained.

Elizabeth was taken aback. Of course, she knew that her mother had escaped war-torn Europe on the Kindertransport in 1938. Hadn't she discovered those postcards from her grandparents before they were shipped off to Auschwitz concentration camp, when Lillian wasn't much older than Freddie?

'Hello, Mum,' her son said, catching sight of her. 'Grandma was showing me the train she came on to England, when she was a little girl.'

'I haven't seen that before,' Elizabeth announced, giving it a closer examination. 'Who was it done by?'

'I painted it myself, many years ago,' Lillian said dismissively.

'It's actually very good, Grandma,' her grandson enthused, going off to find his father.

'It was Charlotte's idea. She was the one who encouraged me to start painting again. So I thought I'd give it a try. Then I must have forgotten all about it,' Lillian said, turning away and putting the picture back in the cupboard where Freddie had found it.

Elizabeth had an uneasy feeling that she might never

have got to know of the painting, had it not been for her son. She couldn't help wondering what other secrets lay hidden with her mother.

'Actually I wanted to speak to you about Charlotte,' she said.

'Darling, can it wait? I'm still tired from the trip and I'm sure Anthony wants to get going.' The look on her face showed she was fully aware that her son-in-law was only there under sufferance.

'It won't take long, and I can always ring for a minicab home,' Elizabeth persevered, aware that there might not be a better opportunity.

'It's your decision,' Lillian said, before going off to enjoy her grandchildren for a little longer.

Elizabeth followed behind to tell her husband and the children that she would be staying on for a while. She needn't have bothered since by the time she reached them they already had their coats on.

'All right, if you're sure,' Anthony replied, needing no further persuasion to go on ahead.

'Goodbye, Grandma, thank you for the presents,' Emily and Freddie called out.

'Enjoy yourselves in Switzerland and remember to take lots of pictures,' Lillian said, closing the door behind them.

Elizabeth accompanied her mother back into the living room where Allen had fallen into a deep sleep.

'The poor old thing is exhausted from the long flight,' she explained. 'Even travelling business class seems to be getting too much for him these days. That's what to expect, I suppose, when you marry a man of nearly eighty.'

'There was the same age difference with Daddy, wasn't

there?' Even after all these years, Elizabeth still found herself looking around for any pictorial evidence of her father Donald.

'Yes, there was, but a gap of ten years doesn't make that much of a difference when you are in your late twenties. Right, I don't know about you but I could do with a sherry,' Lillian announced, going over to the built-in wall units that concealed a well-stocked bar. 'Are you sure you wouldn't like one?'

'No, thank you,' Elizabeth responded, trying to get her thoughts in order.

'I must say, Emily is turning into a right little madam,' Lillian said fondly, settling on her armchair in front of the fireplace with her drink. 'How is she progressing with her piano?'

'Very well, when she can be bothered to practise,' Elizabeth replied, conscious that she was again deliberately downplaying her daughter's achievements so as not to overshadow the girl's less able brother.

'That sounds familiar,' Lillian quipped, taking a sip of her drink.

'You forced me to play, if you remember?' Elizabeth answered back, sitting down opposite her mother.

'With your talent, Mrs Greenfield was convinced you could have gone far, that's all I'm saying. I do wish you hadn't given up.'

Elizabeth didn't tell her mother that she hadn't actually ever given up. Many times she would play when there was no one around, wondering how her life would have changed if she had accepted the place at the Royal Academy of Music. Gaining her financial independence by going out and getting a job, however, had been her only objective at the time.

'So what did you want to talk about?' Lillian asked, enjoying the warmth of the gas fire on her body.

'Why didn't you tell me about that painting before?' Elizabeth asked, her voice shaky.

'There's no need to be upset. It just didn't seem important, that's all,' her mother said, sipping on her drink.

'Important to whom?' Elizabeth replied, trying to stay calm.

'It was a very unhappy time and, once I managed to get it out of my system, I decided there was no point in brooding about it any further.'

'Not even for me?' Elizabeth cried. 'I know so little about my Austrian heritage, and it's not as if there are any relatives on Daddy's side. The only family I've got seems to be the one I married into.'

'I trust all's well with Anthony's parents? I'm really quite fond of William and Margaret,' Lillian said, changing the subject. Elizabeth knew from experience that this was her mother's way of blotting out anything uncomfortable from the past.

She was just having second thoughts about staying any longer, when her mother said, 'Look, I think you should keep Charlotte's flat and put it in the children's name. In the meantime, it would make ideal staff accommodation for some of the well-to-do people that live here.'

'I haven't even thought about what to do with it,' Elizabeth replied, caught off-guard.

'Is something else troubling you?' Lillian asked perceptively.

'Yes, there is. When I started clearing out Charlotte's things, I came across some old letters of hers that I found really disturbing,' Elizabeth said.

'In what way?'

'This will sound totally far-fetched, I know, but Charlotte was not who we were led to believe.'

'Go on,' Lillian said, showing interest for the first time.

'Her real name was Eva Schlessinger and she wasn't Swiss at all. She came from Berlin.'

'Darling, it wasn't uncommon for people to change their names and nationalities after the war,' Lillian replied defensively.

'Mother, this wasn't merely an attempt to become more anglicised.'

'No? Then what else could it possibly be?'

'Charlotte had a love affair with a doctor called Johann Weber. It might be a coincidence, but I'm sure you sent me to someone of that name. More importantly, he served with her father in the Luftwaffe. They were Nazis!'

Lillian just sat in a sort of daze, horrified that her daughter had found out about the family connection between Dr Johann Weber and her best friend Charlotte in Berlin. As for the pair of them having been lovers . . . She was silent for a few moments, thinking how to deal with this, then suddenly snapped out of it.

'That's pure conjecture,' she said firmly. 'Charlotte was special to me . . . and how could you possibly forget the way she doted upon you?'

'And that makes everything all right, does it?' Elizabeth retorted. She was tempted to add that as a lonely child grieving after her father, it was Charlotte who had given her the maternal love lacking from Lillian – but she knew she'd be wasting her breath. Her previous instinct was correct; it really was time to leave.

*

Giving up on finding a taxi, Elizabeth started back on foot, surprisingly less despondent than she had envisaged. She had known all along how her mother would respond, but she herself was no longer prepared just to let matters lie. Quickening her pace around Regent's Park, she wondered whether the discovery at Charlotte's flat and her mother's reaction to it could be linked?

Then it came to her like a bolt out of the blue. It was the off-the-cuff comment that Stephanie had made at the therapy group and which Elizabeth had dismissed at the time. But what if she was right – that the letters had been left there on purpose? It didn't explain why she had been the one nominated to find them, unless Charlotte knew that she alone would make proper use of them. Nor did it explain what Charlotte hoped to achieve by alienating those closest to her. There was a message here somewhere, if only she could find out what it was.

Inadequately protected against the rain that had penetrated her new suede ankle boots, Elizabeth arrived home half an hour later, chilled to the bone but more determined than ever to make sense of it all.

*

Lillian sat quietly in the room at the end of the hallway, a cardboard box lying open on the floor in front of her. She leafed through her collection of photograph albums, pausing each time she came across a photo of Charlotte.

Of course, she was aware of her friend's dark past. It was all in the letter of atonement that Charlotte had written after the painting of the Vienna railway station had left her feeling exposed. Lillian had decided that for the sake of their friendship and for Charlotte's well-being, it was better to let her think she had just ignored it.

Dr Weber, however, was another proposition. In particular, she remembered his air of superiority and the disdain in which he held the British medical profession. But it was the derogatory remark he made about a Jewish colleague while Elizabeth was under his care that had caused Lillian to change the girl's therapist.

*

That night, Elizabeth had a disturbed sleep. For some reason, she couldn't get the image out of her mind of the little girl alone on the train. Why would Charlotte have encouraged her mother to paint that subject if she had been trying to hide her Nazi past? There was something else too. She had missed it at the time but she now recalled there being a third adult in the painting – taller than the rest and lacking their expressions of torment. Instinct told Elizabeth he was her Great-uncle Theo. Apart from crediting him with organising her safe passage out of Austria, her mother had made no further mention of him. Elizabeth wondered what part he had played in the family history. In fact from now on, she decided, she had an obligation to find out the truth about her maternal family, not only for herself but also for the sake of her two beloved children.

The next day, she booked a plane ticket to Vienna.

4

Vienna, Easter 2000

Elizabeth picked up the local directory on her bedside table and searched for any listings of the name Frankl that might give her some clue as to her great-uncle's current whereabouts. It was a long shot but she had to start somewhere. Her search revealed nothing, as the only three listed were all female. What had she expected? If Theodore were still alive, he'd have to be well into his nineties by now, and with no photograph to go on, she had clearly been overly optimistic about finding him.

Admiring the view of the imposing St Stephen's Cathedral from her simple hotel room in the Innere Stadt – the Old Town – Elizabeth realised that it had been a huge mistake to have come to Vienna. Perhaps her mother was right and it was futile to dig up the past.

Her watch registered 6.30 p.m. She'd have an early dinner, Elizabeth told herself, and tomorrow take a tour of some of the city's museums and palaces that lined the famous Ringstrasse, before trying to catch an earlier flight home. At least her family, now in Klosters for the skiing, would be none the wiser about her secret mission. She was glad that when she tried to call the children earlier,

Anthony said they were already getting fitted out at the ski club and were too busy to come to the phone.

Elizabeth took a seat downstairs in the bar, where a few loud individuals were celebrating, and ordered a vodka and tonic. A short while later, a heavy-set man, older than the rest, made his way unsteadily over and plonked himself down on the stool next to her.

'Good evening, Fraulein, would you mind if I joined you?' he asked in English, but with a thick German accent.

'Actually, I was just leaving,' Elizabeth replied, not wishing to get landed with someone who had drunk far too much already.

'Nonsense, I insist,' the fellow replied, refusing to be put off. 'Barman! A beer, if you please,' he demanded, holding up his empty tankard, 'and another drink for the lady while you're at it. I'm Wolfgang,' he announced, 'and you are?'

'Elizabeth,' she replied vaguely.

'Like your Queen of England!' The man roared with laughter. 'We got rid of our monarchy with the Hapsburgs in 1918,' he boasted, taking a huge gulp of beer. 'Strong leaders are what we need, and that is what is missing in our country today.'

'In what way do you mean?' Elizabeth asked, her curiosity aroused.

'We thought we'd got rid of the Jews, but more and more of them are managing to worm their way back here. If we're not careful we'll be overrun with that vermin – and then we'll be back to where we were, goddamn it.'

Elizabeth couldn't believe what she was hearing. She should have got up and walked away, but something persuaded her to stand her ground.

'And where exactly was that?' she said, rising to the challenge.

'Surely you're aware that the Jews control the press and the banks?'

'As a matter of fact, I didn't know that. Perhaps you'd care to explain what you mean,' Elizabeth replied, playing ignorant, whilst trying to control herself.

'Sucking our lifeblood, that's what they do. They brought Austria to its knees once before, and we don't want it to happen again.' The fellow banged a fist on the bar and then drank deeply from his tankard.

'And *I'd* say that trying to discredit people because of their race and because they don't happen to fit in with your deluded ideas of Aryan superiority, is a timely reminder of your shameful past, which *I* certainly wouldn't want to see happening again!' Elizabeth said, raising her voice and uncaring that she was drawing attention to herself.

The colour drained from the Austrian's puffy face. Visibly shaken from the verbal onslaught to which he'd just been subjected, he produced a couple of notes from inside his jacket pocket and left them on the counter. Then, hoisting his ungainly frame off the stool, he staggered back to the relative safety of his colleagues.

Elizabeth finished her drink, leaving the other one untouched, and walked calmly out of the bar with her head held high, determined to deny those who had witnessed the spectacle any glimpse of the turmoil she was feeling inside. Having lost her appetite, she opted for some fresh air. Braving the sub-zero temperatures, she made her way on foot through the quaint local Blutgasse courtyards to the smart shops on the Franziskanerplatz, and soon found herself standing outside Café Mozart in the presence of two young buskers playing the 'Harry Lime' theme song to the movie *The Third Man* on their acoustic guitars. She entered the plush establishment, joining a group of people in evening dress in a hurry to get served. She could see by the programmes they were holding that they had come during an interval of a performance at the Opera House nearby, and were eager to get back for the second half.

Elizabeth felt a stab of envy. *The Marriage of Figaro* was playing – her favourite Mozart opera ever; she loved it even better than *Don Giovanni* or *The Magic Flute*. Ordering a large slice of sacha torte and one of the speciality house coffees, Elizabeth tried to reconcile the two quite different worlds she had entered in such a short space of time. Perhaps this was the real Vienna and the earlier incident had just been a one-off occurrence. However, that didn't explain why her response had been so aggressive. It wasn't as if she had ever been sensitive of her Jewish heritage, but a change was taking place within her; it was gradually gaining momentum and she needed to find out where it would lead.

*

The next day after a light breakfast, putting her plans to return home on hold and armed with a map of the city, Elizabeth set off again, this time taking a taxi to search the Vienna City Archives, located in the mainly industrial 11th district. The place had been suggested to her by the concierge as the usual first port of call for anyone trying to trace their ancestors.

Elizabeth came away disappointed. The huge, former

gas-storage tanks that resembled four turrets of a medieval castle and which had been painstakingly converted to hold the municipal and other records, only went up to 1938 – several decades earlier than she needed. She berated herself for not researching the matter properly. The staff tried to help, suggesting that she might have more luck if she approached the main synagogue on Seitenstettengasse, ironically in walking distance of where she was staying.

Twenty minutes later, making her way up a narrow pebbled street sandwiched between early 19th-century buildings, she came across a premises protected by two armed policemen. A plaque with what she assumed was Hebrew writing indicated to her that she was in the right place.

'Excuse me, could you tell me where I might find records of the Jewish community in Vienna?' she asked the younger of the two, who was rubbing his hands together in an attempt to keep warm.

'You have an appointment?' he quizzed.

'No, I'm afraid I don't,' Elizabeth said.

'Then we can't permit you access. Anyway, the Centre is closed to visitors.'

'There must be a way you can help me. I'm only in Vienna for three days,' Elizabeth pleaded.

'Sorry, Fraulein, it's out of our hands,' the more senior one sympathised.

Just then, a rugged man in a lightweight leather jacket flashed his security pass at the two policemen as he went by. Seeing that he was about to enter the building, Elizabeth instinctively called out to him: 'Please, can you help me?'

'You have a problem?' the unshaven man replied tersely.

'I'm simply trying to find any records of my mother's family, but I had no idea that I needed to write in first for permission,' Elizabeth explained.

'You're from England?'

Elizabeth nodded.

'Show me your passport!' he growled.

Elizabeth rummaged through her shoulder bag but her fingers were so cold that they didn't work properly. Eventually she managed to retrieve it and handed it over to the fellow, holding her breath while the swarthy individual methodically examined every entry in the document.

'McCreary doesn't sound Jewish,' he queried.

'That's my married name. My mother's name was Frankl.'

'Do you have anything to prove you are who you say you are?'

'I have this,' Elizabeth said, handing over a piece of paper that, in the process of time, had gone yellow at the edges. Fortunately, she had remembered to bring her mother's identity card, the one that had admitted her into Britain over sixty years ago and which for some reason Lillian had always kept.

'Is there anything else that shows you're somehow related to this person?'

Elizabeth felt completely frustrated. Obviously nothing was going to convince the fellow that she was authentic; in the meantime, she was practically freezing to death.

'That's all I have. Surely you can see the similarity between us?' she said, pointing to the young girl in the photograph, but there was no reaction. The man's attention was now focused instead on a message he'd just received on his mobile phone. Without any explanation, he abruptly moved away from the building.

'Come on!' he said brusquely.

'Where are we going? I don't even know who you are.' Elizabeth was not happy.

'You'll see. It's not far,' he replied as he strode ahead up the Seitenstettengasse. 'And you may call me Gideon.'

They arrived at what appeared to be a private dwelling. The only clue as to what lay behind the plain exterior was the word 'kosher' so faintly indented in the small front window that it could easily get missed, as was the surveillance camera concealed above the entrance.

Their presence generated the appearance of a small man with a round friendly face who quickly ushered the two visitors into his establishment. After going down a few steps they entered a dimly lit parlour furnished with a dozen or so basic wooden tables. Men of different ages wearing skullcaps sat conversing happily with an equal number of conservatively dressed females. Oblivious to the two new arrivals, toasts of '*L'Chaim!*' ('To life!') rang out across the room. Elizabeth felt she had entered a different world. It then dawned on her that it must be a kosher restaurant rather than an office holding the records she was seeking. It was all very disorientating. She had no idea what was going on.

'Hope you're hungry?' Gideon asked, sitting down in his usual place. His English was impeccable.

'I'm absolutely starving. I haven't eaten anything substantial since I arrived in Vienna,' Elizabeth said, looking at the menu. 'The security here seems really strict,' she commented as an aside.

'Threats are a daily occurrence,' Gideon replied.

'What – even in a place like this?'

'Terrorists prefer soft targets. Since the attack at the synagogue back in 1981, we've had to be extra-vigilant,' he added, checking his mobile again.

'I completely understand,' Elizabeth responded, feeling guilty that she'd probably glossed over the incident. However, it now explained the thorough interrogation to which she'd been subjected.

'My government isn't prepared just to sit back and allow another Hitler to threaten us again,' Gideon said grimly.

'That's a bit extreme, isn't it?'

'With a man like Jörg Haider, it was entirely possible,' Gideon told her, referring to the previous leader of Austria's right-wing coalition. 'Even now, we know he's lined up someone to take his place.'

'I really had no idea things were as bad as that here,' Elizabeth said, shocked.

'You have your own problems in Britain.'

'You mean with the IRA? We thought that was all in the past until that disaster in Omagh last year.'

'And that nail-bombing in Brixton,' Gideon reminded her, 'not to mention the growing influence of white supremacist elements like the National Front.'

'I see you're well informed.'

Gideon shrugged. Then: 'Don't bother with the menu,' he said, changing the subject. Calling the elderly man over, he gave the order in German.

'So I take it you've decided to help me?' Elizabeth probed.

A smile appeared, transforming the man's previously

humourless expression.

'That is why we're here, I assume?' Elizabeth went on, determined to solve the mystery of her presence in this place.

'As you say in English, curiosity got the better of me.'

'I don't understand.'

'It's not every day that someone like you turns up in the middle of winter, wanting to find out what happened to her family sixty years ago.'

'You mean you still don't believe me?'

'Let's just say that I suspect there's more to it than you divulged.'

Elizabeth pondered for a moment. Surely it wasn't normal to be subjected to this degree of questioning? She had the impression that she was being toyed with – but to what purpose?

'And you are not at all what I expected,' she countered.

'I suppose that makes us equal,' the man riposted

Just then, a selection of savoury dishes were placed in front of them, together with two complimentary glasses of vodka.

'I trust you like a mezze? The minced lamb is delicious,' Gideon said, offering her a basket of warm pitta bread.

'That'll be great,' Elizabeth lied, not wanting to admit that she wasn't partial to Middle Eastern cuisine. Then: 'Who are you really?' she asked suddenly.

'Let's just say my government has a special interest in what's occurring in Vienna at the moment.'

'So you're not Austrian?' she asked, picking at her food.

'You couldn't tell by my accent?'

She scrutinised the unshaven man opposite, sensing

something wasn't quite right. True, he spoke the language but his features were not in the least Germanic nor, to her mind, did he fit the profile of an archivist at the Jewish Community.

'I'm Israeli,' Gideon revealed, continuing with his lunch.

It took a moment for Elizabeth to absorb the revelation. Probably, being so familiar with security issues themselves, his country was merely offering their services to Jewish communities outside of Israel, she surmised. But that still didn't explain the over-zealous interest in her?

'Take my advice and go home,' Gideon said, wiping his mouth.

'Why? I really don't understand.'

'Since the fascists entered the government and started spouting their anti-Semitic propaganda, the Jewish Community is feeling vulnerable again.'

'I see,' Elizabeth replied, glaringly unprepared for this type of eventuality. The trouble was, if she left now, the questions and the doubts about the past would continue to haunt her.

'Thank you for your concern, but I really need to complete the task I came for,' she told him after a few minutes.

'That's up to you,' Gideon said casually.

'I'm only here until Sunday, so I'd like to make a start if that's at all possible.'

'Then it's back to your husband, is it?' he enquired.

'Is that your way of finding out if I'm married?' Elizabeth could feel herself blushing.

'Well, you can't blame me for trying. I'm divorced. My job doesn't leave time for a settled family life, which is hard on the children.'

'How many do you have?'

'Two sons, eighteen and twenty. They're in the army and they live with their mother in Haifa,' he said curtly.

'I'm sorry. Mine are slightly younger. My husband has taken them skiing, which gave me the opportunity to come to Vienna.'

'You must trust each other.'

'Yes, we do,' Elizabeth said, draining her shot glass. She often wondered if Anthony had affairs, especially as their love life had never been quite the same since the children had arrived. As far as she was concerned, she missed the intimacy more than the sex, although with her husband, it was just the reverse.

Suddenly, there was jeering outside in the street and then the sound of breaking glass.

'What's that?' Elizabeth asked.

'It's the trouble we were expecting,' Gideon explained. 'I shouldn't worry, it's probably just a group of drunken thugs with nothing better to do.'

The jovial atmosphere in the restaurant had been replaced by looks of concern on the faces of a few of the older diners, Elizabeth noticed, as if it reminded them of a memory from the past. The closure of the Community Centre now made sense, and Gideon's haste in getting her to move away. She looked at the man opposite with gratitude. He had tried to protect her.

Time passed and, as predicted, the hubbub died down. Gideon settled the bill and Elizabeth thanked him and was about to leave when he turned round and said, quite pleasantly, 'I'm sorry that you've had a wasted visit.'

'There's still tomorrow,' Elizabeth said hopefully.

'The Centre won't be open until Monday at the earliest, but you could try the Synagogue. There may be someone there who might be able to help you.'

'I'll do that,' Elizabeth said, glad of the suggestion.

'And you may as well take my mobile number if you are thinking of coming back to Vienna.'

Elizabeth keyed the number into her phone, feeling slightly aggrieved that he hadn't asked for hers.

'Thank you for lunch,' she said again as they parted.

Gideon gave her a lingering smile before he went off in the opposite direction.

*

It was late in the afternoon by the time Elizabeth got back to the hotel. The day's events had left her feeling emotionally exhausted. After a hot bath, she went to bed early, still unsure exactly where her journey would take her but glad she hadn't cut her visit short.

5

Her head covered in a scarf, Elizabeth sat alone in one of the many empty rows within the Stadttempel, in awe of the magnificent oval edifice that surrounded her. Peering up at the two-tier women's gallery, she was reminded more of a theatre in London's West End than of any of the few synagogues she had previously frequented. A young cantor, wrapped in a white prayer shawl, sang a haunting melody from a pulpit facing the Ark, which held the holy Torah scrolls. Thoughts of what must have once been a thriving community passed through her mind. Now she could see it had been left to a paucity of elderly and infirm to keep the tradition going. Elizabeth suffered a sudden pang of conscience. Had she deprived her own children of such a rich heritage? she wondered.

Half an hour later, the service completed, the depleted congregation began shuffling away.

Her attention was drawn to a distinguished elderly couple. Dressed in their finest Sabbath clothes, the man wore a cravat with a pearl pin and his wife a black pill-box hat that rested on her finely shaped head; together, they looked like characters in a winter scene from one of Tolstoy's novels.

'Gut Shabbos,' she said politely, repeating what she had heard the synagogue sexton say at the end of the service.

'Gut Shabbos,' they replied together, the old man tipping his Homburg in a gesture of old-fashioned civility.

'We haven't noticed you before,' the kindly-looking woman remarked in English. 'Are you visiting perhaps?'

'Yes, I'm from London, but I'm only here until tomorrow,' Elizabeth replied.

'You look familiar,' her husband said, visibly trying to remember who she reminded him of.

'I'm sorry, I should have introduced myself. I'm Elizabeth.'

'And you have a last name to go with it?' he came back, quick as a flash.

'My mother was from Vienna. She was a Frankl.'

'Not an uncommon name,' the old man said vaguely.

Elizabeth hadn't considered that there must have been many more Frankls at one time than the handful she had identified in the phone directory. She needed no explanation for their absence.

'So what brings you to Vienna, my dear?' the white-haired lady asked, doing her best to be friendly.

'I'm trying to trace any relations on my mother's side who might still be alive,' Elizabeth disclosed.

'We should be delighted to try and help you, if we can,' the old lady said.

'Thank you, but I shouldn't want to put you to any trouble. It's cold and I'm sure you are wanting to get home.'

'Not at all. In fact, perhaps you'd care to be our guest for lunch?'

'That's extremely kind, thank you,' Elizabeth replied, pleased.

'It's our pleasure. The opportunity, alas, does not arise

that often to entertain. By the way, we're Freda and Ernst Hirschman.'

'Come, Elizabeth,' her husband intervened. 'Our car is waiting.'

'It's a beautiful synagogue,' Elizabeth said, breaking the silence that encompassed them since the start of the journey.

'The Stadttempel holds a very special affection for us. We were married there, almost seventy years ago,' Freda announced.

'And so you attend services every week?'

'We try to make the effort, whenever we can.'

By now, the downtown shopping precincts had given way to the Leopoldstadt, Vienna's 2nd district, a large island surrounded by the Danube Canal and, to the north, the Danube.

'This is where most of the Jewish population lived before the war,' Ernst Hirschman explained, pointing out where the ghetto once stood. 'When the Germans came, they destroyed everything.' There was a grim look on the old man's face as his painful memories came flooding back.

Elizabeth tried to imagine the vibrant life there during a golden period when religious tolerance allowed Jews access to the professions and the arts, which in turn had enabled them to make such a rich contribution to Viennese society. How was it possible that in just a few years, people who had lived there peacefully for centuries found their homes confiscated and livelihoods snatched away from them, then were erased in the most inhuman way from history – as if they had never existed? Even though her mother was only eight when she escaped the holocaust,

Elizabeth was beginning to understand why Lillian never spoke of the ordeal her own parents and brother had had to face.

The car pulled up outside an apartment building that was considerably older than the modern blocks they had passed on the way. It shared many of the same tasteful features, Elizabeth thought, as the period properties in the town centre.

'We're here,' Freda Hirschman announced. She paid the driver, who helped her husband from the back seat of the car, while Elizabeth let herself out of the front. The party of three passed through a heavy iron gate to the entrance, where a caretaker was on view.

'We're on the third floor. I'm afraid there's no lift in the building,' Freda said, taking the steps one by one up the threadbare main staircase.

Elizabeth smiled politely. How the couple were continually able to endure such a hardship – with the risk that they might suffer a fall, she shuddered to think.

'Do come in,' Ernst panted, ringing the bell and trying to catch his breath when they eventually reached their flat. A young fair-haired girl was on hand to take their coats from them.

'This is Joanna – she's from Poland. I don't know what we'd do without her,' his wife gasped.

'Hello,' Elizabeth said, shaking a childlike hand, and entered the tidy abode, where a delightful waft of baking aroused her taste buds. The old-fashioned décor made her feel as if she had entered a time warp. The interior appeared gloomy, even though there was a good view of the Danube Canal from the living room.

'Elizabeth, do sit down and make yourself comfortable,' Ernst said, moving slowly over to a lopsided drinks cabinet that looked as if it could topple over at any minute. 'Can I offer you a whisky or perhaps a vodka before lunch?'

'Ernst! You know the doctor has forbidden you to drink,' Freda cautioned. Turning to their guest, she confided, 'It's not good for his diabetes, but he won't hear of it.'

'We don't want our young guest to think we're being inhospitable, my dear,' the old man said, giving Elizabeth a wink.

'All right, just a small one; otherwise we both know you'll suffer for it afterwards,' Freda conceded, going off to check on the meal.

'I would prefer vodka, if you have it,' Elizabeth said, relaxing back into a maroon velvet armchair.

'Of course.' The old man obliged by pouring a neat measure into a crystal rock glass, which he passed to his guest. Then he cunningly decanted a similar quantity of his favourite Scottish malt whisky which, reluctantly, he now only took out for special occasions.

'*L'chaim!*' he toasted, taking a large gulp before his wife came back into the room.

'*L'chaim,*' Elizabeth responded, enjoying the warm feeling as the spirit went down her throat. She already liked this elderly couple immensely. There was so much she wanted to know about those other Frankls but was afraid to ask. Perhaps the pair had divulged all they could remember. After all, she estimated that they had to be well into their eighties.

She would have lunch with them and then find her way back to the hotel and pack her bag, Elizabeth decided. It was time to go home to her children. There would always be another opportunity to come again; maybe the next time, with her family?

The blonde Joanna appeared with a large soup tureen and platter of assorted cold meats.

'I see lunch is ready,' Ernst said, quickly polishing off his whisky.

The meal passed slowly, interrupted by the occasional wheeze of Ernst trying to clear the congestion from his chest while Freda just picked at her food, seeming to have lost her appetite.

'I used to love to entertain,' Freda told her guest, breaking the silence. 'We'd have dinner parties at least every other week – no, Ernst?'

'Freda had a reputation for her stuffed cabbage and dumplings,' her husband nodded, beaming.

'These days, when it's just the two of us, well . . .' Freda said sadly.

There was no need for her to go on. Elizabeth just wondered how, against all odds, the pair had managed to survive?

There was another short pause while the plates were cleared and a Kugelhopf, a ring-shaped sweetened bread rich with raisins and almonds and dusted with powdered sugar, was brought to the table and served, still warm from the oven, washed down with three tall glasses of lemon tea. It was when Freda started slicing the cake that Elizabeth noticed the number tattooed on the inside of her painfully thin arm. That was a question she couldn't bring up.

'So where did you two meet?' Elizabeth asked instead, as she bit into a large slice of the delicious cake and licked the powder from her lips.

'Ernst and I knew each other as children,' Freda began. 'Our parents were best friends. My father was a psychiatrist – he actually studied under Freud – and Ernst's family ran the most prominent Jewish newspaper in Vienna.' Her eyes twinkled. 'Truthfully, I thought he was far too pompous because he lived in a big house on the Herrengasse.'

'And Freda was too studious for my liking,' Ernst said, coming to life and then, just as quickly, went back to slurping his tea through a sugar cube.

'Only because I wanted to go into medicine and was always attending one lecture or another!' his wife retorted.

A smile passed between the two as they recalled happier times.

'There was a Viktor Frankl,' Ernst then said, completely out of the blue.

'He was my grandfather!' Elizabeth exclaimed excitedly.

'And his wife Anna, such dignified people,' Freda remarked.

'My grandmother,' Elizabeth confirmed. Was this the breakthrough she'd been waiting for?

'Along with the Rothschilds and the Ephrussis, the Frankls were the wealthiest banking families in Vienna,' Ernst revealed. 'Their mansion was easily the size of this apartment block. Rumour had it that their vast gold reserves helped Emperor Franz Joseph in the Austro-Prussian War.'

Elizabeth was taken aback. She had had no idea that they were so wealthy and influential. Her mother had never made any mention of it. All Elizabeth knew about them was what she had discovered for herself: that they lived in a house with a large garden in Vienna.

'I can still see Viktor striding down the Ringstrasse in his top hat dishing out silver sovereigns to the needy, and that bushy captain's moustache of his that curled up at the ends. He was a real character,' Ernst chuckled.

'Anna was much more an introvert,' Freda said.

'According to mother, she was very musical,' Elizabeth replied.

'That's correct. She was such a sensitive person but, alas, not mentally strong enough to cope with what she'd had to face.'

'You mean the war?' Elizabeth said.

'Yes, and the added burden of having to look after a disabled child.'

Elizabeth felt the blood drain from her face. Maybe she had misheard; after all, it was a long time ago. Perhaps they had muddled up her grandmother with someone else.

'I see it has come as a surprise,' Freda said softly. 'You must understand that, however modest they were in their everyday lives and even though they were Jews, the Frankls were treated like royalty.'

Ernst nodded. 'How do you say in English? They were very much in the public eye.'

But Elizabeth barely heard them: she sat in silence, trying to absorb the traumatic revelation that her mother had had a disabled sister – her aunt.

Freda turned to her husband. 'Ernst dear, I think our guest might benefit from a cognac,' she murmured, before addressing Elizabeth again.

'The child was called Erica,' she said gently. 'It was well known that no expense was spared in trying to help the girl, but there was never any improvement. We'd often see her in the Stadtpark with her nurse, wrapped up well and sitting in her wheelchair, looking so cheerful amongst the ponds and pretty walkways. Her favourite place was by the Johann Strauss monument. It was as if she already knew his music by heart.'

'I didn't know any of this,' Elizabeth said, taking a gulp from the balloon glass that had been placed in front of her.

'It's often the case for these things not to be discussed,' Ernst told her, his voice kind. 'You mustn't blame your mother. Imagine how much she's lost and perhaps you'll begin to understand.'

Elizabeth wanted to respond but she didn't know what to say. Slowly, it all began to make sense. She could see it clearly now. The fact that her mother had never been able to bring herself to talk about that period in her life had impacted on their own relationship, creating a barrier of unspoken pain and guilt between them. How ironic that Elizabeth had been the one deemed to be in need of treatment, when the true cause lay with her mother. Lillian had locked away and repressed the past, unaware that the trauma she had suffered by being separated from her parents and her disabled sister, had never been resolved. Elizabeth's thoughts turned to Charlotte. Could it be that Lillian had looked on her dearest friend as the older sister she had lost? Nothing could make up for the losses of the past.

Not for the first time during her visit, Elizabeth was filled with conflicting emotions. Woefully unprepared for what she might uncover, part of her regretted that she'd made the trip in the first place. Perhaps it would have been preferable to carry on living with the uncertainty about her past? No! But what if this was just the start and there was more to come? At that moment, Elizabeth knew she needed to stay a little longer to find out.

Another hour passed. Ernst, feeling unwell, had retired to the bedroom. Alone with Freda, the conversation shifted instead to the old lady wanting to know about Elizabeth's life in London, a city she had never visited. Freda was eager to hear all about her family but reluctant to talk about herself. Then, without any prompting she just came out and said, 'We would have loved to have had children but I'm afraid it wasn't to be.'

'But you were still a young woman when the war ended?' Elizabeth queried.

'I was twenty-six. Many of us who survived Auschwitz were permanently damaged. I was one of the lucky ones but those terrible medical experiments we were subjected to left me unable to conceive.'

'I'm so sorry. I had no idea,' Elizabeth said, taking hold of Freda's hand.

'Looking back, I suppose we could have adopted, but we were so busy trying to get our lives back together; Ernst trying to rebuild his newspaper and I focusing on my psychiatric training. So you see, time seemed to have passed us by.'

'And your families?' Elizabeth prompted.

The old lady shook her head sadly. 'We were the only ones left.'

It was starting to get dark. Elizabeth considered that she had taken advantage of the elderly couple's hospitality long enough. Refusing Freda's offer of the use of her private car company, she said she would make her own way back. Anyway, she was in no hurry to return to spend her last night alone in the confines of that characterless hotel. Saying her goodbyes, she set off to wander around Leopoldstadt and soon found herself at the entrance of the Prater public park. Despite the minus-zero temperatures, she could see that the famous attractions there were busy. The Wiener Riesenrad, a landmark giant Ferris wheel which operated all year round, had Elizabeth thinking of her late father Donald and those wonderful outings to funfairs at the seaside when she was a child; just the two of them because her mother had a fear of heights. She could still feel her heart in her mouth as they sped down the near-vertical tracks, both of them screaming. Trying to relive those moments, she bought a hot chocolate to warm herself and joined the queue for the long, twenty-minute ride.

Elizabeth felt a gentle nudge on her arm and then heard a voice saying, *'Fraulein, geht's dir gut?'* She opened her eyes to see a young park official standing over her.

'I'm sorry, I must have fallen asleep,' she replied in English, deeply embarrassed at having caused a spectacle of herself.

'That's OK,' the youth replied in accented English, smirking all over his spotty face. 'It happens after many beers!' He must have presumed, correctly, that she'd been drinking and it had gone to her head, she thought.

Elizabeth checked the time on her ticket – 5.30 p.m. She'd been out of it for almost an hour, and no one had woken her up. All she remembered, as the wheel first started to turn, was struggling to keep her eyes open.

Learning about the existence of her aunt had had a profound effect upon her. The vivid images of Erica at the train station, missing from her mother's painting, waving weakly to Lillian, the younger sister who she was destined never to see again, played heavily on her mind. And there was something else niggling at her. The trouble was, she couldn't recall what it might have been.

Elizabeth staggered to her feet and joined the latest group of passengers disembarking from the cars. 'I must go and pay for the additional rides,' she said to herself, but she needn't have bothered. The ticket office, admiring her honesty, let her off.

Still feeling disorientated, Elizabeth left the park and more by luck than judgment found a taxi to take her back to the hotel, unaware that she was being followed by the same two men who had been watching her movements since she had attended the synagogue early that morning.

*

Kebabhaus, Innere Stadt

Gideon Halevi wrily observed his two subordinates busily attacking their humus and falafel laffas. More than likely it was their first proper meal of the day, so that was fair enough. However, the new generation of operatives was a different breed from the older ones like him. Hardened by the Lebanon War in 1982 when he was just eighteen, he'd seen enough action in the field to last him a lifetime. Mossad was a piece of cake in comparison.

'So Uri, what did you manage to find out about the woman?' Gideon probed.

'She seems to have hit it off with the Hirschmans,' the young operative replied, wiping his mouth on his sleeve.

'It was a bloody long lunch – and then she had to work it off with an hour-long ride on the big wheel. I swear I couldn't feel my balls by the time we got back to her hotel,' grumbled Beni, his colleague.

'How did you know they'd connect?' the younger one asked perceptively.

Gideon remained silent. He wasn't about to divulge his sources, even to them. The fact was that Freda Hirschman was still sufficiently alert to be of help when the occasion arose. All it had taken was asking her to keep her eyes peeled at the Stadttempel for an Englishwoman in her early forties, travelling on her own, on a mission to trace members of her family, the Frankls. He knew he could rely on the wily old lady to do the rest. Her task was to impart just enough information to persuade the tourist to prolong her stay in Vienna. That was because Gideon needed enough time to establish whether there was any connection between the visitor and a certain prominent member of the Frankl family whom Mossad was keeping under surveillance – or whether it was just a coincidence. True, there was still a chance she would be on the BA flight to London the following afternoon, but instinct told him that the persistent Elizabeth McCreary wouldn't be easily satisfied with what she had learned from the Hirschmans. He'd always found intelligent women a big turn-on and with the looks to go with it, he hoped he was right. Spending more time with her would not be a hardship.

*

Elizabeth ran a hot bath and submerged herself in sky-blue bubbles. The cold had penetrated every bone in her body to such an extent that it had been an effort to get out of her clothes. Slowly, as she thawed out, she began prioritising the things she needed to do. Top of the list was speaking to the children. She wondered how they would be spending their own last evening in Klosters. Knowing them, they would probably go ice-skating and enjoy tackling their final cheese fondue, if experience was anything to go by. She hoped the week's skiing would have benefited the three of them, bringing them together, and prayed there hadn't been any accidents that they were keeping from her, particularly with Freddie, who was always out to prove himself to his father.

After the bath she would pack, order something from the room-service menu and spend the evening in front of the plasma TV that dominated the small bedroom.

Unwittingly, her thoughts turned to her mother. Elizabeth had more or less decided by now to keep what she had discovered about Erica Frankl to herself. For better or for worse, Lillian had found happiness with Allen, so no good could come of digging up the past. More aware now of the traumatic separation her mother had gone through as a child had made Elizabeth more understanding of the reasons behind their often-frosty relationship. The truth was, coming to Vienna had been purely for her own benefit.

Elizabeth stood up and wrapped herself in an enormous soft towel. She was frowning in concentration. The bath had relaxed her; however, she still couldn't work out what had been troubling her when she was roused from her slumber on the Riesenrad. It had something to do with being at the Hirschmans' apartment, she could remember that . . . Maybe it was what Freda had said about her husband being preoccupied with trying to rebuild his newspaper after the war. The word 'newspaper' was the key. Then she remembered: her Great-uncle Theo had been a reporter on a newspaper – that was it! Ernst and Theo would certainly have known each other. She could kick herself for not bringing it up at the time. Was there a reason why Theo was omitted from the conversation? There was only one way to find out, which was to pay the Hirschmans another visit.

6

The next morning after a light breakfast, Elizabeth settled her hotel bill and took her small suitcase on wheels with her when she left, telling the man at reception that she was off to see friends in Leopoldstadt. Since it was still early, there was time to take in a few more of the historical sites before directing the taxi to the Leopoldstadt. Her flight to London wasn't until three in the afternoon and the Hirschmans' flat, she was informed, was on the way to the airport. Assuming there were no delays, she'd still be home before Anthony and the children, who were not due to land at Heathrow until 9 p.m. She had intended to tell her husband what she'd been up to in Vienna while he was away, but realising that her mission was incomplete, she had put off making the call.

Arriving at the main entrance to the apartment block later on that morning, Elizabeth found a small gathering of people outside. They were standing a few feet away from a black limousine with its rear tailgate open, guarded by a solemn-looking man in a Loden cape.

There was a hush and a raising of Tyrolean hats as two undertakers appeared carrying a simple oak coffin. It was carefully placed in the back of the waiting vehicle, which then drove off slowly to its final destination.

Assuming that it was merely the sad passing of one of

the other elderly residents of the building, Elizabeth left her case with the caretaker, who fortunately remembered Elizabeth from the day before and gave his condolences to her and to Frau Hirschman. Wondering what he meant, she climbed the stairs up to the third-floor flat. Finding the door ajar and hearing the sound of subdued voices, Elizabeth entered, suddenly apprehensive. It was then, seeing the group congregated around a tearful Freda, that she understood it was Ernst who had died.

Elizabeth was overcome with emotion. Even though she had met the wonderful old man just once, the warmth of his personality had made a considerable impression upon her.

Waiting in turn to pay her condolences to his widow, Elizabeth was amazed to recognise Gideon Halevi, a few paces in front of her. What on earth was *he* doing here? The Jewish community here was small, so it probably wasn't unusual – but there was something about the fellow that suggested to her that he had an ulterior motive.

As if by instinct, he turned and saw her. 'We meet again – what were the chances of that?' the Israeli said, smiling.

Elizabeth nodded coolly, finding his lighthearted manner out of keeping with the mood of mourning that pervaded the small apartment.

'I thought you had decided to cut your trip short?' he continued.

'I don't think I actually said that. Anyway, my flight's at three this afternoon,' Elizabeth confirmed, wondering what had given him that idea. She found his casual manner unsettling. When he'd suggested she leave Vienna two days ago, she had taken it as concern for her safety.

Now she wasn't so sure.

'The funeral is in forty- five minutes. I'll take you, if you want,' Gideon said.

'How was it possible to organise it so quickly?' Elizabeth asked, surprised.

'Jewish law dictates that a burial must be carried out as soon as possible. Ernst died early last night; there was plenty of time after Shabbos to contact the burial society at the synagogue,' Gideon remarked unemotionally.

'I thought you said the Stadttempel office was closed,' Elizabeth reminded him. Something didn't add up.

'Yes, it is,' was all he said in response.

Elizabeth sensed that she was being played with – but for what purpose, she had no idea.

'I'd very much like to attend if you don't mind dropping me off afterwards at the airport,' she told him.

'No problem, let's go,' Gideon replied tersely.

'But I've just arrived!' Elizabeth protested. She wanted at least to have the opportunity of spending a little time with Freda, whom she had got to like immensely, plus the fact that she, Elizabeth, was probably the last person here in the room to have seen Ernst alive. But it was to no avail because Gideon yanked her by the arm and they were already halfway down the stairs before she could remonstrate further. A few minutes later, she was holding on for dear life in the front passenger seat of a grimy Volkswagen Beetle.

'How well do you know the Hirschmans?' Elizabeth asked.

'Special people,' Gideon grunted.

'I just didn't expect to see you there,' Elizabeth probed.

Gideon gave her a knowing sideways glance which indicated that it was more than just a coincidence.

Elizabeth suddenly noticed that her luggage wasn't there and went into a panic. She remembered leaving it with the front desk, but after that her mind went blank.

'Is anything wrong?' Gideon asked.

'My case – I must have left it behind!' she exclaimed, berating herself for being so careless.

'We might still be able to make it,' Gideon said, unphased at having to change course at short notice.

The small car continued for a few hundred yards then screeched round and sped back the way they had come.

'I assume that Freda and Ernst were able to throw some light on your mother's family?' the Israeli said.

'Yes, yes they did,' Elizabeth replied. 'Apparently they knew them quite well. I learned for the first time that my mother had an older disabled sister. It came as quite a shock. It still hasn't fully registered properly.'

'And it was worth you coming to Vienna just for that?'

'It has helped me to start to come to terms with certain unresolved issues,' Elizabeth said, not wishing to elaborate. She went on: 'Though I'm sure there was more they could have told me. That's the reason I came back, on the off-chance of talking to them again. I should have phoned first but stupidly I didn't take their number.'

'What – there were other relations you wanted to trace?' the Israeli asked, just as they hit a heavy line of traffic approaching the Leopoldstadt.

'My Great-uncle Theo was a reporter on a well-known newspaper before the war. He and Ernst must surely have known each other, but I didn't ask. It was a missed opportunity on my part.'

'And you have no idea what happened to him, this Uncle Theo?'

'The last letters from my grandparents before they were sent to Auschwitz, presumably together with their elder daughter, made no mention of Theo, which is why I hoped that he might have somehow survived. Now I'll never know.' She sighed. 'Perhaps it's for the best.'

The detour completed and recognising several landmarks she had passed when she had set out that morning, Elizabeth was sure they were on the Ringstrasse heading back towards the centre of town.

'I thought we were going to the funeral?' she said, turning to the driver.

'Change of route,' Gideon answered laconically.

Passing the Opera House, they found their progress further impeded by a sign diverting the traffic.

'What's going on?' Elizabeth asked.

'Another far-right rally,' Gideon told her. 'The authorities are obviously expecting trouble, that's why the police are out in such high numbers.'

'What do we do now?' Elizabeth said, panicking.

'Since all the roads out of the centre are more than likely blocked off, it doesn't leave us with much choice. We'll have to sit it out till it disperses.'

'How long will that be?' Elizabeth was now seriously concerned that she'd miss her flight.

'Who knows?' the Israeli shrugged.

They dumped the car nearby and made their way towards a huge throng of people gathered on the Heldenplatz, a large public space in front of the Hofburg Palace.

Suddenly, there were chants of '*Führer! Führer!*' by a contingent of youths in military-style uniform, their shouts followed by Nazi salutes. Attention focused on a tall figure, coat draped over his shoulders, striding confidently up to the ready-made podium for a rapturous reception.

'Who is he?' Elizabeth asked, trying to make herself heard above the din.

'His name is Oscar Gruber. He just got elected to Parliament. Those thugs in caps with red-and-blue-striped bands are his right-wing supporters.'

Elizabeth recalled the boisterous group in the hotel bar and the despicable individual who accosted her; they had been wearing the same ribbons pinned to their jackets. She just didn't understand what any of this had got to do with *her*?

All of a sudden, there was a series of loud bangs; plumes of red smoke filled the area. Then a scuffle broke out with a group of left-wing protestors carrying anti-racist banners who had taken exception to the poisonous views being perpetrated by their bitter adversaries.

'It could get dangerous. We should get out of here,' Gideon announced.

Feeling shaken by the experience, Elizabeth accepted the Israeli's arm as they hastened back to his car.

'Right, it's half past one, we'd better get a move on,' he said, driving off at great speed.

Elizabeth nodded wordlessly. Trying to make sense of the toxic event she had just witnessed was bad enough, but having been confronted by Austria's ultra-right-wing party, so close to when she was due to leave the country, had hardly put her in the right frame of mind to go home. Instinctively, Elizabeth started to try and find ways to extend her stay. Perhaps she should confide in her mother, and ask her to move in temporarily and look after Anthony and the children? After all, at some point Elizabeth knew she'd probably change her mind and decide to share what she had discovered with Lillian, and thereby explain why she had felt she needed to stay for longer in Vienna. However, if past experience were anything to go by, Lillian would revert to type and refuse to revisit the past, irrespective of anything new that had materialised. And she wouldn't want to leave Allen on his own.

Her sister-in-law Jesse adored her niece and nephew, but as Anthony said, she was well ensconced with her life in Paris and, in any case, it would be unfair to ask her to come over and look after them all at such short notice. No, Elizabeth decided, she'd just have to come clean with Anthony and tell him he would have to cope until she got back.

After Gideon expertly negotiated their way out of the Innere Stadt, less than half an hour later, the Volkswagen hurtled towards Vienna International Airport.

Elizabeth came to a decision. 'Gideon, please stop the car, I've got to make a private call,' she announced.

'No problem, there's a place coming up,' he replied. A few hundred yards further on, he turned the car into a motorway service station.

'I'll wait here,' Gideon said as his passenger got out of the car. 'Grab a couple of baguettes and some coffee on your way back, will you?' he shouted after her.

Elizabeth found a table in the roadside cafeteria and, throwing caution to the wind, called her husband on her mobile phone.

He answered. 'Is that you, Elizabeth?' she heard him ask.

'Yes, it's me.'

'The connection's terrible. Where are you calling from – Outer Mongolia?'

'Vienna, actually. How are the children?'

'What on earth are you doing there?'

'It's a long story. I'll tell you when I get back.'

'All right, you can tell me this evening. I reckon we'll be home by eleven,' Anthony said.

'That's the thing, I'm planning on staying a while longer,' Elizabeth responded.

'What? I didn't catch that, there's interference on the line.'

'I said there's something that I need to follow up on!'

'Oh well, in that case I suppose the girl can get the children ready for school in the morning,' Anthony conceded. 'We've had a great time. Emily's already mastered the blue runs, and would you believe it, Freddie's found a couple of chums at ski school. I've hardly seen him all holiday.'

'Francesca's not back from Italy for another two weeks,' Elizabeth reminded her husband.

There was a moment of awkward silence. 'Surely you're not expecting me to take over?' Anthony protested. 'I've got the auditors breathing down my neck and my father's gone awol – this is the last thing I need!'

'You could always ring the agency to arrange some temporary help.'

'This won't do,' he said irritably. 'It's not down to me to supervise the children. I just don't understand what's got into you all of a sudden.'

It was exactly the reaction she'd anticipated. But it was her fault. If she'd objected more forcefully to the tiny part Anthony played in their family life, instead of shouldering all the responsibility herself, it might have been different; but she'd allowed herself to be taken advantage of long enough and now was determined to make a stand.

'Look, there's enough food in the house until I get back and if you're in a fix, I'm sure my mother would be prepared to lend a hand.'

But it was too late, the line was dead. Anthony had cut her off.

Elizabeth was caught in two minds whether to call back again. If she didn't, she risked Anthony turning the children against her and conceivably even jeopardising the marriage. On the other hand, if she caved in, she'd face having to live with herself, knowing that she had forfeited a one-off opportunity to find out who she really was. It was a hard call. Pretty sure that Freddie would have taken his own mobile phone with him, she began composing a text to her son and daughter, explaining the situation. It was important to keep the lines of communication open, irrespective of what their father might say to them. She'd call the landline tonight and put things right.

Frowning, Elizabeth returned slowly to the Volkswagen.

'So it didn't go well?' the Israeli asked perceptively.

'Is it that obvious?' Elizabeth replied, strapping herself in.

'It must have been important, for you to forget my baguette and coffee.'

'I'm sorry,' Elizabeth said, forcing a laugh.

'I assume you've decided against going back to London?'

'What on earth gave you that idea?'

'Your body language? It's my training,' he reminded her.

'Of course, I'd forgotten about the secret agent thing,' Elizabeth said flippantly.

'You don't seem overly impressed.'

'Was I supposed to be?'

'You're an unusual woman, Elizabeth. It takes courage to face up to what you've been confronted with.'

'I suppose I should take that as a compliment?'

Gideon just smiled and squeezed her hand affectionately. Elizabeth turned to him and impulsively threw her arms around his neck. Words were unnecessary; she just needed to feel the closeness of another human being.

After a few moments she moved away, trying to make some sense of her rash action. True, the phone call to Anthony had left her feeling vulnerable – but there was more to it than that. There was something about this man that she found exciting. He always appeared to be one step ahead of her, which made her want to find out more about him.

'Now perhaps you'd be good enough to tell me what's really going on?' Elizabeth queried, as they rejoined the motorway.

'In what way do you mean?' Gideon replied, enjoying the intrigue.

'I'm not naïve enough to believe that we got stuck in that rally purely by accident.'

'You do have a suspicious mind, Mrs McCreary.'

'You have to admit that you've forced me to delay my return to London – not that I have any idea where I'm going to stay.'

'The Hirschmans' flat. It's all arranged.'

'I couldn't possibly impose on Freda with what she's just gone through,' Elizabeth objected.

'It's your choice, though I imagine she'd be pleased for the company.'

Elizabeth pondered for a moment. 'You hurried me out of their apartment, knowing that I'd left my case behind. Why didn't you say anything?'

'Let's just say there was more than one way of keeping you in Vienna,' Gideon said smugly.

Elizabeth was suddenly furious. She hated being manipulated like a tame puppet. It was quite obvious the chap enjoyed running rings around her, and although she grudgingly admired his ingenuity, something didn't add up.

'And why would you want to do that?' she asked.

'I thought that was obvious,' Gideon said, flashing her a smile.

'Why do I sense that I'm being set up?' Elizabeth responded. But there was no response from the Israeli.

Half an hour or so later, they drew up at the block of flats which were now becoming familiar.

'I've got to be somewhere,' Gideon said, letting her out. 'I'll pick you up at seven p.m.' And then he drove off without waiting for a response.

7

Elizabeth marvelled at the cluster of red maple trees forming a guard of honour at the entrance to the park. Gideon was half an hour late and she was becoming impatient. Apart from Joanna, the domestic help, she had the flat to herself. After the funeral, Freda had opted to stay with friends instead of coming home, which was understandable in the circumstances. No doubt she couldn't face being alone without the man she had shared her life with for the best part of seventy years.

Elizabeth went over everything she had learned for the hundredth time, trying to make some sense of it all. At least things were all right at home in London. Freddie had replied to her text, assuring his mother that they were more than able to manage and promising that he would organise everything. This made her feel a whole lot better. Perhaps taking on the responsibility for the family was just what the boy needed to boost his confidence. In any case, having secured an open ticket home at a minimal cost gave her the added comfort of knowing that she could be on a flight home the next day, if necessary.

Elizabeth had just about given up on Gideon when her mobile pinged with a message: *Anton-Frank-Gasse 18th district. Top-floor flat above Café Josef. Gideon.*

How had he got her number? she wondered. He had

his methods, she supposed. Anyway, with the type of controlling individual that Gideon was, she'd expected to be given orders. It was annoying, but having come this far there was little to lose by putting herself out one last time. Muttering to herself, she went off to try and find a taxi.

The journey didn't take long. As instructed, Elizabeth entered through the side entrance of the restaurant and climbed the steep flights of stairs until she reached a narrow landing at the top. She knocked on a plain wooden door without any markings, and few seconds later, Gideon appeared bare-footed, his shirt undone to the waist.

'It's not much, but it's adequate for one person,' he said, showing her into a rectangular-shaped space with roof windows either side. The flat was separated into a kitchen and living room at one end, and a bedroom with restricted head-height at the other. Separate washing and sanitary facilities were accessed through a pair of fan-fold doors next to the entrance.

The distinctive aroma of Chinese food drifted up from the kitchen table. Elizabeth glanced at the two place settings and the open bottle of red wine, wondering if this wasn't what he had intended all along.

'Let's eat,' Gideon said, removing the lids of half a dozen cartons.

'Aren't you going to finish getting dressed?' Elizabeth asked, seeing that she'd go hungry if she waited to be served.

'I didn't think you were that easily embarrassed?' Gideon replied, piling his plate with food.

'Your message came as a bit of a surprise,' she told him, trying hard to keep her eyes off his perfect physique.

'Actually, I very nearly didn't come.'

'So what changed your mind?' Gideon asked, tucking into his chicken noodles.

'I've decided to return to London tomorrow, so I reckoned there had to be better ways of spending my last evening alone in Vienna.' There was little point mentioning that Freda wasn't at home, since he probably knew all about that.

'There's just one thing: I'm intrigued to know how you intended to keep me here in Vienna if I hadn't turned up at Freda and Ernst's apartment this morning.'

'Let's just say it was a well-informed guess.' He wasn't going to divulge how dismayed he'd been when he'd discovered she had already checked out of her hotel. Fortunately, the concierge fell for his sob story about needing to give his sister an important message and mentioned that Frau McCreary had been intending to visit friends in the 2nd district. That could only mean the Hirschmans. The truth was, it was pure luck that Gideon got there before her.

'Well, it obviously worked,' Elizabeth said playfully, as she set about enjoying her first proper meal of the day.

Gideon produced a smile as he filled both their wine glasses

'You're not trying to get me drunk, by any chance?' Elizabeth enquired.

'Invite a woman over for a friendly meal, and that's her response. You obviously don't think very highly of me.'

'Not at all. Remember, I've had rather a lot to absorb over the last few days.'

'It's been worthwhile, hasn't it?' the Israeli probed.

'Finding out about my maternal family, absolutely, if that's what you're referring to,' Elizabeth countered.

'Well, if that's the only reason why you're still in Vienna, the least I could do is to provide you with a little more information before you go on your way.'

'Sounds interesting. About who in particular?'

'Theodore Frankl,' the Israeli said unemotionally.

'Really!' Elizabeth exclaimed, her hopes suddenly raised that her great-uncle might still be alive.

'You need to understand that there were a number of wealthy Jews – and he was undoubtedly one of them – who were prepared to hang on at all costs after the Germans invaded.'

Elizabeth was taken aback, learning about a possible intransigence on her grandparents' part for the first time.

'And I suppose by the time those who stayed behind saw what was happening, it was too late?' she deduced.

'Exactly! But Theo was an opportunist. He had no intention of leaving. You're probably not aware of this, but your great-uncle was involved with an Austrian woman, the daughter of a diplomat,' Gideon divulged. 'She provided him with the cover he required to carry on his business activities without interference from the Nazis.'

'What business was that? I was under the impression he was a reporter on a daily newspaper.'

'More likely that was just a front for his other activities, because it appears that the woman was only interested in his money.'

'And how were you able to find out about this?'

'Since he was one of the handful of Jews who somehow managed to sit out most of the war unscathed, you can be sure there are still a few people around who'd remember him!'

'I really had no idea about any of this,' Elizabeth letting the condescending remark go over her heac else was going to come to light about the enigmatic Theo Frank?

'It was an arrangement that suited both of them, for a while,' Gideon continued.

'What happened?' Elizabeth asked apprehensively.

'This is where it all gets a bit vague. All we know is that Theo disappeared. The chances are that he was murdered with the rest of your relatives.'

Elizabeth swallowed after hearing the harsh words. 'What about the woman?'

'It was only when we were tracking the whereabouts of a low-ranking Nazi officer named Walter Brandt, who'd been in Vienna, that we found out about his wife's identity.'

'You're saying that it was the same person?'

'Yes. Her name was Lise Gruber. At the end of the war, the three moved to Germany, Walter to resume his career in the family business – a heavy-engineering concern of dubious repute regarding its contribution to the Nazi war effort. But being so well established, they were afforded full protection against any wrong-doing by the German government so there was little way we could get to them.'

'You mentioned there were three of them?' Elizabeth said after a brief pause.

'Did I? It must be the wine,' Gideon hedged.

'What happened to them?' Elizabeth asked.

'Lise predeceased her husband; they'd got married, no doubt assuming that they were going to live happily ever after.'

'And did they?'

'Brandt was alive up to about ten years ago, but dementia conveniently struck before we could get to him. You see, we discovered too late that he wasn't quite as low-key as he liked to make out. In fact, we have proof he was complicit in expediting the transport of Jews from the Ghetto to their deaths in Auschwitz.'

Elizabeth didn't want to ask if that was how Theo also met his demise. Perhaps it was a blessing her mother had never known the truth about the one surviving member of her family.

Gideon helped himself to another portion of food and passed the near empty cartons across to his guest.

'Naturally, we know a lot more about Oscar Gruber,' Gideon said with his mouth full of stir-fried vegetables.

'The man who spoke at the rally? He's Lise's son?' Elizabeth speculated.

The Israeli nodded.

'Surely it can't possibly be the same person,' Elizabeth murmured to herself, then: 'I mean, how did he get into politics?'

Without offering a response the Israeli got up from the table to fetch a magazine from the coffee table.

'Here – you can see for yourself,' he said, pointing to the middle-aged Cary Grant lookalike on the front cover and the headline that read *Former Hollywood Actor Challenges Europe's Political Establishment.* ' "Charismatic and extremely persuasive" would probably sum him up. The fact that he's also independently wealthy makes him a formidable foe.'

'With what he inherited, you mean?' Elizabeth said, examining the photograph.

Gideon shook his head. 'The private plane and villa on the Costa Smeralda in Sardinia came from the international media group of which he's still the major shareholder. Being in control of most of the right-wing press in Europe gave him the perfect platform to promote his xenophobic agenda. Here, take it,' the Israeli said, passing the magazine to his guest. 'I'm sure you'll find it makes interesting reading.'

'Do you think that he knows about Theo's existence?' Elizabeth asked.

'I doubt Lise would have broadcasted the fact.'

'I suppose you're right – but what I don't understand is why you didn't tell me any of this before?'

'If I had, you probably wouldn't have believed it. As you explained, there was a lot for you to take in.'

Elizabeth pondered for a moment. What she had heard sounded plausible. She just queried why none of this about her great-uncle had been mentioned when she was at the Hirschmans' apartment for lunch? Something didn't add up.

'Why do I sense there's still more that you're not telling me?'

'I should have thought that was more than enough to make your visit here a success,' Gideon said with a straight face.

'Sounds like you want to get rid of me,' Elizabeth noted.

'I didn't say that. Anyway, this time tomorrow you'll be back to living your comfortable suburban life in London.'

'What if I'm not ready to go?'

Needing little further encouragement, Gideon went over and took her in his arms. They kissed, gently at first then more passionately, this time with the fervour of two bodies aching for each other.

'I'm a married woman, remember,' Elizabeth protested half-heartedly, as she allowed herself to enter forbidden territory.

Lying together, the warmth from their naked bodies the only respite from the unheated room, Elizabeth experienced none of guilt that she ought to be feeling. The truth was, the man with whom she had just made love had awoken something inside of her that had remained dormant for far too long. Maybe this was the other reason she had decided to extend her stay in Vienna.

'You still haven't answered my question,' Elizabeth said, turning to him.

'Oscar Gruber is a real threat,' Gideon said, his voice harsh. 'You saw for yourself the adulation he commands amongst his followers.'

'Yes, it was frightening,' Elizabeth agreed.

'But that's only a small example of what's going on.'

'What do you mean?'

'We know that he's intent on forming alliances with extreme right-wing parties in lesser European countries. But our biggest fear, now he commands a working majority in parliament, is that he will institute a purge of immigrants – and Jews feel they will be top of the list again. We cannot allow that to happen.'

Elizabeth's mind turned to that vile man who had confronted her at the hotel bar; hadn't he alluded to exactly the same thing?

'But the right wing has nothing like the same following in England,' she countered. All of a sudden she could hear her mother Lillian responding in the same dismissive way when she didn't want to hear anything negative about Charlotte. Was she herself similarly closed-minded, Elizabeth asked herself.

'It's the same all over Europe. Trust me. But it just happens to be worse here in Austria – which is why the head of the snake needs to be cut off to teach the rest a lesson that we are not prepared to stand by and let history repeat itself.'

Elizabeth was shocked. She suddenly felt icy cold. 'Surely you don't mean what you are insinuating?' she said.

'All options are on the table. If the man didn't have a ring of steel protecting him, I can assure you we would have taken him out by now.'

'But you can't possibly assassinate him!' Elizabeth said, horrified.

'Why, because it goes against your British sense of fair play?'

'There must be some other way,' Elizabeth tried, a little unsure herself about the stand she was taking.

'We are nearly out of choices and time is running short,' the Israeli stressed.

'Who is "we"?' Elizabeth enquired.

'You've heard of Mossad?'

'Yes, of course.'

'But probably not of Shin Bet, the foreign intelligence unit?'

'No, I don't think so.'

'I'm in charge of their Western Europe operations,' Gideon revealed.

Elizabeth was taken aback. Even though her initial

assessment of the fellow had proven accurate, she hadn't put him down as a Secret Service agent.

'Don't imagine this is some impetuous over-reaction on our part,' he continued. 'You should know it's the result of many months of careful planning by a group of highly trained professionals. It just so happens, you appeared on the scene at exactly the wrong time.'

'So that's the real reason you tried to get me to go back to London?'

'Correct. I didn't want you around if things were going to get heavy.'

'What suddenly changed your mind?' Elizabeth asked.

Gideon took his time before answering.

'Actually, it was my feelings for you,' he said, moving closer to the bare-breasted woman. He didn't divulge that the order had come from the top. He could still hear his boss, Moshe Katan's instruction: 'Use any means at your disposal to get rid of that bastard but avoid an international incident,' he emphasised. 'We can do without any more adverse publicity.' A tough call but Gideon Halevi was no stranger to situations of this sort.

'I'd be surprised if there wasn't more to it than that,' Elizabeth replied sardonically.

The Israeli sighed. 'Don't you ever take compliments at face value?'

'With you, I've learned it's probably safer not to,' she told him.

'There's always a possibility of defusing the situation if the right person could get him to cooperate with us,' Gideon said, focusing his attentions again on the beautiful woman sharing his bed.

'Oh? Such as who?' Elizabeth frowned. She didn't like the way this was going and was beginning to feel extremely uneasy. Suddenly she was aware of an intense look focusing on her, before she was swept away in a sea of passionate embraces.

*

At the same time, over in the luxury penthouse apartment belonging to one of the richest men in Austria, an informal meeting of two people was taking place.

'Now we've reached an historic agreement, my dear Gretchen, I think we should celebrate,' the host remarked, holding up the smart leather-bound document.

'Indeed we should, Oscar – or should I say "leader of the new Austro-German Alliance Party"?'

'A little premature perhaps, but I suppose I can get used to the sound of it,' the man joked, cracking open a bottle of 1962 Dom Perignon, and adding, 'I trust you're not adverse to champagne. It's one of the few things the French are still rather good at.'

'No, not at all,' the matronly woman replied, holding out her glass. 'Though that's more than I can say about that arschloch Pierre Valdron and those juvenile delinquents he relies on for his support. One thing I never thought was that the French lacked finesse.'

'Which is why he's always fallen short of what it takes to be a credible leader,' the host nodded.

'In that case, maybe you should give him lessons.'

'What – and risk that he'd take my place in your affections?'

'If only . . .' The German woman sighed and fluttered

her eyelashes. Then: 'Sorry, Ozzie dear, I forgot you like your women a little younger.'

'I'm sure I could still be tempted – under the right circumstances,' Oscar Gruber said flirtatiously, refilling her glass.

'Careful, *mein lieber*, I might just hold you to it one day.'

The Austrian leader smiled. The evening had gone better than he could have expected. Now he'd secured Gretchen Schwab's Nationalist People's Party in reshaping the European Parliament, none of the others mattered a toss. Those such as Belgium's Thomas Peeters and Ronald Maas in Holland, once they realised where their best interests were served, would join them anyway. Regarding the British, they needed to be forced to make up their minds whether they were in or out. If his instinct proved correct, it would mean the latter, since he couldn't see them dispensing with their precious pound. In any case, in his eyes, they had never been truly European. As for the rest, they could make meaningless alliances between themselves for all he cared.

Naturally, he knew that money talked and the fifty million Euros he'd committed of his own money to the new venture, albeit in strict contravention of EU regulations, was small fry compared to what he was getting in return, a political platform for the millions of people whose opinions his newspapers had successfully influenced. He only wished his mother was alive to see her dream fulfilled.

8

Daylight had just broken into a space barely big enough to accommodate a simple chest of drawers and a fold-up bed. So much about the Hirschmans' modest abode in the Leopoldstadt reminded Elizabeth of Charlotte's flat. When she had returned the previous evening, the similarity sent a shudder down her spine. With so many conflicting emotions swirling around her head, it was hardly surprising that she'd woken feeling exhausted.

Strange that those intimate moments she had shared with Gideon Halevi, albeit wonderful at the time, had paled into insignificance beside the revelations about her Great-uncle Theo. She couldn't bear to return to London until she had found out more. But it was a struggle, as she knew the children would feel that she'd abandoned them if she didn't return soon. Perhaps Anthony was right and she was just being incredibly selfish! There was really no alternative but to ask for her mother to step in and lend a hand. The trouble was, there was so much to say it was difficult to know where to start. Nevertheless, when she felt more alert, she'd explain everything in a text.

Elizabeth reached casually for the *Time* magazine by the side of her bed. Looking at the image of the barefoot man in sunglasses, relaxing on the veranda of his house in Italy with a scantily clad young blonde woman by his side, it was hard to reconcile this bon viveur with a leader of an extreme right-wing party, let alone posing a credible threat to Austria's democracy.

Elisabeth showered, dressed and then went to make herself some breakfast. She was surprised to find Freda sitting in her usual chair in the living room, calmly sipping her tea. The same sense of serenity that she naturally exuded had returned, making it hard to detect that she had suffered such a recent loss.

'Hello Elizabeth, I do hope you slept well?' the old lady said warmly.

'Yes, thank you. It's really kind of you to let me stay but I shall be leaving this morning.'

'There's really no need for you to go and I could really do with the company. Please won't you reconsider?'

'Well, if you are sure … just until I've had the opportunity to delve a little further into the family history,' Elizabeth answered, sounding vague since she still hadn't fully made up her mind what she was going to do.

Freda's smile indicated to Elizabeth that she wasn't entirely convinced by her explanation.

'I thought there might have been another reason for you wanting to stay longer in Vienna?' the old lady said archly.

'I'm not sure I understand,' Elizabeth responded, puzzled.

'It's really none of my business but the two of you seem to get on so well.'

It only took a few seconds for Elizabeth to realise that Freda was referring to Gideon Halevi. It was also clear that when Elizabeth came back after lunch the previous day, Freda had assumed that it was because of Gideon and then, when she observed them sloping off together, it had proven her right. Elizabeth still felt deeply embarrassed that she had missed the funeral because of it.

'We're just acquaintances,' she added, feeling herself blushing. It was clear, however, that there was more to the old lady's relationship with the Mossad agent than she had imagined.

'Gideon has provided me with some interesting insights into my Great-uncle Theo,' she added cagily, hoping to provoke a reaction.

'Well, I hope that has made your journey worthwhile,' Freda said, not taking up the bait.

There was a brief pause. Freda Hirschman then continued, 'Ernst and I had much to be grateful for, due to that young man.'

Elizabeth wasn't sure whether it was a lapse of concentration that had caused the old lady to revert back to the Israeli or whether it was because Elizabeth had hit on a sensitive subject.

'Gideon did mention the security issues facing the Jewish community,' she said, deciding to play along.

'Though that's not the only reason why Vienna has taken on such importance for him,' Freda disclosed.

'Oh, really?' Elizabeth replied, wondering if he had confided in Freda regarding Oscar Gruber.

'Gideon's family was forced by the Germans to leave everything behind as a precondition to be allowed to move to Palestine, as it was called in those days,' Freda revealed.

'They were Austrian?' Elizabeth enquired incredulously.

'Yes, from here in Vienna. The Halevis were well-known intellectuals but alas, Ernst and I never made their acquaintance. The thing was, they never settled in their new country, and Gideon, being an only child, took the brunt of their unhappiness. Not unnaturally, he rebelled. On the one hand, he became fiercely Zionistic and at the same time determined that the fate that the Jews suffered in Europe would never be repeated. So now perhaps you can understand why he feels so protective towards us?'

'Yes, of course,' Elizabeth responded immediately. Now it all made sense. The anger he felt towards the extreme right-wing resurgence was because he and his family had personally suffered at their hands.

'It was wrong of me to pry,' Freda said contritely. 'You have a family of your own and I expect you'll want to get back to them.'

'Yes, I really miss the children,' Elizabeth admitted.

Freda raised an eyebrow but said nothing. Elizabeth could tell what she was thinking. The wily old bird picked up that she had made no mention of her husband. Perhaps she should justify her omission . . . but then she thought better of it. Her mind turned to Anthony. She would like to have felt something, but right now she was running on empty regarding any affection towards him. Maybe it would change when she got home, or was she just not prepared for the real possibility that their marriage might be over?

'I'm sorry. I've prevented you from having your breakfast,' Freda said, getting up from her chair.

'Please don't worry. I'm sure Joanna will show me where everything is.'

'I'm afraid Joanna has left. Her bags were already

packed when I got home last night.'

'That was sudden,' Elizabeth remarked, following Freda into the kitchen.

'The girl was very attached to Ernst and now he's gone, she decided she would go too,' the old lady explained, taking a carton of eggs from the fridge. 'Anyway, I'll manage.'

'Would you consider getting a replacement?' Elizabeth asked, aghast at the prospect of the old lady living all alone.

'Scrambled or would you prefer an omelette?' Freda enquired, seemingly oblivious to her predicament.

'Either would be lovely. I just don't want to put you to any trouble,' Elizabeth responded.

'If you wouldn't mind refilling the kettle and putting a couple of slices of bread in the toaster, that would be a great help.'

A few minutes later, as she was serving up her guest's breakfast of scrambled eggs on toast, Freda announced, 'There was a reason why Ernst and I made no mention of your mother's uncle. I don't know what Gideon told you about him, but it was most probably just the little that he could glean from the official records.'

'So, are you saying that there's more?' Elizabeth said.

'Yes, there is, but I'm afraid it doesn't show him in a particularly favourable light, which is why we were hoping that you wouldn't ask about him.'

'I know about the Austrian woman he was involved with before he disappeared, if that's what you mean?'

'That, my dear Elizabeth, is the least of it. You see, while the Germans were stripping ordinary Jews of their livelihood, Theo Frankl was thriving. He could often be spotted driving around town showing off his latest new motor car, a young woman in tow, or else be seen fraternising in the right circles, seemingly unconcerned about what was happening around him. Where he got his money from, no one was ever able to fully establish. It was well known, however, that he was heavily involved in the black market.'

'That can't be true,' Elizabeth protested, springing to Theo's defence. All her mother had said of him was just that he led a different life from the rest of her family. Nor was there any mention in her grandparents' letters to substantiate Freda's allegations.

By the expression on the old lady's face, she had not changed her assessment of the man. It was also clear that Freda was the source from which Gideon had received his information. Perhaps she would have felt the same way if she had been in their position. Elizabeth was tempted to ask if Freda could confirm Gideon's version of Theo Frankl's disappearance, but that was something she'd have to try and verify herself in the time she still had available. The difficulty was in knowing who to ask, when she'd already reached a dead end.

*

The weather had turned brighter and Elizabeth, hoping she hadn't caused Freda undue distress, decided on a walk in the park to clear her head. Passing the now familiar sight of the amusement park, she began piecing together all the information she'd been given about her great-uncle. Her mind turned to Lise Gruber, the woman with whom he'd apparently been in a relationship. Although it was a long shot, perhaps there was someone somewhere in

Vienna who might have known Lise and would be able to shed some light on what had happened to Theo. The question was, where to start. If, as Gideon suggested, Lise had presented him with a cover, it was fair to assume that she couldn't have been Jewish.

Elizabeth stopped at a park bench and searched for the main religion in Austria on her mobile phone, coming up with Catholic as she'd expected. It was all very well that Lise had married the Nazi officer, but she didn't know exactly when that was. Elizabeth assumed that Theo had met her several years earlier. With nothing conclusive to go on, the first step was to look for the existence of a marriage certificate to substantiate Gideon Halevi's assertions. Recalling that the Vienna municipal archives only originated in 1938, she took a chance and looked up where records of Catholic marriages were held before that time, and saw they were located at the *Erzbischöfliches Ordinariat*, the Archbishop's Palace in the city centre.

Cutting her visit short, Elizabeth left the park and hailed a taxi. At midday, she filled in a registration form, adding details of the marriage she was searching for, presented her mother's details as identification and was directed to the refectory – a stark room with a stone floor, long wooden benches and a particularly severe atmosphere. If it wasn't for a number of computer terminals incongruously placed at regular intervals, she might have entered a time warp. Once she'd logged in the details that had been texted to her, an official document suddenly flashed across her screen. Elizabeth was just about able to decipher the formal German writing, then froze in shock. Scrutinising the document for a second time, there was no mistake.

She was staring at a record of the holy union entered into on 3 November 1936 between Theodore Frankl, 28, and Lise Gruber, 23. It also appeared that the proceedings took place at St Stephen's Cathedral, here in Vienna, so what Gideon said about her great-uncle had only been partially accurate. The question going through her mind was: what else about this enigmatic character would be borne out by fact?

Paying 100 Austrian Schillings for an authorised copy of the certificate and without any plan of what to do when she got there, Elizabeth made the short journey on foot to the Stephansplatz in front of the cathedral. She wasn't going to risk being denied entry so decided to tag on to an official tour that had gathered outside the massive Gothic tower.

At the first opportunity, she broke away from the rest of the group and pretended to be examining a decorated sarcophagus until a church attendant passed by. Discreetly, she asked him in English where she might be able to locate past records of marriages. Listening carefully, she was able to make out that she needed to go to the Directorate of Finance and Administration which was outside, next to the cathedral, and on a higher level. Making her way through the courtyard of the ancient building and climbing three steep flights of stairs, she eventually found the office she was looking for at the end of a long, carpeted corridor.

It was unlikely that Theo could still be alive, but if she were able to establish the priest's identity, there was a chance he'd be able to provide her with a further insight into the true nature of her great-uncle.

Elizabeth rang a bell and, entering through a pair of

stained-glass doors into a wood-panelled room, she approached a well-rounded man in a cassock. He was perched uncomfortably behind an exquisitely carved desk.

'Excuse me, I wonder if you can help me?' she said, trying to catch her breath.

'How may I be of assistance?' the church official said in perfect English.

'I'm trying to establish whether the priest who officiated at a wedding here many years ago might still be alive.' Elizabeth handed over the certificate.

'And what is your particular interest in the matter, may I ask?'

'Theo Frankl was my great-uncle,' Elizabeth explained.

'So I take it you're tracing a family member in Vienna?' came the response, colder now.

'Yes, exactly. However, I haven't been able to learn a great deal about him so far. Just that he was married to a Lise Gruber in November 1936.'

'I see,' the administrator said, pretending to scrutinise the piece of paper in front of him. 'And I assume you have no idea whether this uncle of yours survived the war?'

'From what I understand, he didn't,' she said quietly.

'Hmm, like so many others. It was a tragic time for the Austrian people; they suffered terribly.' And the priest began mouthing a silent prayer.

It was clear to Elizabeth that the man suspected that Theo Frankl was a Jew. Acutely aware again of her own heritage, she felt extremely uneasy in the company of this individual.

After what seemed like an eternity, the priest suddenly opened his eyes.

'I'm sorry, Miss *Frankl*, that you've had a wasted journey,' he said, passing back the certificate without any further explanation.

In different circumstances, Elizabeth would have persevered but she knew it was hopeless.

'Thank you,' she said, noting from the way he had addressed her that her assessment of the fellow had been correct.

Just as she was stepping out of the room, a voice called after her: 'Perhaps with Fraulein Gruber, you may have more luck. At least she was a true Austrian!'

Elizabeth flashed a contemptuous look at the man and closed the door behind her. As she walked back up the corridor, another door opened and an elderly man appeared, holding on to the arm of a young male helper. A maroon cape disguised a painfully thin frame, and the only feature that offered a clue to his identity was the red skullcap sitting proudly on his head.

Still fulminating on the odious church official's parting words, Elizabeth didn't pay the pair any particular attention, apart from a simple *Guten Tag* as she passed by. She was therefore surprised to hear the fresh-faced young man address her formally, and in English.

'Madam, if you are looking for something, maybe I can be of assistance?'

Elizabeth stopped to gather her thoughts.

'I've been trying to gain some information on a relation of mine but it seems that I've reached an impasse. But thank you for your concern,' she said. The truth was, she just wanted to escape the place as quickly as possible.

'Please wait,' he said. 'If you've made the effort to come

to St Stephen's, I should like to help, and if I can't, I might be able to point you in the right direction.'

'That's very kind of you,' Elizabeth responded, encouraged by the contrast between his attitude and that of the obnoxious man she had just seen.

'If I may request you to remain here for five or ten minutes until Bishop Hoffner has his afternoon walk, we'd feel honoured to invite you in for a discussion and perhaps something hot to drink? The current Bishop kindly permits us the use of his apartment when he's away. He and Bishop Hoffner are old friends.'

At this, the elderly man with him smiled and nodded, although he was clinging to his stick and to his young helper.

'Yes, of course. Thank you both so very much,' Elizabeth responded, grateful for any opportunity that might help her to salvage her visit.

9

Another period of prolonged silence had enveloped the small living quarters where Elizabeth sat sipping her mug of black tea, glancing periodically at the old priest opposite, whilst he seemed to drift in and out of reality. She assumed that he must be particularly eminent in the church hierarchy to have been granted use of the private accommodation. She still had no inkling, however, why on hearing the name of Theo Frankl, he had suddenly dismissed his young aide. Elizabeth could only assume that something had resonated with him, going back many years, and with which he was now trying to come to terms.

After a while, he began to speak, 'Elizabeth, my dear child, I cannot tell you how long I've waited for this day. I feared I would not live long enough to see my prayers come to fruition.'

'I'm sorry, Your Eminence, but with respect is it possible that you have confused me with someone else?' Her comment brought a broad smile to the bishop's gaunt, but still handsome face.

'At my advanced age, it certainly would not be for the first time,' he said light-heartedly. 'But not in this case. There was only one Theo Frankl,' he pronounced fondly.

Elizabeth suddenly felt her heart pounding at the thought that she might unwittingly have found what she was looking for.

'You knew my great-uncle?' she asked.

'If you'll excuse my immodesty, I'd like to think we were extremely close friends.'

Hearing this, Elizabeth was too dumbfounded to respond.

'A Jew and a Catholic priest – yes, I can truly say it was an unlikely friendship,' he replied, accurately interpreting the expression of disbelief on his visitor's face.

He went on: 'It's a long story but one which I recall as if it were only yesterday. If you permit me, I'll start at the beginning.'

'Yes, of course, but I shouldn't want to tire you,' Elizabeth said.

'How considerate. Alas, with my health deteriorating, I may not be afforded another opportunity.'

He smiled at her and then he continued: 'We were both junior reporters. Theodore's family were wealthy Viennese bankers, if my memory serves me correctly?'

'So I've been told,' Elizabeth remarked, all of a sudden gripped by the image of her Grandfather Viktor dispensing largesse on the Ringstrasse.

'I, on the other hand, was a lad from a modest village in Lower Austria and had come to Vienna to seek my fortune.'

'But hadn't you dedicated yourself to the Church?' Elizabeth asked.

'I'm speaking of a good few years earlier. Be patient, dear lady, and I will explain. I got a job on the *Arbeiter-Zeitung*, a socialist newspaper, which was where my political affiliations lay. Theo, being far better connected, was a reporter on the more prestigious *Die Presse*. However, he always took an interest in what was going on at our paper. Although he never admitted to it, I'm certain it was because he happened to share many of its views.'

'I really had no idea!' Elizabeth exclaimed, showing her surprise.

'Your mother's uncle was a contradiction in so many ways.'

Elizabeth sat up in anticipation.

'You see, on the one hand he was, how shall I say, a man of sophisticated tastes. Not that he was ostentatious in any way, you understand. It was just that he enjoyed the good things in life. He certainly wasn't going to let something as simple as the Germans marching into Vienna affect the comfortable life he'd created for himself.'

'That was presumably the reason he got married to an Austrian woman?' Elizabeth said.

The remark seemed to knock the old priest sideways. 'I see you've been extremely thorough in your research,' he said hesitantly.

'I found that out purely by accident,' Elizabeth confessed.

'There was a lot more to it than just that. You see, Theo had an eye for beautiful women and, if I may be permitted to say so, the woman you spoke of unquestionably fitted into that category. Moreover, it appeared he was deeply in love with her.'

Elizabeth listened attentively.

'He was, however, playing a dangerous game. This particular woman was working at the time in the Ministry of the Interior; you may not be aware of this, but the officials there were shamefully responsible when the Germans took over for organising forced emigration from Austria.'

Elizabeth nodded sadly.

'Without any regard for his own safety, this put your Great-uncle Theo in direct contact with high-ranking officers of that unsavoury regime but it also enabled him to help a certain Dutch woman who was working tirelessly to help Jewish children escape the terrible fate that awaited most of their families.'

'You mean on the Kindertransport?' Elizabeth blurted out.

'Precisely. Apparently, ten thousand children were saved in that way.'

'One of whom was my mother,' Elizabeth revealed, 'although she never told me how it was that she was included, or who had facilitated her journey.'

'It's likely she didn't know. But you can be certain that your great-uncle had a hand in it.'

Elizabeth thought of the handsome man in the background of the painting at the railway station. Although she had never questioned her mother's explanation that Theo had helped her escape, the impression she now had of him feathering his own nest while his fellow Jews suffered, wouldn't go away!

And however much she wanted to feel convinced by what the elderly priest was telling her, it all seemed so far-fetched and unreal – this revelation coming to light from a chance meeting with a Catholic priest, who had been a close friend of Theo all those years ago.

The old man had drifted off again. The conversation

and the emotion evoked had obviously taken their toll. If there was more to tell, perhaps she could come back again. Just as Elizabeth got up to leave, he stirred and, clearly disorientated, he asked, 'You are who?'

'Elizabeth Frankl,' she said, reverting to her family name.

'I apologise. I get easily confused these days. And we were discussing...?'

'My Great-uncle Theo?'

'Yes, now I remember. And now you are leaving: you must have many other matters to attend to.'

'It's only that I've taken up enough of your time,' Elizabeth replied nervously.

'Not in the slightest, my dear child! Quite the opposite. Your miraculous appearance has provided me with more relief than you can possibly imagine.'

'I'm not sure I understand,' Elizabeth said, sitting down again.

'You will, all in good time. But first I need to explain how our friendship developed.'

'You mean when you were both reporters?'

The priest nodded. 'There was an uprising in 1934. Clashes broke out all over Austria between Fascist and Socialist forces. It only lasted a few days but the consequences were severe. A thousand died and many more were injured; even our beloved Cardinal Innitzer's Palace was ransacked. Order was restored eventually but not before the authorities banned the Socialist Democratic Party and its affiliated organisations including the *Arbeiter-Zeitung*.'

'It must have been a frightening experience,' Elizabeth

sympathised.

'True. What I witnessed had a profound effect upon me. That's when I realised that my calling was to devote the rest of my life to the Church.'

'But that was a huge commitment,' Elizabeth said.

'Not as huge as you may think. Coming from a devoutly religious village which produced more priests than most other places in Austria, I'd intended to follow suit, if I hadn't succumbed to the temptation to travel to Vienna. Like most nineteen year olds, I foolishly believed that the grass was greener here.'

'So what happened?' Elizabeth asked, finding herself caught up in the story.

'Things didn't turn out as I'd expected. Anyway, I only had a year left at the seminary, and with Theo's generosity . . .'

'He supported you?' Elizabeth said incredulously.

'Yes, for two years after my ordination,' the bishop replied with a voice full of emotion. 'It is something I will never forget. Though I was later able to reciprocate in some small way.'

'And how was that?' Elizabeth asked, feeling a genuine admiration for her great-uncle for the first time.

'I had the privilege of performing their marriage ceremony.'

'Wasn't that taking a huge risk?'

'I didn't look at it in that way. With only a few minor irregularities in the paperwork, it didn't attract any suspicion from the Germans. It was the least I could do in the circumstances.'

Elizabeth struggled to take it all in, so implausible did it sound compared to what she had gleaned from Freda and Gideon Halevi. It wasn't their fault; they couldn't possibly have known about Theo's surreptitious friendship with the young priest at St Stephen's Cathedral.

'Did your friendship continue after the marriage?' she enquired.

The elderly man took his time in answering. Elizabeth noticed that by the change in his expression, he was about to embark on a painful episode.

'I'd like to think so,' he said after a short while.

'But all was not well?' Elizabeth asked quietly.

'You're a very perceptive young woman. With the Germans taking full control of the city, events took a turn for the worse, especially for the Jews.'

'And for Theo?' Elizabeth concluded.

'I tried to warn him that he couldn't assume he'd be safe any longer.'

'And I take it that he wasn't receptive to your warning?'

'On the few occasions we were able to meet, he didn't seem particularly concerned. He still said that he had no intention of leaving; remember, it was still just about possible to leave the country at that time, and being a man of means, he could have started a new life in America as many others did.'

Not for the first time over the last hour, Elizabeth experienced another switch of emotions regarding her mysterious great-uncle. Why would he deliberately endanger himself if he had the opportunity to escape, was the question now going through her mind. But then didn't her grandparents also turn down the opportunity to flee, thinking that the upheaval was only temporary?

'There was something else that explained his intransigence,' the bishop said.

Elizabeth waited in anticipation for yet another dramatic revelation.

'You see, Lise was with child.'

'Yes, I found out that she had a son.'

'Indeed she did – but are you aware of the father's identity?'

'Taking the name Gruber, I'd assumed the child was from a former relationship of his mother Lise,' Elizabeth replied. Gideon had mentioned a German officer, though his name escaped her.

'A reasonable assumption in the circumstances, but one that is incorrect.'

'I'm afraid I don't understand.'

'Theo, your great-uncle, was the boy's true father.'

Elizabeth gasped in disbelief.

'I realise this must have come as a shock,' the priest said.

'I had no idea,' Elizabeth mumbled. The other thing was, why neither Gideon nor Freda had mentioned anything about there being a child involved?

'It was of no great surprise to me. They were, after all, a couple who were devoted to each other; at least, it appeared so at the time!'

'Because the marriage didn't last, you mean?' Elizabeth didn't quite follow.

'It was my honour to baptise their son,' the old priest enthused, deftly avoiding the question.

'But surely Theo could have persuaded his wife to leave?' Elizabeth said innocently.

'It wasn't that simple. Lise was a proud Austrian woman

and she intended to bring up her son in the same way.'

'But she was married to a Jew,' Elizabeth butted in.

'And therein, unfortunately, lay the problem.'

'And so they parted?'

'It wasn't Theo's choice.' The elderly man paused for a few seconds before taking up the story. 'Remember, we weren't living in normal times: it wasn't unusual for the soundest of marriages to come under strain,' he explained, choosing his words carefully.

'So Theo remained in Vienna for the child's sake?' Elizabeth asked.

'I wish with all my heart that had been the worst of it. My dear child, please prepare yourself, for there's no easy way of telling you what happened next.'

Elizabeth braced herself.

'Theo came to see me one day. His natural optimism had finally deserted him. He had got hold of a list of names, including those of his family who had been sent to Auschwitz concentration camp, and knew it was only a question of time before he was forced to join them.'

'Couldn't Lise have utilised her connections at the Ministry to help him?' Elizabeth burst out. 'After all, he was the father of her child.'

'I'm afraid those connections proved fatal: they were, in fact, the cause of his demise.'

'In what way do you mean?"

'Theodore confided in me that Lise had met another man – a well-to-do German officer – and he was convinced that this man wanted him out of the way.'

'What – and this Lise just went along with it?' Elizabeth demanded.

'I've often wondered the same thing. Perhaps she was afraid. She couldn't exactly deny the relationship with Theodore when there was a marriage certificate in existence to prove it.'

'In that case, how was it possible for her to have married someone else?' Elizabeth asked, not divulging that she already knew about the other man in Lise's life from Gideon Halevi.

The priest suddenly became pensive. 'Normally it wouldn't have been possible,' he said.

'I'm sorry – once again I don't understand,' Elizabeth told him.

'I was being threatened. You see, I had given Theo shelter – and harbouring a Jew was punishable by death.'

'Here in the cathedral?' Elizabeth asked.

The priest nodded. His face had turned a deathly pale.

'He was no longer living with his Lise and had nowhere else to go. I'd devised a way for him to spend the rest of the war at an abbey in my village. Sadly, the Germans got to him first.'

'So, between them, they conspired to get rid of my great-uncle?' Elizabeth muttered. Despite the over-heated room, she had broken out in a cold sweat.

'Please don't judge the woman too harshly,' the old priest pleaded. 'Self-preservation was very much the norm in those extreme conditions.'

'Even at the expense of innocent men, women and children?' Elizabeth retorted angrily.

'Very much so, I have to confess. However, I was able to make amends in some small way. To avoid any trace of Lise's association with Theo, I was ordered to destroy their original marriage certificate.'

'You mean so it was as though he never existed? But that's dreadful!'

Elizabeth was on the verge of weeping.

'That was the only way the two could get married,' the old priest pointed out.

'And you gave your consent?' Elizabeth was horrified that he would have countenanced such a thing.

'Remember, the marriage entered into by Lise and your Great-uncle Theodore was sacrosanct in the eyes of God. And since the Catholic Church didn't recognise divorce at the time, there was no way that Lise's marriage to the German officer would be valid.'

'So what did you do?' Elizabeth asked, thinking she had been too hasty in her condemnation.

'Firstly, I came up with an excuse why I wasn't able to officiate at the proceedings and gave precise instructions to the young priest who took my place, ordering him to omit certain crucial aspects of the service, so the ceremony was nothing more than a sham.'

'And their marriage certificate?' Elizabeth queried.

'That was authentic enough, at least on paper. I'd kept my side of the bargain, or so they thought.'

'I'm not sure I follow.'

'When it was safe to do so, I switched the certificates back again.'

'How could you do that?'

'I consulted with the Archbishop, who agreed with my interpretation that Lise's second marriage to Walter Brandt was performed under duress and therefore was invalid.'

'That's really unbelievable!'

'What – that a Catholic Bishop was capable of such deception?' the old priest joked feebly.

'No, that's not what I meant.'

Elizabeth forced a smile. Perhaps now she had found out the truth about her uncle, she had achieved her purpose and should leave the old priest in peace.

She was just about to thank the Bishop for a second time and bid him goodbye when there was a knock at the door.

'Enter!' he answered in a frail voice.

The Bishop's carer opened the door. He was holding a metal strongbox, covered with a thin film of dust, which he placed beside his superior.

'Thank you, Franz,' the old man replied. 'If you would do me a kindness and look in the centre drawer of my writing bureau, you'll find a single key.'

The young priest bowed obediently and left, reappearing holding a key.

Elizabeth looked on in puzzlement as the old man, his hand shaking slightly, attempted to open the repository. All of a sudden, the lid sprang open and he carefully withdrew a heavy gauze packet and passed it across to his guest. Elizabeth could see it was sealed with the emblem of St Stephen's and seemed to have successfully stood the test of time.

'This was given to me for safekeeping by your great-uncle, shortly before he was arrested in 1942. He made me vow that it should remain unopened unless anyone of the Frankl family were alive to claim it. You, my dear Elizabeth, are that person. It's now yours for you to do with it as you see fit.'

Overcome by curiosity, Elizabeth accepted the offer of an ivory letter-opener and then, taking great care, she proceeded to slice open the package. It only took a brief moment to see that inside was an envelope addressed to *Ozzie Frankl*, whom she now believed, without a shadow of doubt, was Theo's son. Why she should be the one to take possession of it suddenly seemed wrong and prevented her from proceeding. Surely, if Ozzie were still alive, rightly it belonged to him? In which case, there was nothing stopping the bishop from making contact with him directly?

She was just about to ask for clarification when the novitiate turned to her, saying softly, 'Now my master really needs to rest.'

'Yes, of course.' Still trying to fully absorb the revelations of the last hour, she got up from her chair and moved over to the old priest a few feet away.

'Your Grace, I really don't know how to thank you.'

'It's you whom I should be thanking, my child. You have relieved me of the terrible guilt that I've been carrying all these years,' he said remorsefully.

'But from what I heard, you did everything possible for Theo.'

'It's kind of you to say so, but I fear it's not the truth. I shall always regret just standing by when the Germans took him away.'

'You mustn't blame yourself,' Elizabeth said shakily.

'So I have your forgiveness?'

'Yes, of course, with all my heart,' Elizabeth replied, trying to make the old man feel better.

'Thank you. Thank you so very much, Elizabeth.'

The elderly man sighed heavily and closed his eyes. The tormented expression present up until a few minutes ago had now been replaced by a look of serenity.

*

It was early evening when Elizabeth returned to the flat in the 2nd district. Relieved that Freda wasn't around, she made straight for her room. She was in no mood to be sociable. Having accomplished more than she could ever have imagined possible a mere twenty-four hours earlier, she should have felt upbeat, but instead she felt depressed. Perhaps it was because she was no longer able to justify extending her stay.

The text she'd received from her mother earlier, most probably at the behest of her children, asking her to call, persuaded her that she should go home.

Elizabeth stretched out on the bed and placed the envelope back in the metal deposit box open next to her. That was when she noticed something that resembled a secret compartment. Easily sliding it open, she fished out the several velvet pouches carefully lining the perimeter. Methodically untying each of the drawstrings, Elizabeth saw that the pouches contained a number of diamonds and other precious stones. Now she understood why the bishop was so insistent that she take the box with her, since he must have known all along about the treasure trove hidden in the cathedral vaults. This was obviously all that her Great-uncle Theo had managed to spirit away before he met his inevitable demise. Elizabeth realized now that it behoved her to share all she'd discovered about him that afternoon.

There was, however, something else troubling her

about his son – something that had lingered in her mind although she was unable to bring it into focus.

All of a sudden, it hit her! Since the boy had reverted to using his mother Lise's maiden name at some stage, she hadn't grasped the fact that Ozzie Frankl and Oscar Gruber were one and the same person. The leader of Austria's ultra-right-wing political party was her second cousin!

The shock took her breath away. Slowly, everything started to fall into place. But then she asked herself why she and not Oscar had been chosen to take possession of the old box. Perhaps the Monseigneur had concluded for some reason that he wasn't the person best placed to reveal the truth to Oscar about his father. Elizabeth's thoughts then turned to Gideon Halevi. She wouldn't have put it past him to have known about the connection all along. It was just like him to feed her enough little snippets of information to keep her from returning to London – but this was a far more serious matter. It had seemed strange at the time for him to have readily divulged the highly sensitive nature of his mission in Vienna, but she could see now that it was no accident.

Her blood went cold. Reaching for the phone, she had to find a way of stopping the Israeli from carrying out his mission before it was too late!

10

Elizabeth stood in the middle of the Jewish Ghetto feeling mixed emotions. Freda had taken to her bed with a heavy cold and Elizabeth had made the short journey from the Prater on foot. The meeting with Bishop Hoffner had left her with a great desire to find out more about her Jewish heritage. Hoping to see some remains where half a dozen synagogues once stood, she had to do instead with a gentrified area of pastel-coloured buildings and fashionable restaurants inhabited by artists and musicians. The scene bore little resemblance to the picture she had conjured up.

Meeting in the Karmelitermarkt Square, where they would draw less attention to themselves, was the Israeli's suggestion. He must have detected from the tone of her voicemail that it was important. She didn't delude herself that his prompt reply had anything to do with the episode of passion they had shared. For herself, however, and despite the fact that she knew he had an agenda, she found herself thinking about their lovemaking often. Now, with everything she'd discovered about her great-uncle and his son, was she a step ahead of the Mossad operative?

Elizabeth was beginning to give up hope when she saw a tense-looking Gideon Halevi striding towards her.

'What did you want to talk about? I'm short of time,' he

said brusquely, keeping his distance.

Caught off-guard by the lack of warmth, Elizabeth had difficulty in summoning a response.

'Very well. Why didn't you tell me that Oscar Gruber was Theo Frankl's son?' she said, coming straight to the point.

A wry smile appeared on the Israeli's handsome face.

'Come, let's walk and talk,' he said, taking Elizabeth by the arm. 'I can see you haven't been idle since we saw each other last.'

'What did you expect?' she returned, as brusque as he had been.

There was no response.

'Look, if I had told you, you wouldn't have believed me, would you?' Gideon said eventually, taking the long way around the square.

'So you admit you were just stringing me along?' Her tone was angry.

'Elizabeth, you're an exceptionally intelligent woman.'

'And that's supposed to make me feel better, is it?'

'So, are you cross about the fact I misled you – or maybe it's something else?' he said, smirking.

'You're a real bastard!' Elizabeth countered, trying to divert her gaze from the man who she found it so hard to resist.

'In that case, I am a bastard with whom you'd best not get involved,' Gideon retorted.

'Whether I like it or not,' Elizabeth said tightly, 'we seem to have been thrown together. I've come here to say that you can't carry out your plan to assassinate Oscar Gruber.'

'It's not as simple as that.'

'I don't understand. Didn't you tell me that if the right

person could get to him, you might call it off?'

'I was talking hypothetically.'

'Please, give me the opportunity of seeing what I can do first,' Elizabeth asked passionately. She was perfectly aware that relying on the proof she'd obtained to enlighten Oscar Gruber on his Jewish background – and to show him that she was his second cousin – was unlikely to make him renounce his political affiliation . . . but for the sake of her mother Lillian and the family she'd lost, and the family Oscar had lost, and for the sake of the wonderful Bishop who had protected Oscar's father for as long as he could, she owed it to them to make the effort.

Gideon spoke patiently. 'Elizabeth, with the greatest respect, you really don't know who you are dealing with.'

'You are wrong. I'm the only who does!' she hit back. At this point, there was no way she was going to expose herself by revealing the contents of the metal deposit box.

'All right,' Gideon sighed. 'Suppose we agree to go along with this fantasy of yours, how do you intend getting to Herr Gruber? Because you can't very well go up and ring his intercom and expect to be greeted with open arms.'

'I might ask you the same thing,' Elizabeth said.

'You don't expect me to discuss the details of our plan. That's top secret!'

'I would have thought it was a reasonable trade, don't you?' Elizabeth said, feeling emboldened.

'You really are something else.' Gideon laughed out loud.

'So you've said, but that still doesn't answer my question.'

'All right. Look, I'm willing to share certain information that could provide you with access to him,' the Israeli conceded. He knew he was taking a hell of a chance, but if it avoided an international incident, it just might be worth it.

Elizabeth took a deep breath in anticipation of what was coming next.

'We have it on good authority that the leader of Austria's far-right party will be hosting an informal gathering to celebrate the anniversary of his election to parliament tomorrow evening.'

'So what's that got to do with me?'

'We know who is on the guest-list – or should I say who's *not* on it.'

'You're not making yourself clear,' Elizabeth said impatiently.

'Let's just say that one of Gruber's Eastern European friends has been taken ill at the last moment and will be sending his deputy in his place. It so happens the individual in question is single, so it won't look suspicious for a female to accompany him.'

'Surely you're not suggesting me?' Elizabeth blurted out.

'You're English, so that's an advantage and there's no one else who'll be attending from the UK to quiz you about who you are.'

'Tell me under what pretence I am supposed to be there?'

'That's for you to decide,' the Israeli said tersely. 'I'm just facilitating your entry. The rest is up to you.'

Elizabeth couldn't believe what she was hearing. It sounded more like a film plot than a real-life situation; the problem was, she couldn't come up with a better solution – and if it meant putting off the assassination of Oscar

Gruber, she had to give it careful consideration.

She frowned. 'And my escort for the evening is who, exactly?'

'Lukas Petronis, vice-president of the Lithuanian Nationalist Movement.'

'And I assume he's aware about this?'

'Once you agree, he'll be informed.'

Elizabeth pondered for a moment. Everything felt so contrived, as if she'd been set up from the day she had first met Gideon Halevi. He had accurately predicted that she would follow the scent until she'd learned everything about her Great-uncle Theo and his son – information that Gideon already knew. Now, when she had foolishly believed she was in control, Gideon had once again exposed her naivety by recruiting her to do his dirty work.

'And if don't agree?' Elizabeth said, both of them knowing full well she wasn't going to decline.

The Israeli smiled briefly and marched off in the opposite direction before stopping abruptly. 'Wear something revealing,' he said, without turning around. 'Oscar Gruber has an eye for a good-looking woman.'

Elizabeth grimaced. What had she got herself involved in? All of a sudden, she felt a strong temptation to pack up and go home. There was no way Gideon could keep her in Vienna against her will. She'd found out more than she'd ever dreamed to, about Theo Frankl; the rest she would forget. What Mossad got up to with regards to Oscar Gruber was really none of her business – or was it? She didn't doubt the Israeli's ruthless plan to carry out his threat, if she just walked away.

*

Gideon waited till he was out of view and tapped the number into his mobile phone. *Ben Zona!* Son of a whore! He swore when there was no response from the other end. He needed to get hold of the Lithuanian thug in order to tell him of the change of plan, and prayed that he wasn't already too late!

*

The smartly dressed man checked himself again in the passenger mirror then eased himself out of the chauffeur-driven limousine. Oscar Gruber entered the ATV studios at precisely midday, unaware of his image in the telescopic viewfinder of the high-velocity rifle positioned on him a few minutes before. He could have done without making the diversion to the Media Quarter, but the chance of appearing on Kurt Brunner's prime lunchtime TV show was hard to turn down. With the show's audience mainly consisting of good Viennese Hausfraus, he could use the opportunity to increase his popularity and tell them what they wanted to hear. His office had been supplied with a list of topics for his approval beforehand, but Oscar was wary: he had it on good authority that the openly gay presenter was a shit-stirrer who enjoyed being controversial.

At 12.45 the intro music started, followed by shouts of approval from the invited audience as the cameras homed in on the slight figure of a man with high-lighted blond hair, reclining in an oversized leather armchair.

'Hello, and thank you,' the man said, trying to make himself heard above the continuing applause before a raised arm brought it abruptly to an end. He then switched his attention to the expensively dressed man positioned on a low settee a few feet away,

'My first guest's face appears on billboards and posters all over Vienna, not forgetting the film-star status afforded to him everywhere he goes. Seen by many as Austria's next President-in-waiting, welcome Oscar Gruber!'

'Thank you for inviting me,' Gruber responded, accompanied by enthusiastic shouts of approval from the studio gathering.

'May I begin by asking how you obtained that disgustingly healthy suntan?' Brunner began playfully.

'I've had a few weekends away in Saint Anton,' the guest replied casually.

'You have your own place in the village there and a few other homes besides that in Italy and New York, I believe?'

'I do, yes, not that I get to use them as much as I would like.'

'Since you've devoted all your energies to the Freedom Party, do you mean?'

'That's right, Kurt. I didn't realise fully what was involved beforehand.'

'So I am fascinated to find out what drew you into politics at a relatively late stage in life?'

'It was really just a natural progression from what we've achieved through G Medien.'

'Your group of newspapers, which our researchers inform us has one of the largest readerships in Europe right now!' the host announced, resulting in a short burst of applause.

'We're really proud of the number of people whose views we've been able to influence,' Gruber replied. 'Now we simply feel we've secured a mandate to carry out their will.'

'Would you mind elaborating for us and for those watching at home, what exactly your policies are?'

'Certainly. It's well documented that our prime objective is to restore the national pride of the Austrian people.'

'I wasn't aware that we'd actually lost it,' Brunner said facetiously as an aside to a couple seated in the front row.

'There are many people in this country who are extremely concerned about their jobs, who wouldn't necessarily agree with you,' Gruber came back at him.

'Could you be more specific?' Brunner replied, intent on drawing his guest out.

'With pleasure. When you have an open-border policy that allows an unrestricted influx of people willing to work for considerably lower wages than our own workers – in our factories, for example – naturally it's going to cause resentment.'

'You're not suggesting that Austria would be better off out of the European Union you signed up for, are you?'

'No, not at all, it's just that we have a responsibility to—'

'And with the fact that unemployment in Austria at 4 per cent is one of the lowest in the world and currently less than half of the rest of the EU, aren't you only fuelling the fire of resentment?' the interviewer interrupted.

'Kurt, you've asked an important question; at least extend me the courtesy of allowing me to give you a response.'

'You're right, I apologise,' the chat-show host retracted.

'I'm aware of the figures but the trend is upwards. I'm merely stressing that we must be seen to do more to protect the livelihoods of Austrian citizens,' the politician resumed, retaining his composure.

'Very well, I think it's pretty clear where you stand on *that* subject. Let's turn to more about Oscar Gruber, the man. By your own admission you came from very comfortable beginnings, so I'm curious to learn what contributed to your unbridled drive to succeed?'

'You can probably put that down to my failing as an actor.'

'Failure's not a word you would normally associate with Oscar Gruber!' the host came back, quick as a flash.

Gruber shrugged. 'But that's what happened. I'd gone over to America in the 1960s.'

'After you finished university in Berlin, wasn't it?'

'Yes. My family moved to Germany when I was very young.'

'Although you retained your Austrian nationality?'

'My mother was Austrian.'

'And your father?'

'He was German. I didn't see very much of him, growing up. He was away on business a lot of the time.'

'And what business was that?'

'Nothing terribly exciting. The company was in engineering.'

'And you were an only child. It must have been lonely?'

'Not really. I was always closer to my mother and had some good friends.' Oscar always wondered whether that was the cause of the hostility his father demonstrated towards him. Strange, that after all this time, it still caused him pain.

'We got side-tracked. You started talking about America?' Brunner said.

'I didn't know what I wanted to do after university. I

loved the cinema and had taken a few acting lessons so I thought I'd go where the action was and see if I could make it in Hollywood.'

'How old were you at this stage?'

'Twenty-two.'

'And your parents didn't object?'

'They weren't overly pleased, but since I was prepared to pay my own way, there wasn't much they could do about it!'

'It sounds like you had a point to prove.'

'You're right, although I wasn't conscious of it at the time.'

'But surely it wasn't easy just to uproot. Wasn't there anybody special in your life at the time?'

'I didn't claim I went on my own,' the guest countered, and then regretted it.

'I assume they didn't approve of whoever it was then?' the interviewer probed.

Oscar didn't offer a response. He was damned if he was going to let that little shit go any further. He'd made a point of stressing that his private life was definitely out of bounds.

'I thought you wanted to talk about what happened in Hollywood?' he said, cleverly changing the subject.

'I'm getting there,' Brunner replied with a wry smile that indicated he was still the one in charge of proceedings. Then, taking a sip of water from his glass, he continued, 'All right then, so tell us how the change of career came about.'

'I was at a party at the Hollywood home of a man by the name of Seth Robins. You might have heard of him?'

'You're referring to the owner of the San Francisco Bears, not forgetting the largest newspaper chain on the West Coast?' Brunner confirmed.

'That's right. Anyway, I was friendly with his goddaughter and she thought he'd help me.'

'So would you say you were disillusioned with acting at that stage?'

'I'd given it a fair whack for a couple of years without being offered any decent parts and quite frankly, I'd got pretty fed up sharing a room with two other guys and long hours serving in diners to make ends meet.' Oscar smiled charmingly at the camera.

'So you were on the look-out, as it were?'

'That's right, though I didn't really know what I wanted to do. I had a business degree but was more interested in the way media shaped public opinion.'

'We've learned from bitter experience how easily we Austrians can be influenced, especially in the wrong hands, have we not?' Brunner said provocatively.

Oscar Gruber gave the interviewer a disdainful look. He deeply resented the clumsy reference to the Nazi era but wouldn't allow himself to rise to the bait.

Ignoring the jibe, he went on: 'I must have created a favourable impression because he offered to back me, so I went ahead and purchased an old-established newspaper in Vienna, still living on its pre-war reputation, and managed to turn it around. A few other acquisitions followed and it wasn't long before we had a meaningful presence in the industry.'

'And the rest is history, as they say, and it's all thanks to that man Seth for giving you your first break, and of course, his goddaughter. By the way, what did happen to her?'

'She probably ended up marrying someone else,' Oscar replied casually.

'And you didn't?' the interviewer said slyly.

'A bit like you, Kurt, I've never quite got around to it,' the guest said.

'Touché,' the slight man responded, hiding his discomfort. 'Well, it's been fascinating. Thanks so much for making time in your busy schedule to drop by and talk to us. Oscar Gruber, everyone!'

11

Elizabeth entered the elegant building opposite the opera house accompanied by a lanky fair-haired man in an ill-fitting suit who looked completely out of character for the role that had been assigned to him, not that she had any idea what he'd been told. The prospect of spending the evening with a man who spoke little English and stank of stale cigarettes wasn't exactly appealing. After her initial resistance, Elizabeth had taken on board Gideon's comments and purchased a tight-fitting red taffeta dress that left little to the imagination. If that's what it was going to take for the host to notice her, then it was an effort worth making. If she did manage to get to Herr Gruber and talk to him, she just hoped he wouldn't dismiss her and what she had to say.

Giving their names to a beefy man on security, the pair were superficially frisked for any dangerous objects then directed to take the lift to the penthouse suite. Here, on arrival, they were supplied with tastefully designed nametags.

Swarmed on by a posse of female servers armed with exotic cocktails and trays of hot canapés, Elizabeth helped herself to a Kir Royale and passed on into a space of ballroom-size proportions, packed with middle-aged men with large stomachs and bejewelled female partners, all speaking in a number of different languages.

Feeling completely out of place, she wondered what had possessed her to come. The phone conversation with her mother, earlier in the day, had stayed with her. Far from reprimanding her for abandoning her family, Lillian was full of praise for her daughter for having the resolve to do what she herself had never had the courage to do. She wanted to know everything that Elizabeth had discovered about the Frankls. Eizabeth told her a little, but explained that there was more, and that she would tell her the whole story when she was back.

Elizabeth asked how the family were getting on without her. The only point of concern wasn't Emily and Freddie, Lillian said, since they were faring well without their mother, but with Anthony. Lillian said he seemed unusually preoccupied: perhaps it had to do with some problem or other at work. Strange, Elizabeth thought, because her husband normally confided in her, and he hadn't mentioned anything about a problem before he went skiing. Still, having already decided, come what may, that this was going to be her last night in Vienna, she'd find out soon enough, assuming he was still talking to her!

Taking the initiative to go over and introduce herself to her host, she was stopped in her tracks by a loud explosion and the sound of shattering glass. Thick smoke filled the room that had been thrown into darkness; it was impossible to determine what had occurred. Knocked off-balance by the force of the blast, Elizabeth covered her head in her hands, expecting a second device to go off at any second. But there was no repeat, just an eerie silence interrupted by the sound of bewildered and distressed voices. Her first thought was that Gideon had carried out his threat, followed by berating herself for being prepared to put her children at risk.

Suddenly, there were shouts of: '*Achtung! Achtung!* Don't move! Stay where you are!' coming from the floor below, which only seemed to increase the panic of those guests desperate to find their way out. The blare of sirens just moments later provided Elizabeth with the reassurance that help was on its way.

At the same time, the emergency generator kicked in, light was restored and the true extent of the damage became evident. The front of the triple-aspect room had buckled under the impact but, miraculously, no one appeared to have suffered serious injury.

Elizabeth looked around for Lukas but he was nowhere to be seen. She found, instead, a dazed Oscar Gruber in the middle of the room, clutching his shoulder. They exchanged glances, neither able to find words to express what they'd just experienced.

Half a dozen special officers from the EKO Cobra counter-terrorism unit, expecting the worst, were the first to arrive with their hands at the ready on their automatic weapons. A team of paramedics equipped with resuscitation equipment and stretchers followed them a few minutes later. Meanwhile, a television crew, intent on being first to capture the breaking news, had camped outside on the pavement and were just about to start their broadcast.

'Good evening from ORF News,' began their bright-eyed spokesperson. 'I'm standing outside a luxury apartment block in the centre of Old Vienna. Approximately an hour ago, at seven this evening, a large device was detonated at the home of the leader of the Freedom Party, Oscar Gruber, who was entertaining a gathering of political leaders from Eastern Europe at the time; they had been invited to celebrate the first anniversary of his election to parliament. Suspecting a terrorist attack, officers from the EKO Cobra counter-terrorism unit were called and arrived a short time afterwards. Despite extensive damage to the property, miraculously, there were no serious casualties and most of the guests, although understandably shaken, were with the assistance of the security services able to find their way to safety. At this stage, there's no indication as to the identification of the perpetrators . . . Sorry, I'm hearing on my headphones that a phone call was made to our station a few moments ago from an individual belonging to MLT, an extreme far-left organisation that is outlawed in Austria, claiming responsibility for the explosion and predicting that further devices will follow until the present government is overthrown. That's all we have at present. We'll bring you further developments as and when they occur. This is Paul Schmidt, ORF News.'

*

Elizabeth joined Oscar Gruber in a sparkling new ambulance, taking them to the Vienna General Hospital, two and a half miles away. She'd hoped to be allowed to go back to the Hirschmans' apartment, but the officer in charge, a surly individual with a military-style shaven head wouldn't hear of it, saying that she needed to be checked over and then questioned by the authorities before she was free to go.

'I don't think we've been formally introduced,' her fellow passenger said jovially, despite appearing to be in a great deal of discomfort.

'Elizabeth McCreary,' she replied hesitantly.

'You're from the UK?'

'Yes, from London,' Elizabeth replied.

'And how was it that you attended this evening?'

'I came with Lukas Petronis,' she divulged, not expecting to have to justify herself.

'And who was *he* exactly?' Gruber asked.

Elizabeth froze. Apart from the spiel they had rehearsed that the young man was the rising star among his country's growing far right and that he held up Austria as the perfect model, everything else she had committed to memory about the fellow was now a blur.

'It'll come to you, don't worry,' her companion said. 'It's the shock, isn't it. Anyway I have to say, whoever he is, I admire his good taste.' He beamed at her.

Elizabeth felt herself blushing. Oscar had assumed she was from an escort agency – but since she didn't have another explanation and couldn't exactly divulge the true nature of her mission, perhaps it was best to let him carry on thinking that way until a more appropriate opportunity presented itself. At least it would make her ignorance of the person she'd accompanied appear more plausible.

'He's vice-president of the Lithuanian Nationalist Movement,' Elizabeth suddenly recalled.

'Ah yes, that's correct. My good friend Aleksas Vardas couldn't make it so he sent his young deputy in his place – I remember now. Presumably he was in that stampede to the fire escape? Pity I didn't have a chance to meet the fellow, though it can't be all bad if it threw us together,' he remarked flirtatiously, then winced with pain as the ambulance hit a bump in the road.

'Do you think the shoulder is broken?' Elizabeth enquired, directing the conversation away from herself.

'Dislocated, more likely. When you've done it once, it only takes the slightest fall for it to come out again. That's why I gave up skiing.'

Elizabeth was about to mention that her husband and children had just returned from Switzerland but stopped herself just in time.

'I don't suppose you have any idea who was behind the attack?' she asked.

'Could be any one of many. There's no shortage of fringe elements wanting to try their luck,' the injured man said.

'You seem quite relaxed about it,' Elizabeth remarked.

'Maybe it's because it hasn't quite sunk in yet; although I'm actually fatalistic when it comes to these things.'

'You mean it's happened before?'

'Fortunately not, but I doubt this'll be the last time. It's part of the risk of being in the public eye.'

'And tonight wouldn't influence you to alter your position?'

'I don't think that would go down too well. Our electorate expects strong leadership, not someone who caves in at the first attempt at intimidation. Why, you seem surprised? Unless of course, you know something I don't.'

The comment caused Elizabeth to recoil. All of a sudden, it felt as if the man could see straight through her.

'Don't worry, I was only teasing,' he retracted.

Elizabeth breathed a sigh of relief. 'It's just, if it were my home that got destroyed in an attack, it would certainly lead me to question certain things about myself,' she said, attempting to plant a seed of doubt in her co-passenger's mind.

'The place is insured. Anyway, the building was in need of refurbishment,' he added unemotionally.

'So what will you do in the meantime?'

'My company has a suite at the Imperial that might come in useful. Which reminds me, I don't suppose you have a phone on you? I need to get hold of the Filipino couple who work for me and tell them to start moving a few things over straight away.'

Elizabeth reached into the evening bag she had managed to hang on to and handed across her mobile. Then, just before they approached the hospital, she said, 'I really am perfectly all right. I hope they won't keep me long.'

'A quick examination is prudent. You can never tell,' the man next to her replied, his voice kind.

'But the officer I spoke to said that the police will want to question me?' Elizabeth said innocently, knowing she had absolutely nothing to hide.

'If it'll put your mind at ease, just tell them you're a friend of mine. I doubt they will trouble you any further.'

'But you hardly know me, Herr Gruber.'

'Let's just say that my instinct tells me there's more to you than you've made out.'

'Well, thank you,' Elizabeth replied, feeling that she had already established a rapport with the leader of Austria's Freedom Party.

'What are your plans for the rest of your time in Vienna, if I may ask?'

'I'm staying with friends in the Leopoldstrasse and

returning to London in a day or so.'

'Perhaps we might see each other again before you go back?' Oscar said as he was helped down from the ambulance.

'I'd like that very much,' Elizabeth said, with a smile.

12

Elizabeth arrived back from the hospital just before midnight, feeling quite upbeat considering the ordeal she'd endured. Treated for nothing more serious than a few minor cuts to her neck and hands, she was warned, however, to expect a delayed reaction Thankfully for her, Oscar Gruber had proven as good as his word and the police didn't even bother with an interview, unlike the rest of the guests who apparently were being contacted, one by one, in order to delete them from the list of possible suspects.

She wondered what Gideon's reaction was going to be, regarding the events of the last few hours. Not for the first time, it occurred to her that she was holding all the cards as far as the Israeli was concerned. She would get back to him when she was good and ready.

Elizabeth fell into bed and immediately entered a deep sleep. She dreamed she was trying to escape huge flames that had engulfed the penthouse apartment she'd been at just hours previously, but all the exits were blocked. The only alternative was to jump. As she did so, a faceless man came running towards her and, holding out his arms, he managed to cushion her fall. It was then that she saw his face and recognised him as her husband Anthony.

*

The next morning, Elizabeth was awoken by the sound of familiar voices. Thinking they were part of her dream, she turned over and tried to go back to sleep but was finally roused by a loud knock on her bedroom door.

'Who is it?' she called out groggily.

The door opened, and standing there was a worried-looking Gideon.

'You didn't return my calls,' he said petulantly. 'Check your phone!'

It was then Elizabeth realised that Oscar Gruber must have forgotten to return her mobile when they were in the ambulance.

'I'm sorry about that, but as you may have heard, there was rather a lot going on last night,' Elizabeth said, yawning and rubbing her eyes.

'I'm not referring to the attack!'

'Oh, was there something else that I missed then?'

'I was referring to Lukas.'

'How silly of me – I thought you were concerned about me.'

'The police are looking for him all over Vienna,' the Israeli grumbled, ignoring her comment.

'If he hadn't made a beeline for the exit instead of staying to see if I was hurt, I might have been more sympathetic,' Elizabeth snapped.

'That wasn't in his brief.'

'And what's *that* supposed to mean? I think you owe me an explanation,' she said angrily.

'Lukas isn't who you think he is.'

'You told me that he was standing in for the other chap from the Lithuanian People's Party.'

'That part of it is true, but he's one of our men.'

'You mean Mossad?' Elizabeth said, sitting up.

Gideon nodded.

'So why did you invent that whole story, letting me think I would be able to influence Oscar Gruber to see the error of his ways?'

'All you need to know is that the device going off at his apartment wasn't on our agenda.'

'Gideon, you're not making yourself clear.'

'There was a change of plan. Our orders were that the original directive had to be implemented without any further delay.'

It took a few seconds for Elizabeth to fully absorb the implications of what she'd just heard. But there was no mistake, the person she had innocently thought was her entrée to Oscar Gruber's reception was his intended assassin – and she was to be his cover rather than the other way around!

'And what was my fate to be in all this?' she demanded, her voice shaking with rage.

'We would have got you to Israel with a change of identity. It's not the first time we've had to arrange such things at short notice,' Gideon said.

'How reassuring of you. And what was I supposed to do about my husband and children – just abandon them?' Elizabeth said, raising her voice.

'There were a few options.' The man shrugged.

'Gideon, if you've got something to say, say it because I'm tired of all this beating around the bush bullshit!'

'I should have thought that even you have had more excitement than you bargained for. But if you insist on finishing what you started with Oscar Gruber, I'd advise you to do it sooner rather than later.' Then turning his back on the semi-naked woman in the bed, he walked back up the narrow corridor. A few seconds later, there was the sound of the front door of the apartment slamming shut.

Elizabeth didn't need anyone to explain the meaning of his final words. It was now a question of who could get to the leader of the Austrian Freedom Party first: the lost relation he never knew he had, or the Mossad agent wanting his head. After what could so easily have ended as a fatal escapade, surely the sensible thing would be to just walk away? But there were wider issues at stake, Elizabeth decided, like preventing the spilling of blood of a man denied truth about his father. Closer to home, there was also her desire to clear her uncle's reputation. At least she had the perfect excuse of going to get her phone; she just hoped that Herr Gruber hadn't accessed any of her texts in the meantime.

*

Elizabeth got dressed quickly and decided to have breakfast out. She hadn't spoken to Freda in person for a couple of days, although she had sensed her presence in the background when Gideon had turned up unexpectedly. The old lady must have let him in – unless he had a key.

Psyching herself up for the difficult task that lay ahead, she stuffed the entire contents of the deposit box into her Louis Vuitton shoulder bag, left the flat and went across to the café in the Prater. If time really was running out, she was well prepared to provide Oscar Gruber with the proof about his past. Running her eye down the self-service menu, she chose an almond croissant and Americano and sat down at a table in the window. Reflecting on the terse conversation with Gideon, she was convinced that someone was following her every move. After a few minutes she left the restaurant and, after peering around for any likely suspects, she waved down a taxi and asked the driver to take her to the five-star Imperial Hotel.

A supercilious concierge at the front desk informed her that no one by the name of Herr Gruber was residing in the hotel. She'd been naïve in thinking that he had told her the truth about where he was taking refuge, and on reflection she wouldn't have blamed him after the attempt on his life a short time before; or else it was added security measures he had put in place. Unsure what to do next, Elizabeth's attention was diverted to a small oriental man who had just entered the hotel, laden with a full complement of freshly laundered items. Recalling Oscar mentioning a Filipino member of his staff to whom he'd given the night off, she impulsively got to her feet and went over to him.

'Excuse me,' she said, 'my name's Elizabeth. Are you by any chance employed by Herr Gruber?' But before she had a chance to say anything further, the young man sped back into the street with the shirts still over his arm. Realising that her hunch had proven correct, Elizabeth gave chase, catching up with the man at a bus stop.

'Please, I don't want any trouble!' the frightened fellow said in German.

'I'm really sorry, but I need your help,' Elizabeth said in slow, clear English.

'You don't want my papers?' the man replied in the same language.

'No, of course not. I'm only a friend of Herr Gruber's.'

'So you're not from immigration?'

'You really have nothing to worry about. I just want to get a message to your employer.'

'OK,' the little fellow replied, a broad smile lighting up his face. 'Come with me.'

The two then made their way back to the hotel lobby.

'You wait here!' the Filipino said, hastening over to the bank of lifts.

Watched suspiciously by the concierge, Elizabeth hovered by the lift until the domestic reappeared, flanked this time by two unsmiling bodyguards.

'You claim to be a friend of Herr Gruber?' the older one said, again in German, inspecting Elizabeth up and down.

'Yes, that's correct. I was at his home last night,' she managed to reply in her schoolgirl German.

'And what has led you to believe he's in this particular hotel?' the other one intervened.

'We were in the ambulance together that took us to hospital after the attack; he mentioned it then.' She gestured to the dressings on her neck and face. 'He took my phone and I really need it back.'

The two guards exchanged a look and then, satisfied, the first one said, 'Fraulein, please accompany us.'

They entered the lift and when they came out, she was ushered through a pair of heavy wooden doors by another one of their colleagues who was standing watch outside the rooftop suite.

Elizabeth found a relaxed Oscar Gruber sat at the breakfast table and, apart from a heavily strapped-up shoulder, he showed few ill-effects from the previous evening. The scent of perfume and a woman's silky robe strewn on the floor leading to another room with a closed door led her to believe he hadn't spent the night on his own.

'My dear, what an unexpected pleasure to see you – or is it, as I suspect, merely to pick up the phone you'd forgotten?' he asked, gesturing over at the mobile on the sideboard. 'Either way, won't you join me and have some breakfast?' he offered, politely getting up and, utilising his good hand, pulled out a chair for his visitor.

'Thank you, I would love a coffee,' she replied, hoping it would calm her nerves.

'I trust you've recovered from last night's fun and games?' he asked.

'Yes, I was fine after a good night's sleep, and thank you for sorting out the police for me.'

A dismissive wave of a hand was the only response.

'The papers are full of it this morning,' he said, glancing at the headline in front of him.

'You read the British papers?' Elizabeth asked.

'Of course. You may not be Europeans, but the content of your newspapers is far less parochial than our own – and I should know, since most of them are mine,' he chuckled. 'Also, I spent quite a few years in the States and I still read the *New York Times* every day. Old habits die hard.'

'And the UK – how do you feel about us?' Elizabeth said casually, accepting the cup of coffee he handed her and adding a little hot milk to it.

'I'm fond of London. It's probably the best place of all to do business, but politically, you Brits are hard to get to grips with. At least with Americans, you know exactly where they stand.'

'Really, in what way?' Elizabeth enquired, sipping her excellent coffee and trying to draw the fellow out.

'First of all, it's a myth that the English are moderate. They are as extreme as the rest of Europe except it's disguised; in fact, some I could name put us on the right to shame.'

Elizabeth thought about her father-in-law. Didn't he fit that mould completely?

'But surely, that's why you were targeted,' she tried.

'No doubt, but I've always stood up for what I believe in. Haven't you?'

Elizabeth pondered on the question. It was a good one. Tracing back how much she had changed in a short time, it was a question that would be hard to answer right now.

'In any event,' Oscar went on, more businesslike, 'I doubt you've come here to talk politics. I suspect it's something far more pressing. Am I right?'

'Herr Gruber, you are most perceptive.'

'I think we can dispense with the formality. Do call me Oscar. We are friends, are we not?'

'Yes, yes, of course.' Dispensing with everything she'd carefully prepared, Elizabeth threw caution to the wind and went straight to the point.

'I came to Vienna a week ago to trace family on my mother's side.'

'Ah, so now the truth comes out,' he beamed.

'Please, Oscar, if you will allow me to explain . . .'

'OK. Go ahead!'

'I needed to trace a certain member of my mother's family.'

'She was Austrian?' Gruber was surprised. 'It was just

that I took you for an English Rose.'

'I'm actually the daughter of a Holocaust survivor.'

The room fell into an uncomfortable silence before Oscar said: 'Well, this *is* turning out very differently from what I expected.'

Elizabeth knew she must press on: there was nothing to be gained in holding back.

'What I discovered had a profound effect upon me,' she continued.

'In that you found relations who were still alive?' the host remarked, showing a glimpse of interest.

'Yes, that comes into it, but before that I learned I had an aunt I'd known nothing about beforehand.'

'Your mother's sister?'

'Yes, her older sister – and I learned that she was disabled. That helped to explain an awful lot about my mother's behaviour that I had to deal with, growing up.'

'And was that all?'

'No, there's more.' Elizabeth looked down, summoning up her courage because she was about to embark on the main purpose of her visit.

'My mother had an uncle, called Theodore Frankl.'

'And he's still alive?' Oscar enquired politely, with no idea of the revelation to come.

'Unfortunately not, but I discovered some important things about him that I would never have known, had I not come to Vienna.' She cleared her throat and looked Oscar in the eye. 'You see, Theo was involved with an Austrian woman, a Catholic, just before the war.'

It was hard for her to tell what the man opposite was thinking since he showed no reaction.

'Go on,' he said.

'The relationship didn't last.'

'And why was that?'

'She went off and married someone else, a German officer stationed in Vienna at the time.'

'What's so unusual about that?' Gruber frowned.

Elizabeth sensed he could tell she was skating around the issue.

'The thing is, my uncle suddenly just disappeared.'

'And you've assumed that this woman and the new man in her life conspired to get rid of him.'

'She may have been under a great deal of pressure, from what I established.'

'You're saying that she had no choice in the matter?'

'She was living with a Jew.'

'But she must have known that was a risky business?'

'Perhaps they were in love and she couldn't help herself,' Elizabeth mumbled, just saying the first thing that came into her head.

Oscar picked up his newspaper again. 'It's a sad story, Elizabeth, but unless I've got lost along the way, I'm not sure what this has to do with me.'

Elizabeth took a large gulp of coffee before continuing. This was the part she'd been dreading the most.

'There was a child involved,' she told him.

'It's normal for married people, no?' Oscar teased.

'Of course, but it was from an earlier relationship.'

'With your uncle, perhaps?'

'Yes.'

'And I suppose if that child were still alive, he or she would be your cousin – no, your second cousin,' Gruber deduced, appearing to enjoy making the pieces of the puzzle fit.

Elizabeth paused to allow the Austrian leader time to absorb the meaning of her words and her expression. He suddenly turned a ghostly white.

'What I assume you are insinuating is completely ridiculous, woman!' he hissed. 'It's insane!'

Elizabeth was trembling. 'Oscar, I didn't believe it myself until I met the one person who was able to verify everything.'

'And who is this person?'

'An old bishop at St Stephen's Cathedral.'

'And what was a Catholic priest's unlikely role in this fantasy, may I ask?'

'Bishop Hoffner was a close friend of my uncle; in fact, he officiated at their marriage.'

'Marriage to whom? You've lost me.'

'Lise Gruber,' Elizabeth said bravely.

'Elizabeth, I'm warning you ... I know that's impossible because I've got my parents' marriage certificate!' was the angry response.

'I'm sure you have, but I'm afraid to tell you it's invalid,' Elizabeth declared.

'That's quite enough!' the injured man shouted. 'Look, I don't know who you are or what game you are playing, but I really think it's best you leave. Go on – get out!'

The argument attracted the attention of the bodyguard outside in the hall, who stormed into the room ready for action. Oscar irritably shooed him away.

Elizabeth had accurately predicted Gruber's reaction, but having come this far, she was determined to stand her ground.

'Oscar, I quite understand that you're upset and that all this has come as a shock – but ask yourself, what would I have to gain by making this all up? Putting my life and that of my family at risk, unless there was a very good reason? That would have been completely insane!'

While Gruber looked on suspiciously, Elizabeth reached into her bag for the old brown envelope and passed it across the table.

'What's this?' he demanded.

'Proof that what I'm telling you is true.'

Gruber examined the letter from the outside. 'This is from the man you are trying to convince me is my real father, right?'

Elizabeth nodded.

'How did you get hold of it?'

'When the bishop was certain that I was a Frankl, he had his assistant bring up a metal box from a vault in the cathedral.'

'He must have written this just before he was arrested,' Oscar muttered, running his eye down the missive from sixty years ago.

'There's more to it than just that,' Elizabeth divulged.

Gruber looked up.

'You see, she was still married to Theo Frankl until the day she died.'

'But that's impossible!' Gruber retorted.

Without saying a word, Elizabeth passed him the copy of the marriage certificate she'd obtained from the Erzbischöfliches Ordinariat.

'But how was it possible I didn't know of its existence until now?' Oscar Gruber blurted out, unable to hide his surprise.

'It was hidden by the same bishop until after the war, when it was swapped back with the one you have in your possession.'

The Austrian leader fell silent. Elizabeth could see he was having difficulty absorbing what she had just revealed and what must have sounded like a wild invention.

'Until now, I never knew much about my real father apart from the little my mother told me,' he divulged quietly, after a short while.

'Ah, so you knew about her relationship with Theo?' Elizabeth said.

'No, not by name. I was told that it was a casual love affair when she was very young, and that the relationship had just fizzled out. At the time I believed her, but she always seemed close to tears when she spoke about him. And later, when I was older and seeing how unhappy she was with Walter, my stepfather, I'd often wondered whether there was more to it than that.'

'And now you've been proven right,' Elizabeth said.

There was no response.

'But your parents' marriage can't have been all bad if Walter was prepared to take on another's man's child?' Elizabeth tried.

'Walter was in love with my mother but it wasn't reciprocated. No doubt that's why the bastard took his frustrations out on me!' Oscar said angrily. 'And the fact they couldn't have children together only made my predicament worse.'

'Presumably that's why you changed your name to your mother's maiden name – Gruber?' Elizabeth said.

'Correct. I didn't want anything to do with him or his

family's tainted money!'

'Sorry?' Elizabeth said, picking up on something untoward.

'Never mind about that,' Gruber backtracked.

'So, you went off and made your own fortune. There was a piece about you in *Time Magazine*,' Elizabeth revealed.

'Yes, for which Walter never forgave me.'

'He resented your independence?'

'Precisely. Because his father hadn't given him any choice, he thought he had a right to expect the same of me – total obedience.'

'And how did he react to you going into politics?'

'With disdain.' Gruber snorted. 'He looked on it just as a publicity stunt and in a way he had a point, certainly initially.'

'What changed?' Elizabeth wanted to know.

'Simple. I saw an opening and decided to take advantage of it.'

There was a momentary pause, allowing Elizabeth to collect her thoughts. How did Oscar, she asked herself, the leader of Austria's far-right party, fool himself into thinking he was any different from his predecessors?

Gruber must have interpreted her sceptical expression correctly because he sighed, then tried to explain.

'Despite its past, Austrians are proud of their heritage. At least *we've* learned our lesson,' he said, which sounded to Elizabeth like a further dig against the British!

She came back with: 'But inevitably you attract followers who hold the same extreme views of those leaders I assume you've just condemned? I witnessed them in action myself at your recent rally.'

'I'm aware of a lunatic element who dream of going back to the good old days of the Anschluss, but I can assure you that's only temporary.'

'How can you be so sure?'

'They wanted a platform for their extreme views and they think we provided it for them, that's really all there is to it.'

'I don't understand,' Elizabeth frowned.

'You've heard of the expression "playing to the crowd"? Well, that's exactly what we've done. First, appeal to the lowest common denominator, wait till you're in power, then perform a U-turn and become more moderate. It is a tried and tested method.'

'And do you feel any differently now, after our conversation?'

Oscar Gruber glanced at the letter next to him, addressed to *Ozzie Frankl*. 'Let's just say, what you've told me has come as a surprise – assuming it's all true?' he said, using a knife from the breakfast table to carefully open the faded envelope.

Elizabeth flinched – but it would have been unrealistic to expect this man to simply take her word for such a momentous revelation into his past. Even though her German was sketchy at best, she regretted that she hadn't given in to her impulse to read Theo's letter herself first, for she was certain it would have substantiated her claim. But it was not addressed to her. And anyway, now it was too late and she'd have to rely on her newfound cousin's conscience to take the necessary steps to defuse the predicament of the Jewish community. The fact that his life depended on it only increased her unease.

'Apparently Theo wanted me to do something on his behalf,' his son announced eventually, examining the missive in his possession.

Elizabeth braced herself for what was coming next.

'For the survivors of families he'd been unable to save,' Oscar went on. 'Look, he made a list of them.'

'There must be fifty names here!' Elizabeth exclaimed, thumbing through several sheets of paper. She'd had no idea that Theo's influence extended beyond the Kindertransport. Now her doubts about her great-uncle had been allayed, it came as a huge relief, knowing for certain that Freda and probably others in the Jewish community had also misjudged him.

'Apparently, he'd been betrayed by an immigration official, which put an end to providing those people with an escape route,' Gruber said, glancing at the letter again.

Elizabeth was almost certain about that individual's identity but she held back from voicing her suspicion. Far better to let him carry on thinking of his mother as a victim of blackmail rather than a willing party to his birth father's demise.

'So what now?' Elizabeth asked after a short pause.

Gruber burst out laughing, catching her completely off-guard.

'First, you turn up last night at my home under some false pretence and, for your information, my enquiries have drawn a blank on that fellow Lukas, or whatever his real name is. Next, I expect you'll try to tell me that he was behind the attempt on my life!'

Elizabeth held her breath. With the progress she was making, she'd hoped to avoid bringing that subject up. But that had been optimistic, she now saw. And Oscar hadn't finished.

'You can't expect me to suddenly abandon everything I've built up because of what's come to light after sixty years. Quite frankly, I could just as easily carry on as if none of this had ever happened,' he told her.

'Don't you think the same thought went through my mind?' Elizabeth retorted forcefully. 'You seem to forget that I gave up a perfectly safe life with my family in London to embark on this journey. There were several times I could or rather should have walked away. I had my plane ticket and my bags packed!'

'So why didn't you just walk away?'

'For the same reason I believe that you won't. Like you, I had discovered things about my past that I needed to come to terms with. And with that new knowledge also came a certain clarification of identity that I now realise was missing.'

The comment knocked the man back, causing him to reflect for a while. Then, recovering his poise, he said: 'Theo mentioned something about there also being a quantity of valuable stones?'

'Yes, I have them,' Elizabeth confirmed, producing the half-dozen small drawstring pouches.

'Although he didn't give precise instructions, it's pretty clear for whom they're intended,' Gruber said.

Elizabeth nodded. She wanted to ask whether her mother was included amongst the beneficiaries but Oscar was immersed in rummaging through a small stack of official forms, threaded together with a thin scarlet ribbon.

'Is something wrong?' she asked, conscious of his pensive expression.

'Just looks like some title deeds from the old Ghetto,' he said.

'But I thought the Germans confiscated all Jewish property in the war?' Elizabeth said.

'That's what one would have assumed,' he replied, seeming somewhat distracted.

Elizabeth didn't see any merit in pushing for more explanation. Although it appeared the revelation about his true father and the contents of his letter had had a profound effect on him, whether it was enough to make him climb down from the extremist position currently held by his Party was another question.

There was only one way of finding out – and that was for him to meet the only person able to make that assessment: Gideon Halevi!

*

Gideon checked his watch for the umpteenth time that afternoon.

Elizabeth could read his thoughts. Oscar Gruber obviously wasn't going to show. He'd probably needed more time to digest what had been sprung on him about his past and had had second thoughts about coming here. That was understandable, but a shame because two days ago she had taken the trouble to arrange for him to meet Gideon – a meeting which could save his life – at the attic flat in the 18th district, a rendezvous that was sufficiently out of the way not to attract undue attention. Had she done enough to get the edict against her second cousin overturned?

'I take it you'll be going back to London,' Gideon said, breaking the uneasy silence.

'I've got a flight tomorrow morning,' Elizabeth replied despondently.

'Don't feel bad about Gruber – you did your best.'

'That's not much of a consolation if his life is still in danger.'

The Israeli shrugged, leaving Elizabeth with the impression that Oscar's absence might not have been entirely accidental.

Indeed, Halevi wasn't about to divulge that the meeting in the hotel room had been bugged. Now that Elizabeth McCreary had paved the way with her long-lost relation, the ball was now firmly in Gruber's court to take the necessary steps to protect the Jewish Community.

*

Earlier that day, Oscar Gruber came away from the cathedral he'd become so familiar with. His mother had always talked with such affection about the priest whom she'd encountered during the war in Vienna and, as a result, who had provided him with the same guiding influence throughout most of his life – not that he had disclosed anything about that to Elizabeth McCreary. However convincing the evidence was that she'd presented, Oscar wanted to hear it from the old priest himself that Theo Frankl was his real father. He also wanted an explanation of why neither the priest nor his mother had thought to mention it to him before, rather than have the news come from a relation he hitherto knew nothing about. Had he known years ago, at least then he could have made up his mind about who he really was and maybe have chosen a different path to follow in his life. But now it was too late. With Bishop Hoffner's recent death, he'd been denied that opportunity.

The other problem was how to reconcile his political profile with his newly discovered Jewish identity: there was no getting away from the fact that they didn't sit at all well together. Furthermore, the sudden surge in his popularity, now the alliance with Gretchen Schwab had gone public, had given him no choice but to reconsider the relationship with Elizabeth McCreary, the woman who claimed to be his second cousin.

Returning to his refuge in the Imperial Hotel, he didn't expect to find that the door to his suite had been prised open, footprints on the carpets and his own security nowhere in sight. The words *Judenliebhaber,* Jew lover, daubed in black paint indicated that he might already have been too late!

PART TWO

13

Central London, late April

Anthony sat in his office overlooking Waterloo Bridge, staring into space. The auditors' report, delivered by hand while he was lunching at the Savoy, had contained the words *material discrepancy*, and this made him feel uneasy. Normally, something like this wouldn't have bothered him in the least. Accountants always found anomalies – that was their job – but the fact that their bookkeeper Ronald Bassett had suddenly decided to take early retirement after thirty years made it feel a lot more serious.

As he pondered, a squat individual in an ill-fitting suit and thick-rimmed spectacles entered the office carrying an absurdly large attaché case.

'Barry, good of you to drop by,' Anthony said, trying to appear relaxed. Not easy when he was well aware of the man's reputation as the City's most ruthless reporting accountant. Barry Levinson was called in by the Solicitors Complaints Bureau whenever there was the slightest hint of wrongdoing, and Anthony knew the chap wouldn't leave any stone unturned.

'I assume it has to do with this?' Anthony asked, holding up a thinly bound document.

'There are certain irregularities which have been highlighted by your auditors and which require further investigation,' the accountant said unemotionally.

'I can assure you that all entries in the client account are checked thoroughly,' Anthony stressed.

'The auditors' comments don't relate to a simple arithmetical error but to what the account is being used for,' the man replied.

'And what's that supposed to mean?' Anthony snapped.

'Perhaps you can explain how, on three separate occasions over the last twelve months, sums amounting to exactly three million pounds were received from the private Bruden Bank in Switzerland and were then transferred in smaller denominations to a number of different accounts in the Channel Islands?'

'I've absolutely no idea,' Anthony protested, visibly shocked by the size of the deposits. The truth was, he *didn't* check the client account on a regular basis. He had no reason to. Even if he had, the chances were that he wouldn't have detected anything untoward. He wondered whether this had anything to do with what his sister Jess had been trying to tell him. Whatever it was, he suspected he was in a great deal of trouble.

'I'll look into it and get back to you,' Anthony said, showing the fellow out.

'Please do. I'm sure you don't need reminding that money laundering is a criminal offence and is looked on particularly severely where professional firms are involved,' the accountant replied, not mincing his words.

Anthony tried his father's mobile again. Perhaps William could provide some answers. The thought crossed his mind that it might have been more than just a coincidence that his father had sold his shares to the other partners at the beginning of their financial year. Bugger it! Still no answer! It began to feel very much like he'd been left carrying the can, responsible for whatever had been going on behind his back.

Taking the longer route on foot to Bank tube station to calm his agitation, Anthony pictured his career in tatters, no longer able to provide for his family. There and then, the issue of his errant wife fell into insignificance, and for one incoherent moment, he even contemplated taking the easy way out and ending it all.

*

Barry Levinson stayed late in the office. He knew from experience that he was at his most productive when no one else was around. He glanced at the email that had just come through on his desktop computer. His intuition – that there was something fishy going on at McCreary's – had proven correct. The funds in question had come in piecemeal denominations from three subsidiaries of the highly respected Crediton Trust, innocuous enough on the surface, except that on further investigation it turned out that the ultimate destination of the funds was the British Independent Party. The reason for the subterfuge was obvious: first, the Crediton Trust had hoped that they could remain as hidden donors, and secondly, small donations to a political party wouldn't have to be made public.

Anthony McCreary had every reason to be worried. Solicitors were strictly prohibited from providing banking facilities for their clients through the client account and this, at the very least, would result in a severe censure. But then, if he'd been a solicitor worth his salt, he would have known that! There were only two possibilities: either the fellow was completely inept or he'd put on a convincing show and knew a lot more than he let on. However, Barry's instinct told him that there were some bigger issues at stake and he knew just the man to help him find out what they were and who was involved in them.

Rick Overton and he had been students together at the London School of Economics. There was no doubt in Barry's mind that there was no better investigative journalist in the country.

*

The 9 a.m. British Airways flight from Vienna landed at Heathrow Terminal 1 on time. Elizabeth reached into the overhead locker for the bag of presents she'd bought at the airport and tentatively made her way down the steps of the Boeing 737 aircraft. She'd purposely remained vague with the children as to when she was coming home, and Anthony had agreed not to tell them since she wanted her return to be a surprise.

It was the first time they'd spoken since he had put the phone down on her – something that now seemed a lifetime ago. In contrast to his petulant tone of voice when on the line from Switzerland, this time he was positively civil. The fact that the family had coped so well without her had actually left Elizabeth feeling somewhat peeved. Her one regret was that she hadn't had the opportunity of spending more time with Freda Hirschman, who'd done so much to make her feel welcome. She consoled herself with the thought that she might go back to Vienna; after all, there was unfinished business there – although she didn't want to admit that it might also afford another opportunity to see Gideon.

While sitting in the back of a black cab caught in heavy traffic on the M4 to Central London, Elizabeth found that the nearer she got to home, the more she began questioning what she really wanted. With everything she'd discovered about herself in Vienna, she couldn't envisage returning to the mundane life she'd left just over a week earlier. At least her mother had shown some genuine understanding of what she'd been through. They'd talked for over an hour on the phone the previous evening. Through a sea of tears she'd held back for more than sixty years, Lillian wanted to know everything about her older disabled sister Erica, whose place she had taken on the Kindertransport. Elizabeth now understood that the figure of a girl in so many of her mother's childhood drawings was Lillian's way of keeping the memory of Erica alive.

Beyond skating over the fate of her Great-uncle Theo, Elizabeth resisted going any further, which proved especially difficult when her mother mentioned in passing the attempt on Oscar Gruber's life that had made front-page news in the British press. Lillian had more than enough to take in and Elizabeth hadn't wanted to add to her anguish.

Arriving in Primrose Hill at just before midday, she spotted her husband's car in the drive and immediately assumed he was unwell. She let herself into the house to find him sat at the dining-room table poring over several pages of a computer print-out.

'Hello, darling. I'm home!' she called.

'I didn't hear you come in,' he muttered, not bothering to look up from what he was doing.

'Is something wrong?' she asked. Elizabeth could never recall him taking time off from work before.

'No, just some stuff that needs sorting out. I'll be with you in a few minutes,' he said brusquely, as if he were addressing one of his juniors in the office.

Elizabeth stood with her coat on at the entrance, her luggage beside her. She felt deflated – but what had she expected? A welcome with open arms wasn't in her husband's nature and it hadn't bothered her up until now. She decided she needed to give it time and, in any event, there were the children to think of. She wondered whether they at least would be pleased to see her. She certainly hoped so.

*

Three weeks passed during which Elizabeth tried to re-adapt to the domestic routine. But at night her sleep was interrupted by vivid dreams. One morning, she jolted awake after another disturbing dream, feeling exhausted. She had dreamed that it was the depths of winter and she was standing shivering in a long line of shaven-headed men and women in their concentration-camp striped uniforms, bearing the yellow Star of David on their breast pockets. They were waiting while their names were shouted out by a Nazi officer. Looking closer, she saw that the officer was Oscar Gruber. What did it mean? she asked herself, now she was awake. They hadn't seen each other after that time in his hotel suite. Perhaps that was the meaning of the dream: she needed reassurance that he would make positive use of his newly discovered heritage to safeguard Vienna's Jewish community.

She looked across at the vacated side of the bed and sighed. She hadn't heard Anthony get up. For a moment, she even wondered whether he'd come to bed at all. It had been the same scenario ever since she got back from Austria. Even at the weekends, they barely had two words to say to each other – and then it was only to discuss the children or the odd social invitation that needed responding to. Right now, they seemed to be married in name only. Anthony remained aloof, unprepared to share the problem he was encountering at his law firm with her – if that's what it was. Of course, it did occur to her that he might have found someone else and didn't know how to break it to her. For her part, she felt listless and was finding it hard to settle back into her former life. It was difficult to prevent the tense atmosphere in the house from being noticed by the children, especially Freddie, who was too perceptive to be fobbed off with lame excuses that everything was all right.

Elizabeth was prompted to seek help from Marlene Katz, on a one-to-one session; she had no wish to share her issues with the rest of the group. Sat in the therapist's pretty cottage in Hampstead, surrounded by a sea of greenery, she could still hear Marlene's words:

'But Elizabeth, haven't you considered that perhaps *you're* the one who's changed?' And then: 'You said it was your choice to go to Vienna . . .'

Deep down, Elizabeth knew the woman was right. Possibly, had she envisaged the dramatic effect that searching into her past would have upon her, she might have thought twice about making the journey. Part of her wished she had stayed at home!

She talked to Marlene about her brief fling with Gideon and said that she had the urge to confess it to Anthony. Marlene made her question the wisdom of that: was a break-up of the marriage what she really wanted? And was she prepared for the fall-out from her children if, as was likely, they were to attach the blame solely to her? The answer was a resounding no!

But it was Marlene's observation that she might be suffering from post-traumatic stress following that potentially fatal incident at Oscar Gruber's apartment, which stayed most in Elizabeth's mind. It hadn't occurred to her before that she wasn't well, and that her judgment might be impaired. As yet, she was unsure whether or not she would take up the offer of a referral to an expert in the field.

Still not fully awake, Elizabeth put on her robe and went downstairs, thinking she would catch the children while they were having breakfast. But there was no one around. Anthony must have left for work early, and then, remembering that Freddie had gone on a school trip to the war graves in Belgium and that Emily was sleeping over at her friend Katie's, on reflection, she was glad to have the house to herself.

Retreating to the kitchen with a solitary item of post addressed to Anthony and marked *Strictly Private and Confidential: To Be Opened by the Addressee Only,* Elizabeth made the decision to open it whatever the consequences. She needed to see if it could explain what was going on with her husband and causing his bad moods and strange behaviour. Carefully, she withdrew the letter and immediately saw the terse wording from the Office for the Supervision of Solicitors requiring the presence of Anthony McCreary at a hearing to answer serious charges of breaches of the professional body's code of conduct.

Elizabeth was deeply shocked. So that was the reason for her husband's quite understandable preoccupation. And she had been thinking only of herself. Ashamed, she vowed to try and put things right when he returned home that evening.

*

The following afternoon, Anthony entered the RAC Club on Pall Mall and made his way down the grand marble staircase to the basement that housed the famous Grecian-style swimming pool and health spa. Knowing from experience that his father frequented the Turkish baths there in the afternoons when he was in Town, he wasn't surprised to find the older man in one of the cubicles lying prostrate, his huge body swathed in towels.

'Hello, my boy, don't just stand there – get undressed!' William McCreary boomed, peering up from his tankard of lime cordial at his son hovering over him.

'I'm not here for the baths; we need to talk,' Anthony said levelly, keeping his distance. Accustomed to being intimidated by his father, the frank talk with Elizabeth the day before had cleared the air between them and left him feeling unusually emboldened. How absurd of him, he thought now, not to have believed that she would wholeheartedly support him with regard to this awful predicament that was none of his making. He was truly lucky to have a wife like her – and to think he might have lost her in that terrorist attack! Even though she had tried explaining the circumstances to him, her presence in that dangerous situation was still a mystery.

'Huh?' His father struggled up to a sitting position. 'So – what's so important that it couldn't wait until the weekend? We've got a longstanding arrangement in the country, according to your mother.'

'A serious problem has arisen that won't go away on its own,' Anthony responded, hoping to draw his father out.

'The professional world is always full of new challenges. We just have to man up and confront them face on,' William said carelessly, not taking the bait.

'I'm not referring to normal day-to-day staff issues or a difficult client,' Anthony said tightly.

'In that case, I don't have the slightest idea what you're getting at.'

'So you have no knowledge about the irregularity in the company accounts that the auditors have discovered, and which is why they've been unwilling to sign them off?'

'Should I?' the older man replied guardedly.

'Well, it does seem odd that it happens to have coincided with Ronald applying for early requirement, and you having effectively washed your hands of anything to do with the firm of late.'

'It was merely the right time for you to stand on your own two feet,' the naked man said firmly.

'I doubt you'll be able to claim you weren't involved,' Anthony replied, trying to call his father's bluff. He wasn't to know that he, Anthony, was the only name on the summons, although he was pretty certain that the misuse of the client account had gone on for some time; thus making the former senior partner jointly and severally liable for any wrongdoing.

William McCreary's expression suddenly became darker.

'That blithering idiot of a bookkeeper; it was all his fault,' he bleated. 'If he'd followed instructions none of this would have blown up.'

Anthony couldn't believe what he was hearing. Feeling constricted in the airless space, he took off his jacket and loosened his tie.

'And you never once thought of mentioning it to me?' Anthony said angrily, raising his voice and attracting disapproving looks from members in the adjoining cubicles.

'The less you knew, the better – and it should have continued that way.'

'And what way was that?' Anthony demanded, wanting his father to confess to the full extent of his impropriety.

'The funds, to which I assume you're referring, should have been paid into the firm's bank account, not the client account. That way, like any other commercial transaction, no questions would have been asked.'

'But it wasn't just a straightforward commercial transaction, was it?' Anthony pressed.

'How much do you know?' William said, adopting a far meeker tone.

'That the monies came from the Crediton Trust.'

'Nothing wrong with that; they're long-standing clients.'

'How about the fact that you're also one of the trustees?'

'I doubt anyone's going to be that worried about a possible conflict of interest,' his father shrugged.

'No, not now that it's been established where the funds

ended up,' Anthony replied coolly.

The older man twitched nervously as he tried to think up an appropriate response, now that he'd been exposed.

'It's no secret that I've been interested in politics since my Cambridge days,' he said after a moment, recovering his equilibrium.

'But why the British Independent Party?' his son wanted to know. 'You always voted Tory.'

'You saw the results of the last election,' William said disgustedly. 'Blair won with a landside! The highest proportion of seats since the war and the Conservatives lost more than half of theirs. The party's gone soft. Extreme measures are what are needed to combat New Labour's wishy-washy policies of kowtowing to Europe.'

'So you're happy aligning yourself with Fascists?' Anthony was shocked. 'Elizabeth was right.'

'There's no need to bring *her* into it,' William McCreary said nastily.

'And what's that supposed to mean?'

'I've never been overly fond of the Jews. If you look back in history, they've been at the forefront of stirring up most of the trouble that very nearly cost us two world wars.'

'You can't say things like that!' Anthony protested half-heartedly.

'All right,' William retracted, sensing he'd overstepped the mark. 'But you can't escape the fact that letting in all those other immigrants has made the England that I grew up in and which I love, totally bloody unrecognisable.' William shifted and groaned, going on: 'More to the point, what do you intend to do about that small spot of bother you're in? Take my advice, play the white man and insist it was a simple bookkeeping error.'

'That's easy for you to say. After all, you're the one who gave the instruction,' Anthony reminded him.

'You will find there's no record of that. So I'm afraid, my boy, you're on your own with this one.' With that, William McCreary shifted his large frame off the narrow bed and trundled off back to the steam room.

Even though Anthony had suspected the outcome, it still hurt to receive the confirmation that he was being offered up as the scapegoat.

14

Elizabeth left her car keys with the attendant on the third floor of Selfridges car park, took the lift down to street level and proceeded on foot to her lunch arrangement in Mayfair, a short distance away. Scott's seafood restaurant was her mother-in-law's preference and she was happy to oblige. There was far more at stake than just the choice of restaurant. Passing the landmark American Embassy that dominated one entire side of Grosvenor Square, Elizabeth wondered what Anthony would say if he knew what she was doing. After that vitriolic encounter with his father a few days before, he had taken the decision to sever all ties with his parents. It had been left to Elizabeth to try and keep the lines of dialogue open, if only for the sake of the children.

Entering the exclusive establishment, Elizabeth gave her name to the maître d' and was promptly led to the centre of the dining room, where a large woman with short, wavy grey hair sat at her usual table with a bottle of the Chablis that she liked.

'Hello, dear, glad you could join me,' the older woman said, slurring her speech. 'Forgive me for starting without you, but I was just gasping for a drink.'

'That's quite all right,' Elizabeth replied. Because of the formal nature of their relationship, she was never quite sure whether a kiss or shaking hands was more appropriate, deciding on neither before taking her place opposite her mother-in-law.

'How are the children?'

'They're both fine. That is to say, Freddie is stressed about his GCSE mocks in a few weeks' time.'

'And Emily?' The woman's face brightened as she enquired after her favourite grandchild.

'You know Emily, takes everything in her stride. She's fortunate that she doesn't have to work hard and yet still manages top grades.'

'She's lucky to have a mother like you,' Margaret remarked, taking a large gulp of her drink. 'I never spent time with either of mine on their schoolwork,' she admitted sadly.

'Well, they seem to have managed quite well despite that,' Elizabeth replied, feeling a sudden sympathy for the woman.

'Jessica could have gone far,' her mother revealed. 'She wanted to go into law but naturally William wouldn't hear of it. He's always had a thing about women in business.'

'I didn't know that,' Elizabeth said, wondering why her sister-in-law had never mentioned it to her.

'Hard as it is to believe, William's simply terrified of his daughter.' Margaret McCreary smiled ruefully. 'Probably because she's the only one who is prepared to stand up to him.'

To Elizabeth, hearing these words, it now seemed obvious why her husband had been the one to take prime position in his father's law practice: it was because he could be easily manipulated. That meant that Jess never stood a chance, which helped to explain their lack of a close sibling relationship. Elizabeth was disgusted with her father-in-law for taking advantage of his children in that way.

Then, in a sudden change of mood, Margaret said to the waiter who'd come to take their order, 'I'll have a dozen oysters, followed by the turbot.'

'Just the turbot for me,' Elizabeth said, devoid of an appetite but not wanting to appear impolite. 'And may we have some water, please?'

'Oh, and Giuliano, put another bottle on ice, will you?' Margaret McCreary added. 'Now,' she said, filling Elizabeth's glass, 'I assume you want to talk about that unfortunate business at the firm.'

'I was hoping that you might be able to talk to William,' Elizabeth responded.

'That *would* be a first!' The older woman produced a raucous laugh that briefly turned the heads of patrons at the adjoining tables.

'My dear,' she went on, 'I can't recall the last time my husband took my advice about anything like that. William assumes females are an inferior species that should remain out of view and only be brought out on rare occasions.'

'That's awful, but—'

'Why have I put up with it for so long, you were going to ask? And here's my answer: for the same reasons most people of our generation stay together – to avoid disrupting the family and admitting to the outside world that the marriage has failed. Ridiculous, of course. In my case, however, I should like to feel the satisfaction of seeing William falling flat on his arse, first hand. It would serve him right for what he's put us all through.' The waiter approached at that moment and Margaret was served her oysters while the waiter refilled their glasses and replaced the empty bottle.

Elizabeth was speechless. She couldn't believe the words that had come out of her mother-in-law's mouth. She had had no idea the woman felt that way, nor that she would be willing to be so frank about it. The fact was, however, that none of this helped Anthony's predicament.

'You don't know the half of it,' Margaret confided now, this time lowering her voice. 'It wouldn't surprise me in the slightest if William has got another family tucked away somewhere. He was never around much when the children were growing up. On the other hand, perhaps it's just that he bats for the other side?' She chuckled and sipped her wine. 'He's always admitted to preferring male company.'

'But surely you'd have known about something like that?' Elizabeth said.

'Not having had anything that resembled sex for twenty-five years, you'd certainly have thought so. But then you don't know him as well as I do. He's quite capable of keeping something like that quiet.'

'You mean like his involvement with the British Independent Party?' Elizabeth put in, trying to draw her mother-in-law out.

'Oh, you know about that, do you?'

Elizabeth nodded.

Margaret grunted, 'The idiot's got himself into that up to his neck and now he can't extricate himself.' She frowned. 'Daddy would have had a heart attack if he'd still been alive. He'd fought tooth and nail against fascists all his life. He tried to warn me off William but I was a fool and didn't want to listen.'

'What in particular did your father dislike about him?' Elizabeth asked, anticipating that she was about to hear a further revelation.

'For a start, he didn't take to William's air of superiority and the way he ran down the country at every opportunity. I wouldn't mind if he'd actually served in the forces. The only action he saw was a stint of officer training at Sandhurst – and that ended abruptly. From what I gathered later on, he got thrown out. Knowing William, it was probably for insubordination; he never did like taking orders from anybody.'

'You're making him sound like a major disappointment,' Elizabeth dared to say.

'Only to himself. Believe it not, he's always suffered from low self-esteem. But there I was, refused to listen to my father.' Margaret sighed. 'I was no oil painting, but at last I had someone who wanted to marry me – and frankly, that seemed good enough at the time.'

Elizabeth was filled with pity for the woman sitting next to her. Impulsively, she wanted to delve further into the circumstances that had brought the two together but then thought better of it. And then their turbot arrived and for a while they both concentrated on the meal, which was delicious. Elizabeth stuck to water after her one glass of wine, while Margaret downed the Chablis with gusto.

'Fortunately, William was sufficiently bright to have qualified as a lawyer,' she resumed eventually, as if there had been no hiatus. 'He joined his father's firm and worked hard to build it up to what it is today.' There was an unmistakable note of pride in her voice.

'But then, didn't his decision to go into politics seem a bit strange?' Elizabeth enquired.

'The episode at Sandhurst left him with a terrible chip on his shoulder. Instead of putting it down to experience, the fool allowed it to fester.'

'But in every other way, he made a success of his life?' Elizabeth said.

'Don't you think I tried telling him that? But I was wasting my breath. It was as if he'd made up his mind that if he couldn't be Commander-in-Chief of the armed forces, he'd make his mark on the political landscape instead.'

Elizabeth mulled over the things that her mother-in-law had said. It was extraordinary that it had taken all this time for her to find out from Margaret about William McCreary's true character. She would never have gleaned the same insights from Anthony – probably because, up until now, he'd been in such awe of his father that he would never have dreamed what William was capable of.

'The thing is, he's left Anthony to take the blame,' Elizabeth stressed, returning to the main purpose for the lunch.

'I'm fully aware of the situation but there's little I can do,' the older woman said, greedily spooning up the last of the sauce on her plate.

Elizabeth tried hard not to show her disappointment; she had known it was a long shot to expect help from the woman. Now she and Anthony would just have to go it alone.

'There is one bit of advice I *can* give you,' Margaret said.

Elizabeth perked up, but her hopes were soon dashed.

'Don't underestimate William. He won't let anything – *or anyone* – stand in his way.'

Elizabeth felt a chill run down her spine at the clear warning.

The two women left the restaurant shortly afterwards – Margaret McCreary in good time for the four o'clock train from Paddington station to the Cotswolds, and Elizabeth for Regent's Park, neither of them mentioning their long-standing arrangement for the weekend in the country.

15

Two weeks after the lunch at Scott's, Elizabeth waved goodbye to Emily at the school gates and went back to her car. She wondered how long it would be until, like her older brother, the girl would insist on making her own way to school. Hopefully, it wouldn't be for a while yet, now her mother was glad to be back in her old routine.

The three sessions with Marlene had restored Elizabeth's belief that she was a good mother, but more than anything else, it was Anthony's difficulties at work that had brought the family back together. There were even signs that the intimacy which had been absent between the couple for so long was slowly getting back on track.

As she unlocked the car, Elizabeth checked her phone and noticed that she'd received an unexpected message from Gideon Halevi, asking her to call him. Her initial reaction was to delete it. The last thing she needed was another complication. However, she knew how persistent the fellow could be and that he would keep on trying until he got hold of her. The question was, whether part of her wanted him to?

*

Elizabeth glanced at the Victorian clock above the fireplace as the chimes rang out at 9 p.m. Still no sign of Anthony. She guessed that the meeting with counsel, who were representing him, must have gone on longer than expected. Convinced he would get off with the usual perfunctory censure, her husband appeared to have regained much of his cheerfulness – to the extent that the couple had talked about taking a family holiday in the summer to Disney World Florida. But despite his outwardly stoical appearance, she could tell that the split with his father over the case was eating him up inside.

Returning to her paperwork and the music degree module she'd been trying to get to grips with since she returned from Vienna, she was put off her stride by a new text on her mobile.

Stopover in London en route to New York. Meet at Excelsior Hotel Heathrow, 10 a.m. tomorrow. Gideon.
Before she had a chance to formulate a response, there was the familiar sound of a key in the front door – and then Anthony staggered into the living room. His tie was halfway down his shirt and his face had been drained of its colour.

'Hello? Something wrong?' he said, slurring his speech and blissfully unaware of his appearance.

'We've been worried, wondering where you've been,' Elizabeth told him. 'Emily wanted to stay up and Freddie hung on for as long as he could before going over to Gus's house to work on their Geography projects.'

'I need a drink,' Anthony blurted out, appearing unsteady on his feet.

'Looks like you'd be better off with a black coffee,' Elizabeth said, getting up and making her way to the kitchen, wondering what had brought this on. He was in quite a state.

'I'd prefer something stronger,' he grumbled.

'Don't you think you've had quite enough?'

Without offering a response, Anthony flopped down on the sofa next to where his wife had been sitting. Returning with the coffee a few minutes later, she found him holding the mobile phone she'd left behind. Elizabeth's heart sank. He must have read the text from Gideon.

Sitting down and passing him his mug of coffee, she waited for him to say something. Instead, he just sat there with a glum look on his face. Finally, he spoke.

'It's over,' he said resignedly.

Elizabeth's first thoughts were that he was referring to their marriage.

'Struck off!' he lamented. 'I still can't believe it.'

'But the hearing wasn't supposed to be till next week,' Elizabeth objected, relieved that she wasn't the cause of her husband's distress.

'It was today. I didn't tell you because I didn't want you to worry.' He passed a shaking hand over his brow.

'We're in this together, darling, remember?' Elizabeth said, taking hold of his hand.

'Really?' Anthony said dully.

'Of course. What else did you expect?' Elizabeth replied, still afraid that he had caught sight of her lover's message and was about to use it against her.

'We'll have to sell the house,' he said, 'and there's no way we'll be able to afford private-school fees. As it is they are three thousand a term each. We're not going to be able to afford that.'

'Anthony, listen to me! They can't stop you from working. That's just not fair.'

'I'm the one responsible – that's what they said. I'm the one responsible,' he muttered, unaware that he was repeating himself.

'We'll appeal,' Elizabeth argued. She hated to see him defeated like this.

'They claimed I should've known what was going on. They're right. I'm not fit to run a law practice,' her husband rambled on, consumed with self-pity.

'That's ridiculous and you know it. You're a first-rate corporate lawyer. Your father often said—' Elizabeth stopped herself from continuing.

'Don't mention that bastard! *He* did this to me!' Anthony screamed.

'Darling, please, you'll wake Emily. I know you're upset. Perhaps I should talk to your mother again,' Elizabeth fretted. But she knew it was a long shot, especially as she hadn't come away with anything positive from the recent lunch at Scott's.

'Waste of time!' Anthony slurred. 'She's scared of him; always has been. Lillian is more use than Mother has ever been.'

'You've never said that before,' Elizabeth replied, surprised.

'We get on well, your mum and me.'

'Really?'

'Couldn't do enough, when you were away. Perhaps she thought you'd done a runner?' He gave a long sad sigh.

'I doubt that,' Elizabeth said hesitantly. Apart from when she first got home, she and Lillian hadn't seen much of each other. It was as if the initial interest her mother had shown in Vienna had all been forgotten and she'd reverted to type by once again putting her older sister Erica out of her mind.

'Jess was always his favourite,' Anthony said, right out of the blue.

'Jess? That's it!' Elizabeth exclaimed.

'What?'

'Didn't you mention that she and William had an awful row about something?'

Anthony leaned back and shut his eyes, appearing to drop off to sleep but managing to say, 'Apparently she'd stumbled on some private papers in Father's study in the Cotswolds that she wasn't supposed to find.' He yawned hugely.

'And didn't you also say that he was still supporting her after she moved to France?'

'Yes, that's right,' Anthony mumbled.

'You don't think there's any possibility that the two things are connected? That he's paying her off?'

'I suppose there might be.'

'If we could provide evidence to the tribunal that they acted too hastily,' Elizabeth thought aloud, 'the judgment against you could be quashed.'

'Must be worth a shot.' Anthony sat up, grasped his mug with hands that still trembled and took a cautious sip. 'Jess has been waiting to get her own back for the way she was treated.' He put the mug back down, and said more clearly, 'I'll call her tomorrow when I clear out my office, assuming they haven't already put a block on my phone.'

'So who is going to run things in the meantime?' Elizabeth asked, taking a gulp from her own mug.

'Mustafa's the only one who's qualified.'

'That'll no doubt please your father!' Elizabeth quipped.

Anthony saw the irony. It was the first time he had smiled that day.

'You're the best. Do you know that?' he said, drawing his wife close to him and kissing her forehead.

*

Earlier that day, no one paid any particular attention to the man sat unobtrusively making notes during the hearing at 1, Fenchurch Street in the City. Although the panel hadn't yet passed judgment, Richard Overton's instinct told him that there was more to this disciplinary action than just a breach of solicitors' code of practice. This was why he'd used his personal connection with the clerk of the court, with whom he was on first-name terms, to gain entry to the otherwise closed-door proceedings.

For one thing, he asked himself, why were they in such a rush to condemn the defendant, Anthony McCreary, and have the case done and dusted? In addition, the Crediton Trust had received only a passing mention, inferring they had done nothing wrong. Naturally being a FTSE Top 100 company and therefore considered beyond reproach, it wasn't surprising they were unrepresented on such a trivial issue.

Then there was the matter of the British Independent Party. Richard knew all about that elite group of upper-class racists. Even now he shuddered at the thought of their secret manifesto: purely by chance, he had managed to obtain a copy. What were they doing, accepting huge donations from undisclosed sources, unless they had no intention of declaring them? But it was the result of his digging around that revealed how William McCreary had a foot in both camps – and yet he too had somehow conveniently escaped any charges. This had convinced Richard that there was a cover-up somewhere, bringing with it the potential for an exposé, written by himself, which would shake the very foundations of the British Establishment.

Unsurprised by the verdict, delivered just thirty minutes later and which had ended the defendant's career, the journalist slipped away and hailed a cab to Euston station. With luck, he'd still be in time for the 6.40 p.m. fast train to Manchester Piccadilly. He hadn't been home in a while to see his folks in Cheadle, and he wanted to pick his father's brains; plus, it might present an opportunity for them both to go and watch United at Old Trafford on Saturday!

Raymond Overton was a university don and an expert on European Economic History and just might be able to provide Rick with some leads on what he knew about the origins of certain multinational pharmaceutical companies in Britain. It was public knowledge, for instance, that Crediton was established after the Second World War and had become a fully quoted company in 1969, but apart from establishing that its seed capital had been provided by a conglomerate of German pharmaceutical firms, there wasn't a great deal of information available. What had made the company decide to move to England and reinvent itself as a research charity in a remote town in Devon was anyone's guess.

16

Heathrow Aiport, May

Elizabeth spotted Gideon in the coffee shop, the moment she arrived at the airport hotel the next day. She couldn't explain to herself why she had decided to turn up, especially after that near-miss with Anthony seeing her phone messages. Surely she couldn't put it down to still being in need of excitement? On the other hand, the last few months had taught her that she didn't know herself quite as well as she'd previously supposed.

'Hello,' she said, going up to the banquette where he was having breakfast.

'I didn't think you'd come,' he said, looking up from a large bowl of muesli.

'Let's just say I was curious.' Elizabeth sat down opposite him and took in his appearance. She was still attracted to him, she found, still hadn't managed to fully get him out of her system.

'So what brings you to London?' she asked casually, trying to hide her feelings.

'I wanted to see you.' The Israeli spoke bluntly.

'Really?' And then Elizabeth caught sight of the two large suitcases beside him.

'Yes, because I shan't be returning to Vienna.'

'So, I assume Oscar Gruber is no longer a priority?' Elizabeth enquired, voicing her relief. She wasn't going to mention that she'd expected to hear in the news that he'd been assassinated.

'There's nothing new on that front apart from a few newspaper articles concerning Vienna's forgotten Jews and the same old talk of reparations, which we've all heard before,' Gideon said sourly.

Elizabeth remembered Freda Hirschman saying that Gideon's parents had been Austrian Jews from the Leopoldstadt: this explained his strong affinity with the community. She regretted not having discussed it with him at the time.

'And who do you think may be behind the renewed interest?' she asked.

'Wouldn't surprise me if it wasn't your second cousin, just to drum up extra support for his next power grab.'

'What do you mean?' Elizabeth was puzzled; aware she must have missed something.

'You obviously haven't read yesterday's papers,' Gideon said, producing a copy of the *Vienna Times* with Oscar Gruber's image on the front page.

'So are you saying he's no longer a target?' Elizabeth wanted to know.

'Herr Gruber has announced that he's decided to run for President, the next time around. With the money he has at his disposal for his campaign, he may well succeed,' Gideon said, deftly avoiding the question.

'That was a bit sudden.' Elizabeth frowned. 'He didn't mention anything when I was there a few months ago.'

'Don't assume it was an impulsive change of direction on his part. He was probably keeping it under wraps in order to gain maximum impact. That man understands the power of the press better than anyone; that's what makes him so dangerous.'

'And so you are implying that to alter his views would prove politically divisive?'

'That's the way my superiors see it.'

Elizabeth thought for a moment. All that effort in discovering that she and Oscar Gruber were related, and her subsequent attempts to convey that discovery to him, along with the proof – and at enormous risk to herself – now seemed to have been in vain.

'But you didn't come all this way just to tell me that,' she said flatly. 'Why am I here, really?'

'I came to warn you.'

'About what in particular?' Elizabeth was by now thoroughly confused.

'My replacement may not have the same "distraction" that I had,' Gideon said in a low voice, forcing a smile.

It took Elizabeth just few seconds to comprehend that he was referring to her.

'I suppose I should take that as a compliment?' she said.

'One that cost me my job!' the Israeli retorted.

Elizabeth felt her heart pounding on learning that their attraction hadn't been purely one-sided.

'So what exactly is your replacement's brief?' she asked.

'First of all, Major Livni is a *she*, and secondly, it's classified information,' Gideon answered tersely.

Elizabeth looked around before asking, 'You are saying Mossad still want Oscar to be assassinated?'

'I'm no more privy to their plans than you are. I just thought you should be aware that it's still a possibility,' Gideon said, finishing off his muesli.

Elizabeth had a sudden sensation of déjà vu – but this time she felt less inclined to do anything about it. She had done her best in Vienna; there were now more important priorities closer to home that required her attention.

'And what are your plans, may I ask?' she wanted to know, more than a little hopeful that she was going to be part of them.

'I've got a job in New York with a private security firm,' Gideon revealed.

'So we shan't see each other again?'

'Not unless you intend on following me there.'

'It might have been nice to be asked.' Disappointment was plain in her voice.

'Elizabeth, you and I know it wouldn't work out,' the Israeli said, repeating the exact same words she had used when they were last together.

An uncomfortable silence ensued as Elizabeth saw all hope of rekindling their romantic relationship disappear.

'How's Freda?' she asked, realising she had been remiss in not enquiring earlier after the old lady who had afforded her such wonderful hospitality.

'Not great, the last time I saw her. She's not eating much these days.'

'I noticed that when I was staying in the apartment but I thought it was just the effects of her heavy cold.'

'She's never completely recovered from losing Ernst,' Gideon divulged.

'And how did she react about *you* leaving Vienna?'

'Freda said she understood.'

'It must have been difficult.' Knowing how close the two had been, Elizabeth suspected it must have been an awful wrench for the old lady. 'Anyway, I'm sure you'll keep in contact,' she said as an aside.

The Israeli's expression told her that it was unlikely.

With nothing left to say, they parted shortly afterwards.

*

Elizabeth drove home, feeling a mixture of relief that it was now over with Gideon and of shame that she had left herself perilously open to straying again. The important thing was that she could now concentrate on supporting her family during what was bound to be a testing time. She would pull her weight by going back to work; in fact, she'd already put a few feelers out with some old contacts at EMI, who had responded positively about rejoining the musical publishing company she'd worked at twenty years before.

*

Gideon Halevi went up and shook hands with the heavy-set man outside the Israeli Embassy in Kensington Gardens, who handed over a thick packet and then briskly moved away. It had taken time, but as the Head of their European surveillance operations, David Goldstein was well placed to provide the verification he needed to absolve Elizabeth McCreary from any personal involvement with the pro-Nazi British Independent Party.

*

Early that afternoon, a black cab pulled up outside the pretty Crescent opposite Primrose Hill and a svelte woman with bleached-blonde hair and a long Afghan sheepskin coat got out, paid the driver and proceeded up the pathway of number 22 and rang the doorbell.

Elizabeth drew back the living-room curtain to spot a familiar figure standing on the doorstep.

'Jess! It's really lovely to see you,' she said, opening the door and throwing her arms around her sister-in-law.

'Anthony sounded distraught on the phone so I jumped on the first plane,' Jessica explained, entering the home she'd practically lived in before she moved to France.

'I was just going to make myself some lunch. Do you fancy joining me?' Elizabeth asked, leading the way into the rustic designed kitchen.

'It's OK, I had something on the plane,' Jess answered, unbuttoning her coat.

'Still watching your weight?'

'You know me too well.'

'I wish I had your will-power,' Elizabeth countered, opening the door of the fridge.

'And I'd like to have a sexy figure like yours,' Jess replied, planting herself on a stool at the breakfast bar. 'But you can't have everything!'

'Emily and Freddie will have a nice surprise when they get home from school. How long do you intend on staying?' Elizabeth spooned out a healthy quantity of cottage cheese into a wooden salad bowl.

'As short a time as possible,' Jess replied. 'I do have a life away from here, thankfully.'

'By the way, how is Aisha?' Aisha was the stunning

Pakistani partner that Jess had been with for the last three years.

'Great! We want to get married, but it's not possible in France, or Britain at the moment.'

'Why, what's the problem?'

'Apart from the fact that it's against the law, that we're gay and that one of us is a Moslem, you mean? Paris is even more racist than here, at least on the surface.'

'But I thought the reason you chose to go there in the first place was because it was a clean start and Aisha spoke French?'

'I left because I couldn't bear to see my family being torn apart.'

'Nice of you to warn me what I was getting myself into,' Elizabeth said drily.

'I didn't know about it then. Remember, I was also only in my twenties and the only important thing in those days was partying and getting laid.'

'Lucky you. More than ever happened to me,' Elizabeth remarked.

'I don't know – you seemed pretty keen on that guy with a house in Knightsbridge and a yacht in Monte Carlo.'

'You mean André? Oh yes. Good God! It's been ages since I last thought about him.' Elizabeth laughed. 'He's probably married with grown-up children by now.'

'I hate to break it to you but he was married *then*. You were merely his bit on the side.'

'You're not serious,' Elizabeth gasped, enjoying herself. 'How did you know?'

'Remember that time he said he was entertaining business associates at Annabel's?'

'Yes, and I'm still pissed off I wasn't there,' Elizabeth replied.

'That was because it was really his wife's birthday party. I don't think she would have been all that thrilled if you'd been on show.'

'So – come on, how did you find out?'

'Female intuition, plus the fact I saw him purchase an expensive piece of jewellery when I was working at Asprey's, to be engraved *To My Darling Wife*.'

'I'd forgotten about your stint at that respectable establishment.'

'It was my mother's idea of where a debutante should be spending her time before getting married off. Unfortunately, she was wrong on both counts.'

'No wonder Margaret and William didn't take too kindly to your change of lifestyle.'

'That's their problem – although it wasn't a bowl of cherries either, trying to convince them that I wasn't the daughter they'd envisaged.'

'I suppose that's what made you leave home?'

'No option, more like it.'

'It must have been hard.'

'What, working nights in a café in Gospel Oak and living in a one-bed above the Jolly Mariner? You must be joking. It took a little getting used to but I was *sooo* glad to be away.' Jess looked at her sister-in-law, adding, 'Anyway, at least you've got the balls to stand on your own two feet without them telling you how to live your life.'

'That sounds like a dig at Anthony,' Elizabeth said.

'He needed someone strong, who was prepared to stand up to his father,' her sister-in-law replied.

'Yes, I can see that now,' Elizabeth agreed. 'To be fair though, I have to say they've always been perfectly civil to me.'

Jess pulled a face.

'You're not convinced?' Despite her words, Elizabeth couldn't help feeling she hadn't been sufficiently warned before walking blindly into the McCreary family set-up. Her mother's best friend, Charlotte Brown, known as Elizabeth's Aunt Charlotte, had not liked them, and her intuition had proven accurate. Elizabeth recalled the first time they had met at her engagement party. William had had more than his fair share to drink and spent the evening grilling her aunt about her *foreign* accent. Lillian came to her friend's rescue just in time. On reflection, maybe William tolerated her as a daughter-in-law because it suited him to do so?

'Look, it's not what I think of my father that matters,' Jess said, taking up the conversation again. 'My brother needs to get back to the firm for the sake of his state of mind, which as I'm sure you are aware is not good at the moment.'

'Are you saying that you think he's depressed?'

'My brother isn't as resilient as he makes out. It's just a front he puts on to hide his insecurity.'

'Really?' Elizabeth was put out to be hearing things about her husband for the first time, things which she should have noticed herself. Of course, she was aware that Anthony was in awe of his father, but she had had no idea that it affected him to such an extent.

'Anyway, I think I can help him,' Jess concluded.

'That would be wonderful because I didn't get very far

with your mother,' Elizabeth explained.

'It was brave of you to try.' Jess grinned.

'We had lunch in town, you see, and—'

'Don't tell me, Scott's in Mount Street.'

'That's right. How did you know?'

'There's a table permanently reserved in her name but it's no wonder she couldn't be of any use because she always gets so pissed!' Jess screwed up her face. 'Once when we were kids, the four of us were sitting there, Mother got up to go to the loo and fell flat on her face – and none of the guests at the other tables batted an eyelid.'

'You're not serious?'

'The management got quite used to it. One time, she got up off the floor to a round of applause, like some impromptu house entertainment.' Jess chuckled. 'The truth is, I feel sorry for her having to live with that monster for the last thirty years. Did you know they've never shared the same bedroom from the day they were married?' Jess yawned. 'How Anthony and I were ever conceived is a mystery. In fact, I'm sure she had to get him pissed to fuck her!'

'That's not very nice,' Elizabeth responded.

'You don't get it, do you – *he's* not very nice. It wouldn't be so bad if it was only because he just didn't fancy her but he's a bully and richly deserves what's coming to him.'

'Like what, for example?' Elizabeth asked, curious.

'Let's just say I've got some dirt on Daddy dear that will prove that he's not been exactly whiter than white. I hadn't intended on using it until my bro told me what the old man had been up to. Now he's given me little choice.'

'Does Anthony know about this?'

'No, not yet. I thought we could discuss it over an Italian this evening?'

'Sounds good to me. I know of one or two places but we'll need to reserve a table,' Elizabeth said, going to get her Filofax for the telephone numbers.

'Great. Then you can fill me in about Vienna!' Jess called after her.

The comment stopped Elizabeth in her tracks. Perhaps she was overreacting due to having just seen Gideon, but it had become apparent that Anthony had kept in closer contact with his sister than he had admitted. It made her feel uncomfortable knowing that she, more than her father-in-law, had been the main topic of their recent conversations.

*

Anthony McCreary strode confidently into a grimy building south of the river and took the stairs to the accountant's office on the third floor.

'So Anthony, you said it was important?' Barry Levinson greeted him coolly and with not so much as a word of sympathy for his visitor's current troubles. As far as he was concerned, he'd had a job to do and that was that. It was only out of curiosity that he'd made himself available this morning, not because he'd envisaged anything materially new having turned up.

'Here's proof that my father acted on his own,' Anthony said, handing over copies of the bank statements belonging to the British Independent Party. Thank heavens that Jess had had the nous to photograph them.

'I agree, it looks as if he intended to keep his involvement secret,' the accountant responded after perusing the contents.

'It goes further than that!' Anthony exclaimed excitedly.

Barry sat back in his tattered leather chair, a sceptical expression appearing on his chubby face.

'My sister claims that he bought her silence.'

'Oh, did he now?' the accountant muttered, looking up.

'Father had gone out of his way to make Jess's life unbearable because she has a female partner and he didn't approve of her choice of lifestyle.'

'So you're saying he wanted her out of the way?'

'Yes, because of the harm it would do to his political profile if it got out that his own daughter was a lesbian: it's against everything his party preached,' Anthony confirmed. 'Then, when she accidentally came across these papers in his study at his house, by all accounts he went berserk and threatened her with all sorts of nasty things.'

'That must have been hard for your sister,' Barry replied, giving the statements he'd received a second glance.

'She's a tough nut, is Jess, and not that easily intimidated.'

'But how on earth did she get hold of these without her father noticing?'

'I've no idea, but then Jess can be resourceful and more than a little devious when the occasion warrants it,' Anthony explained admiringly.

'So what happened then?' the accountant asked.

'They reached an accommodation: Jess would keep quiet about what she had discovered and in return, he wouldn't discontinue her allowance.'

Barry Levinson pondered for a moment.

'For what it's worth, I believe you were not party to the dealings in question,' he told Anthony, 'but what went on between your sister and her father was just a domestic arrangement that I'm afraid won't stand up in court, if you are intending to appeal, as is your right. The fact still remains that, being in a position of authority, you should have known what was going on in the firm.'

Anthony slumped down in his seat feeling completely deflated. This was his one chance to clear his name and he'd failed.

'Look, all's not lost,' Barry Levinson said. 'I've got someone investigating Crediton's involvement which, with a bit of luck, might produce some interesting results.' But his words had fallen on deaf ears. The man in front of him, drained of all the optimism that had been present just thirty minutes earlier, had become completely forlorn.

17

Elizabeth entered Southwark police station just after midday and gave her name to the officer in charge. She was directed to a seating area already filled with anxious-looking people and found a seat next to two tramps clasping mugs of sweet tea, no doubt grateful for the first hot drink of the day. The phone call she'd received barely forty minutes earlier had sent her into a panic. In it, she was told simply that a man identifying himself as Anthony McCreary was being held and appeared to be in some difficulty. Jess had offered to accompany her but Elizabeth had declined. Anthony was her responsibility. She would look after him. It was just such a shock. Last night over dinner at La Famiglia in Chelsea, he had been in such good spirits, convinced that the governing body had been over-zealous in handing down their judgment – but it didn't matter, he said. With the new information his sister had provided, it would be certain to reverse its decision. It was only a question of time until he was reinstated, he had told them.

Elizabeth wondered what on earth had happened in the meantime to have caused such a change in him.

A surly-looking uniformed officer eventually appeared. 'Mrs Elizabeth McCreary?' he boomed in his sergeant-major's tone.

Elizabeth tensed up, anticipating the worst, while the tramps and everyone else who was waiting there stared at them.

'Come with me, please,' the fellow said, looking straight ahead.

Elizabeth followed the policeman into a small room furnished with a simple wooden table at which sat her husband. Still smartly dressed in his grey flannel suit, it took her a few minutes to detect what was different about the man who had left home just a few hours earlier. It then hit her. The left side of his face was badly distorted. He tried to speak but the words came out slurred and she was unable to discern what he was trying to say.

'We found him wandering in the middle of a busy road by London Bridge,' the policeman divulged. 'How he wasn't killed is a miracle. Fortunately, a passer-by helped him to the side of the road until our lads arrived on the scene. To begin with, we thought he was drunk like those two tramps outside.'

'He was fine when he left home this morning,' Elizabeth said, deeply shocked. 'I think we need to get him to hospital,' she added, wondering why they hadn't used their initiative to get the police doctor to take a look at him.

'Probably the best thing to do,' the policeman agreed. 'Apart from a few shaken-up motorists, no one has come to any harm; so now you're here, we can release him into your care.'

But Anthony had certainly come to harm! Elizabeth helped her husband to his feet. Her immediate priority was to get them both away from this dreadful place that made her feel as if they'd committed some awful crime.

'Just make sure to keep a good eye on your hubby, Mrs McCreary. We won't be wanting a repeat performance,' the policeman said, showing them out.

*

Elizabeth sat waiting patiently in the out-patients department of Guy's Hospital. Although the queue wasn't long and Anthony had been seen straight away, he'd been gone for over two hours and she had begun to worry. Fortunately, Jess had delayed her return to France and was able to pick Emily up from school.

Just then, a young male doctor with fine oriental features appeared.

'Mrs McCreary, I'm Dr Chang,' he said, introducing himself. 'Your husband has been assigned to me.'

'Anthony is going to be all right, isn't he?' Elizabeth asked nervously.

'We've looked at the results of the brain scan, and I think it's safe to say your husband has not suffered a stroke. The more likely scenario is a mild palsy. Are you familiar with the condition?'

'No, I can't say I am. Is it serious?'

'That depends more on the underlying causes than the neurological disorder itself. Let me explain. Has your husband been under any particular strain recently?'

'A great deal actually,' Elizabeth replied. 'Why, could that have had anything to do with it?'

'The condition is consistent with a sudden shock to the system but it could also have been building up over a few weeks.'

'I see,' Elizabeth said pensively. She had obviously misinterpreted Anthony's slurred speech when he came home the other evening as being drunk when, in fact, it was something far more serious.

'I just don't understand why he didn't go straight to a doctor if he wasn't feeling well?'

'A logical question but it's likely he was feeling more confused than in any degree of discomfort.'

'The police did say that he was found wandering on London Bridge, but he wasn't able to tell me what on earth he was doing there.' She could only imagine that he'd received a setback regarding his chances of an appeal, and that this had finally pushed him over the edge.

'The palsy may well have increased his sense of disorientation so that would make sense,' the medic nodded.

'So what now?' Elizabeth asked, fearful for what the future might hold.

'A combination of steroids and antiviral drugs should increase the probability of facial-nerve function recovery within six months,' Dr Chang replied. 'In the meantime, aspirin or ibuprofen will provide pain relief but make sure he gets plenty of rest.' He passed Elizabeth the prescription he'd made out. 'And I'd like to see Mr McCreary again in two weeks to check his progress,' were his parting words as he moved on to his next patient.

A few minutes later, a nurse appeared, accompanying Anthony, who was proceeding tentatively towards her. The vacant look was still there but at least he still recognised her. No words passing between them, just relieved to have her husband back, Elizabeth took hold of his arm, collected her car from the car park and drove home.

*

The *Herald*'s Editor sat his athletic six foot six frame back in his chair, gazing down at the paperwork he held in his hands – the carefully researched piece that the man sitting a few feet away had just presented to him.

Rick Overton had no reason to feel confident. No one need tell him that he was holding a hot potato, which was the reason why most of the other dailies had already turned him down. At least in Lance Edwards, there was a chance. The Australian, a former cricketer, had never shied away from contentious issues and Rick knew they rarely came more controversial than this.

He still couldn't quite get to grips himself with the extent of what his father Raymond had eventually uncovered, but it was now as clear as day how the founders of the Crediton Trust had managed to amass their fortune. An unspectacular family concern had prospered substantially from its surreptitious activities under the Nazi regime!

'So Lance, are you prepared to run with it?' Rick said, coming straight to the point.

'You're not asking a lot, are you, mate?'

'Didn't think *you'd* have a problem sticking your neck out,' Rick replied.

'Bloody explosive, that's what I'd call it,' the other man said, his claw-like hand sprawled across the typed pages. 'That's more than likely why you came to me last, eh?' he added perceptively.

Rick knew better than to argue; they both were fully aware that this was his last chance to nail what could be an incredible story. Of course, there was a worse than evens chance that taking on a corporation of worldwide repute could result in a series of expensive law suits, which might well ruin his own reputation and career, but that was a risk he was prepared to take.

'Tell you what, matey, get some proof that these allegations are not some made-up load of old bollocks, OK? – and I'll look it at again. That's the best I can do. Now bugger off 'cos I've got a lunchtime deadline to meet.'

Rick suspected as much. However, he'd been given a glimmer of hope and that was all he needed to keep him focused. Leaving the building in Fleet Street, he decided to walk to the Balls Brothers wine bar on Old Broad Street for the prearranged lunch with Barry Levinson. His accountant friend was sure to be interested in what he'd dug up on Crediton, but as far as Rick himself was concerned, this was only one side of the coin. In return, he was looking to Barry for enough dirt on William McCreary and his British Independent Party.

*

Elizabeth was in a determined mood on that Friday morning as she entered the same dreary building south of the river, just as her husband had done forty-eight hours previously. She'd managed to get Anthony to tell her about the last appointment he had attended, and she was resolved to find out exactly what had transpired there: since whatever it was, had caused him to become seriously ill. Anthony had resisted her coming here but she was resolute. She was starting as she meant to go on in proving her husband's innocence and having him restored as senior partner at his law firm.

'It's Elizabeth McCreary for Mr Levinson,' she announced to the receptionist.

'You can go in, it's over there,' the woman said after

making a quick call. She pointed to an office with the door open, a few feet away.

Contrary to what she had built up in her mind, Elizabeth was disappointed to find an unimpressive individual sat behind a cluttered desk. If this was the man who had reduced Anthony to such a state, he certainly didn't fit the part.

'Good morning, Mrs McCreary, please make yourself comfortable. I'll be with you in just a second,' the accountant said, returning to the file he was working on. 'Have you been offered tea or coffee?'

'That's quite all right,' Elizabeth replied, pulling up a chair. She just wanted to get on with it, have her say about the despicable way her husband had been treated and to make it clear that from now on in, *she* would be the one fighting to clear his name.

'Right, I assume you've come here on behalf of your husband?' Barry said, ready to give his visitor his full attention.

'Yes, that's correct. Unfortunately, Anthony has been taken ill.'

'I'm very sorry to hear it, but it's hardly surprising with the ordeal the poor chap has been subject to lately.'

'Yes, thank you,' was all Elizabeth managed to say, caught temporarily off-balance by the unexpected sympathetic reaction.

'Although I'm not sure if you're fully aware of Anthony's predicament?' the accountant added cagily.

'Enough to know that it was you who instigated the proceedings against him,' Elizabeth responded angrily, having recovered her poise.

'I make no excuses for the job I had to do, which in this case unfortunately went against your husband.'

'Worse still,' she said passionately, 'when he came to you with evidence that clearly showed his father had acted alone . . .'

'I assume you're referring to the bank statements?' Barry interrupted.

'That you dismissed out of hand, saying it wouldn't stand up in court!'

'I'm afraid that's so – at least, not on their own.'

'What are you implying?'

'Mrs McCreary, I've recently discovered that there's considerably more to this unfortunate episode than I had originally imagined.'

'Oh really? Perhaps you'd care to explain.'

'Did Anthony ever mention the Crediton Trust?' Levinson asked her.

'No. Should he have had?'

'I take it you're familiar with the name?'

'Of course, isn't everyone? They're one of our largest philanthropic concerns.'

'Quite so. However, there's another side to them which they have been very careful to keep under wraps.'

'I'm not sure I'm with you.'

'For some time, it appears they have been the main providers of funds to extreme right-wing political parties in the UK.'

'I see. So – how is any of this relevant to Anthony?' Elizabeth asked, genuinely bewildered.

'The right-wing parties include the British Independent Party, where his father William is Treasurer,' Barry informed her. 'Granted, this would be pretty insignificant in the overall scheme of things, except it would cause them considerable embarrassment if the City were to discover where its shareholders' capital was being deployed.'

'What are you saying?'

'When I discovered what they were up to, I called on the services of a trusted reporter friend to do some digging around on the company. I have to say, what he came up with was quite astounding.' Barry passed across the report from Richard Overton that he had been perusing when his visitor arrived.

There was no mistake. It was clear in black and white about the connection with the Nazis, but what really shook her was the strong implication of the Crediton Trust's involvement with medical experiments on victims of the Holocaust. For some reason, her mind turned to her mother's painting of the railway station in Vienna. The possibility that her grandparents – or worse, her disabled Aunt Erica – might have been subjected to the same acts of cruelty, sent a shiver down Elizabeth's spine.

Barry said, quite gently, seeing that she was distraught, 'So, Mrs McCreary, you can see that this runs far deeper than your understandable concerns over your husband.'

'Perhaps I've missed something, but I'm still unsure how all this connects to Anthony,' Elizabeth replied pensively.

'Elizabeth, if I may call you by your first name, the Holocaust is still an extremely emotive subject; so much so, that if these findings were ever to see the light of day, the fallout could well be catastrophic.'

Elizabeth stared at him wide-eyed. 'Meaning what, specifically?'

Barry leaned forward. 'To start with, the City's reputation would be in turmoil having one of its largest companies on the Stock Exchange facing such serious allegations.'

'Sounds to me as if you're making a case for that not to happen,' Elizabeth frowned.

'On the contrary,' Barry said, 'I'm interested in establishing the truth, not in cover-ups. And especially not about something like this.' He sighed. 'The only thing is, we would require firm evidence of what Crediton were purported to have been involved in, otherwise bringing an action against the company probably wouldn't get off the ground.'

'It's been so long since the war, what proof could there still be?' Elizabeth wondered.

'I should imagine that the International Criminal Court in The Hague – the jurisdiction for prosecuting war crimes – should first have to locate any survivors who might be willing to testify.'

Elizabeth pondered a moment. Something had resonated with her, to do with medical experiments. Then it struck her. Of course, Freda Hirschman! Hadn't the old lady mentioned that she'd suffered the same fate? In which case, she could be well placed to know whether any other such persons might still be alive, especially in Vienna.

'There is an Austrian woman who I met a few months ago who might be able to help,' she said.

'Do you think you could get in contact with her or, better still, pay her a visit?' the accountant asked.

'With Anthony in his current state, it's just not going to be possible,' Elizabeth shrugged. There was no way she could leave her husband at the moment.

'I understand, but do have a think about it. It may just be the best chance of having the charges against him quashed.'

'How so?' Elizabeth asked, thinking she might have reacted too quickly.

'If the action brought against Crediton were to succeed, I can't see the Solicitors Regulation body being too bothered about what Anthony knew or didn't know and, for what it's worth, I'd do everything possible to see he was reinstated.' Barry didn't mention the welcome addition it would almost certainly bring – of a nail in the coffin of William McCreary's British Independent Party!

'You'd really do that?' Elizabeth realised that she'd judged the accountant prematurely.

Barry gave her a warm smile.

'Now, I'm afraid I have to go off to a meeting,' he said, getting up to show his visitor out. 'I'll leave it to you to get in touch, even if it's only to give me an update on Anthony's state of health.'

18

It was a warm June afternoon a few days later, and Elizabeth felt on edge as she crossed the road by the London Central Mosque on Regent's Park Outer Circle and made her way to the boating lake. Why was it, she wondered, that she always came away from visiting her mother feeling guilty? True, they hadn't seen much of each other since Easter, but there were perfectly good reasons for that, namely Anthony's recent health problems and the fact that Emily and Freddie nowadays had their own social arrangements.

The call from Barry Levinson the same afternoon had surprised her by the speed at which he had managed to arrange the rendezvous with the reporter he'd mentioned at their meeting, as well as his belief that her acquiescence to it would be a foregone conclusion. Due to the highly sensitive nature of their discussion, it was agreed between them that a Royal Park bench on a weekday morning might be the safest place to meet.

Even from a distance, she could see the man waiting for her. Barry had described him perfectly. Taller than average and in his early forties, he was casually dressed in a short-sleeved shirt and chinos, and had a copy of *Private Eye* in one hand and an ice cream cone in the other. He resembled any other tourist frequenting the capital at that time.

'Hello,' he said, peering over his Ray-Ban sunglasses at the woman a few feet away.

'Mr Overton?' Elizabeth enquired.

'That's me. But do call me Richard or Rick, whatever you prefer.' The man smiled at her.

'Very well, Richard,' Elizabeth said, taking an immediate liking to the fellow with a kind expression.

'So how do you suggest we play this?' he asked.

'How do you mean?' Elizabeth replied, a bit lost.

'Well, we can either stay here or if you prefer, we could take a stroll in this lovely weather. It's up to you,' he said, pushing the last bit of cornet into his mouth and then wiping his lips on a napkin.

'I'm fine where we are,' Elizabeth responded, sitting down but keeping a small distance between them.

'Let me begin by saying that I never for one moment believed your husband deserved to be struck off,' Rick Overton said sincerely.

'I wasn't aware that you had followed the case,' Elizabeth said.

'Let's just say, when I got to hear about the high-profile parties who were involved, I knew there had to be more to it.'

'You're implying that Anthony was just a scapegoat?'

'Yes, Elizabeth, in a way he was. Look, there's no question that he exercised a lack of professional judgment – but to take the rap for what was really going on was completely out of proportion. To my way of thinking, it was a rush job to satisfy the Solicitors Regulation Authority in order to appear whiter than white, whilst the real culprits were permitted to continue unimpeded.'

'But that's entirely wrong!' Elizabeth blurted out.

'I totally agree with you but, as I'm sure you already know, your husband is up against some seriously heavy hitters. William McCreary is the driving force behind the British Independent Party – but even that couldn't have been possible if he hadn't had access to substantial lines of finance. It costs millions to fight a general election, and that, even for someone of his means, would normally be well out of reach.'

'I had no idea that William's political aspirations were so advanced,' Elizabeth said, dumbfounded.

'That's understandable because, up to now, he and his cronies have been careful to keep a lid on publicising their activities, especially in the media. But make no mistake, behind the scenes they've been extremely successful in recruiting a large number of the electorate who share their fanatical views. That's why the high-level connections within the Crediton Trust didn't come as a surprise.'

Elizabeth couldn't believe how naïve she'd been. True, her father-in-law's bigoted views reared their head from time to time, but by remaining oblivious to what was going on in her immediate family, she knew she was just as guilty as Anthony, who had been oblivious to what was going on in the firm of which he was in charge.

'Barry Levinson informed me of what you managed to uncover,' Overton went on grimly. 'It's almost beyond belief that an institution renowned for its philanthropic deeds in the fields of medical research would have partaken in such cruel practices during the war.' He looked at Elizabeth. 'Mind you, I'm not claiming that the present board of directors knew what was going on. Most are far too young, but a few of the older ones might have done – if they're still around.'

Elizabeth couldn't help feeling impressed by the depth of the research the man next to her had undertaken but she had to wonder what lay behind his interest.

'Barry Levinson also told me that you were seeking proof from any survivors who might have been subjected to those inhuman experiments?' she said.

'None of the main newspapers will go to print without it,' the reporter confirmed.

'I understand,' Elizabeth responded, disappointed by the answer to her question. Foolishly, she had thought that Overton had purely been influenced by the gross injustice that had befallen her family.

'Which is why I wanted to meet you,' Richard told her.

'Because I can help you to get a good story, you mean?'

'There's that – I'm not going to lie – but there's also something so much bigger at stake: the chance to expose some undesirables in politics and big business for what they really are. That is what really interests me.'

'Sounds like you've got something to prove,' she said daringly.

'Elizabeth, you don't know me very well but the reason I've remained a freelance journalist is because it gives me licence to go after stories that my colleagues employed in the industry daren't touch. Unlike them, I don't have to follow the party line. So, if there's any possibility that this woman you mentioned to Barry may have suffered at the hands of those bastards, then I think we have a duty to get them to pay, don't you?'

'Yes, of course,' Elizabeth nodded, convinced by the man's genuine passion.

'Who are we talking about, by the way?' Richard asked.

'Her name is Freda Hirschman. I met her a few months ago when I visited Vienna.'

'Just on the off-chance, when you were on holiday?'

'No, there's more to it than that. I had planned to take three days in Vienna in order to find out more about a certain member of my mother's family – an uncle who helped her escape on the Kindertransport.'

'So you are Jewish, Elizabeth?' Overton asked.

'Yes, and my mother's family name was Frankl.'

'I see. So you might say that being Jewish, and in these circumstances, your motivation is a good deal greater than my own.'

'For me it's never been about revenge,' she tried to explain. 'More about finding out about my maternal family history.'

'You mean it was deliberately kept from you?'

'No, not intentionally – it's complicated. Let's just say the gap in my knowledge in turn created a void in my life that needed filling.'

'And were you successful?' Richard asked, intrigued.

'Yes. It was an amazing few days. In fact, I discovered far more than I had ever bargained for.'

'I'd love to hear about it one day,' Richard said, and he meant it. 'Although I have to say that with the rise again of the far right under that chap Gruber, you were brave to have ventured there.'

Elizabeth began to reflect on her visit, thinking how, with all the drama going on in London, it seemed to have fallen into insignificance.

'As it happens, I got to know Oscar Gruber,' she

disclosed, completely out of the blue.

Overton looked at her, startled. 'Don't tell me he's the long-lost relation you were mentioning?' he quipped weakly.

'Yes, as a matter of fact he is,' Elizabeth revealed. 'It turns out that he is my second cousin.'

'Come on – I wasn't being serious!'

'It came as much of a surprise to me too, I can tell you.'

'How on earth did you establish that this man who is being touted as Austria's next President is related to you?' the reporter asked, staring at her with a hint of disbelief on his face.

'It's a long story,' Elizabeth replied, not wishing to elaborate. 'All I can say is that it was as a result of a number of surreal coincidences – one of which nearly cost me my life.'

'Surely you're not referring to the terrorist incident on Gruber's home?'

Elizabeth took a few moments to respond. Although the nightmares had ceased, she still had anxiety attacks that she put down to the traumatic effects of that evening. 'Yes, I did happen to be there,' she said in a low voice.

'Was that before or after you found out that you were related?' Richard quizzed. He was relentless, she thought.

'It doesn't really matter. I just wanted the opportunity to get to know the man better and I was able to wangle an invitation to the event he was hosting.'

'And were you able to pursue that, with everything else going on?'

'Not then, but we met again afterwards.'

Richard Overton let out a slow whistle. How could he

ever have predicted this twist to the story . . . 'So how did he react?' he asked. 'I assume you were the one who found out about the family connection?'

'Yes, it came from me. Not unexpectedly, he took what I said with a degree of scepticism at first, but then, when I provided the evidence I'd managed to come by, he became more interested.'

'And have you remained in contact?' Richard asked.

'Not since I returned in April.'

'Incredible! You should write it down one day,' Richard advised her, still in a state of shock.

Elizabeth just shrugged.

After a pause, Overton resumed, but taking it slowly: 'Going back to that woman – Freda, wasn't it – what do you think the chances are of an interview?'

'I really can't say. You see, she'd suffered the loss of her husband while I was in Vienna and I found out subsequently that she hasn't been too well.'

'So you have communicated with her?'

'No, not directly, just through a mutual friend I met up with in London a few weeks ago.' An image of Gideon Halevi fleetingly passed through her mind. She wondered how she might have reacted if he had asked her to join him in New York.

'It's up to you but if I were in your position I wouldn't hang about. No one knows how long any of the survivors are going to be around. Here, take this. Call me any time if you want to discuss your plans, or just want to talk,' the freelance reporter said, handing across a grubby business card. He then got up, smiled at the beautiful red-headed woman he'd rather taken to, and walked away, confident that it was only a question of time before he heard back from her.

Elizabeth remained seated for a while, flipping through the discarded magazine next to her whilst trying to bring her muddled thoughts into some semblance of order. She had to deal with two separate issues. It appeared that Anthony's fate depended upon the successful outcome of a case brought against a multi-billion-pound organisation. That just seemed unrealistic. Margaret McCreary had proven unable to give a hand, so it was now solely down to Elizabeth to help Anthony get back on his feet. And with the way they had already started eating into their savings, that must happen sooner rather than later.

The other issue was the discussion with Overton, which had stirred her conscience. If nothing else, she needed to find a way of reminding Herr Gruber of his obligation to the Jewish community. Regarding Freda Hirschman, she would have to think carefully of how to approach the sensitive subject of her traumatic past. It was a shame that Gideon Halevi was no longer in Vienna since he was the one person who would have been perfectly placed to assist the elderly woman in seeking retribution.

19

Hampshire, south-east England

The BMW 7 Series turned off the M3 motorway, took the Hook exit and then proceeded fast in a north-westerly direction on the B3349.

'You certainly handle her well,' Richard said nervously, at the way Elizabeth was negotiating the narrow country lanes.

'Sorry if it's a bit fast but I only get the opportunity to drive Anthony's car when mine is being serviced,' Elizabeth explained, confidently overtaking the car in front. 'Rotherwick is only a couple of miles away now. We should be there shortly.' She slowed down at a light, saying: 'And you're sure it's a good idea, making out that we're researchers for a feature on the Crediton Trust?'

'Couldn't think of anything better; anyway it's partially true,' Overton said. 'The important thing is that it got us a foot through the door.'

'Who is it that we're seeing again?' Elizabeth asked.

'A man called Jacob Holtz. He retired seven years ago which, according to the records, would put him at nearly eighty; although he sounded alert enough when I spoke to him. Strangely, he didn't seem at all surprised by the call.

It was as if he'd been expecting it somehow.'

'What was his position in the company?'

'Head of Research and Development.'

'Sounds like it could be promising,' Elizabeth remarked, genuinely impressed by the progress that had been made in the few days since meeting Richard Overton for the first time.

'We'll see,' he said, not wanting to get either of their hopes up. The truth was that they were rapidly running out of options since he'd been unable to make contact with the only other person, Joachim Kroll, who'd retired a year earlier and seemed to have disappeared or perhaps had died in the meantime.

Before long, they drew into the car park of the Coach and Horses, a quaint pub in a stunning rural setting. Not having a description to go on, the pair had little trouble in picking out the white-haired man in blue blazer and tie at a table on his own amongst a bunch of locals enjoying a few lunchtime beers.

'Mr Holtz? I am Richard Overton and this is my assistant Elizabeth Saunders,' the reporter said, introducing them and using Elizabeth's maiden name to avoid any association with William McCreary.

'It's just on one o'clock, so you're on time. That's very good,' the elderly man announced, consulting the pocket watch in the palm of his hand. 'May I offer you some refreshment after your journey?'

'Please allow us,' Elizabeth stepped in, glancing at the menu.

'That's very kind but my appetite isn't what it once was. Must be my age catching up with me. They do, however, offer a fine selection of sandwiches. The chicken ones are simply delicious.'

'That's perfect for us,' Elizabeth confirmed, sure that she could detect a slight foreign accent in the older man's speech.

Richard nodded his approval.

'And what would you like to drink?' Elizabeth asked the men.

'Guinness is my preferred choice but I can rarely manage more than a pint these days,' the old man said dolefully.

'Great idea. That would do for me too,' Richard added.

Elizabeth went off to the bar to place their order, highly amused by the elderly man's sudden recovery of his appetite. She did have her doubts, however, whether there was more to this fellow than the offer of a free lunch – although he had held a very important position within the Crediton Trust. Looking over her shoulder, she could see Jacob Holtz and Richard in lighthearted conversation. If there was anything at all to be gleaned from the fellow, Richard was sure to uncover it.

'We were just discussing how much the world of big business has changed since Jacob's time,' Richard remarked as Elizabeth returned with a tray of drinks.

'Do you know, by the time I retired, our company bore absolutely no resemblance to the place I joined all those years ago,' Holtz said, shaking his head.

'When did you start working for them?' Elizabeth asked, sipping her shandy.

'Summer, 1943. I remember it as if it was yesterday,' Jacob said, a touch of nostalgia in his voice.

'Things must have been very different then,' Elizabeth said encouragingly.

'You're absolutely correct, my dear. It was just a family business in those days. Research Assistant was my first job after leaving university in Hamburg.'

'I would never have guessed you were German,' Richard said, feigning surprise.

'Living in the UK for over forty years, sometimes I have trouble reminding myself,' the man joked.

'Sorry, Jacob, I interrupted. You were talking about when you first joined the firm, in 'forty-three. Do go on. You were saying?'

'*Jah*, I remember my boss, Otto. He was a fine man, from whom I learned a great deal.'

'What did the company actually specialise in?' Richard probed.

'We were the leaders in pharmaceutical research for the mentally and physically handicapped,' the German said, as proudly as if he were still part of the team.

Just then, a pleasant-looking young girl appeared carrying a tray on which sat a large plate heaped with a selection of sandwiches, three smaller plates and some napkins. She put them on the table, then hurried back to the bar.

Elizabeth and Richard exchanged looks. They were sufficiently in sync to be able to tell what the other was thinking; namely, that 'pharmaceutical research' was more than likely a euphemism for 'medical experiments'. How to get the former Research Assistant to admit to something as incriminating as that would be no simple matter, Elizabeth knew. But they had to find a way, since she could sense that he had more to give. Peering at the man's almost empty glass, she decided that, despite his previous protestations, another Guinness might do the trick.

'So what happened to the company?' Richard asked, suspecting that he already knew the answer.

'Otto wanted to retire; he knew Moritz wasn't up to running a business.'

'Moritz?' Elizabeth interjected.

'His son! A lazy good-for-nothing – only ever interested in what he could sponge off his father.'

'Didn't he have a profession?' Elizabeth wanted to know.

'Only as a second-rate architect, but his father knew the boy wasn't capable of taking over the company he'd built up from scratch.'

Hearing those words, Elizabeth was reminded of William McCreary voicing the same unkind doubts about his own son!

'So you see from his standpoint, Otto had no choice – he had to sell. Not that there was any shortage of suitors wanting to get their hands on the company, you understand! We were leaders in the field. In the end, Otto received a good price but we lost our independence. Swallowed up by one large concern after another, things were never the same after that.'

He sighed, drained his pint and then, without any warning, he got up from his seat and said, 'I've so enjoyed chatting with you but now I must get back home to feed Erich, my German Shepherd. He doesn't like to be left on his own for long.' And with a simple bow of his head, he slipped away.

'Well, that was unexpected,' Elizabeth remarked. 'Perhaps we said something to frighten him off?'

'More likely the other way round,' Richard grunted, also draining the last of his Guinness.

'What do you mean?'

'The old boy actually told us an awful lot. Perhaps he thought he had gone far enough.'

'Don't you think it was a little odd, that he didn't ask anything at all about us?' Elizabeth said, helping herself to another sandwich.

'Shouldn't think he was that interested.'

'So why do you think he came?'

'More than likely, he lives on his own with Erich the dog, and he looked on it as an outing.'

'And an opportunity to delve into the past, perhaps?'

'He likes an audience, that's for sure,' Richard agreed.

'Everything was going so smoothly, I was just expecting more,' Elizabeth bemoaned.

'Look, he was hardly likely to divulge what they got up to in the war, was he?' Richard said reasonably.

'Unless he could be forced into it somehow . . .' Elizabeth pondered.

'Surely you're not suggesting some sort of blackmail, Mrs McCreary?' Richard said with a straight face.

'No, of course not. It's just that if we had taken him into our confidence, he might have had . . .'

'What? An attack of conscience after sixty years? I hardly think that's likely,' the reporter scoffed. 'Unfortunately, that sort of thing just doesn't happen.'

'All I'm saying is that if he knew what was going on, he just might have wanted to rid himself of the guilt he'd been carrying for all this time.'

'It's a possibility, but my impression was that he was far too canny for that. He was no pushover – remember that before he retired he'd been Head of Research and Development at Crediton, not the little assistant he'd been when he'd started.'

Elizabeth nodded, but she couldn't help feeling that they'd missed an opportunity. Anthony was becoming restless being stuck at home all day and talked of little else than picking up the reins again in trying to clear his name. Now, with nothing definite to report at her end, she wondered how much longer she could keep him at bay.

'So Richard, what now?'

'We need to talk to that Hirschman lady you met in Vienna,' he replied assertively, indicating that he'd already decided on their next step. Elizabeth had hoped the visit might have been avoided since she had no wish to return to Vienna, especially after the trauma she'd suffered there. Not for the first time she was feeling compromised.

Richard didn't notice her lack of enthusiasm. 'What we're looking for is to somehow get survivors to talk about their experiences in the camps,' he went on. 'It would only take one of them to recall the name of a doctor or the name of the drug company that the doctor used to administer those dreadful experiments, for us to get back on track.'

'Fine, but how is this relevant to us?' Elizabeth queried.

'Let's just say there may be other ways of getting what we need,' Richard said, leaving a five-pound note as a tip for the waitress.

Elizabeth smiled, her spirits suddenly restored.

*

Back in Primrose Hill, a couple of weeks later, Elizabeth checked the three table settings. It was a particularly warm evening and she had decided they should dine outside on the patio. Most of the summer had already come and gone. She couldn't recall the last time they were in England at the end of July but then this wasn't a normal year. Fortunately, the children didn't seem to mind staying at home. She was lucky particularly with Freddie who, in the main, understood the challenges they were facing as a family and just wanted to help.

The dinner was also an opportunity for Anthony to hear, first-hand, the progress Richard Overton had achieved on their behalf, especially as they had only met briefly on one previous occasion. Elizabeth too was anxious to hear the results of his trip to Vienna.

Elizabeth gazed at her husband, who had dozed off in front of the television. Even though it had only been a month since his collapse, his condition had improved considerably, and it was only just possible to detect that his left eye still drooped slightly. Equally important was the positive change in Anthony's mental state. Apart from suffering the odd bout of fatigue, he'd recovered his resolve sufficiently to want to correct the injustice to which he'd been subjected.

Despite his suggestion that she go back to Vienna with the reporter since he had taken a special interest in the case, Elizabeth was hesitant. Part of her reticence was on account of the mischief she had got up to previously – and she didn't altogether trust herself to be alone with Richard, an attractive younger man.

Straight after their visit to meet Jacob Holtz, Elizabeth

had smoothed the way for Richard's visit to Vienna by telephoning Freda, who was very happy to hear from her and only regretted that Elizabeth herself wouldn't be coming too. Elizabeth explained the background to the visit: that the journalist was planning an exposé into a large British – formerly German – pharmaceutical company with a dubious wartime past and that Richard Overton would be very interested to hear in person about her two and half years in Auschwitz, if she was willing to talk to him. Elizabeth knew that Richard was hoping to learn the name of the doctor who was carrying out those awful experiments, and details of the surgeries that were performed. It would be a traumatic conversation, and Elizabeth prayed that it wouldn't have a further detrimental effect on the old lady's health.

Oscar Gruber, on the other hand, hadn't returned any of her calls since her return to London. Whether this was due to his decision to stand for the presidency and him not wanting anything to do with the past that might queer his pitch, she didn't know. Whatever the reason, she felt let down. It was obvious he'd forgotten all about her, about the family he had recently discovered and the obligation to make good his word to Vienna's Jewish community.

As she brooded, there was a ring at the doorbell that was answered by Freddie on his way out of the house.

'Hope I didn't keep you waiting,' Richard Overton said, appearing with a large bouquet of white lilies.

'Richard, you shouldn't have! They're gorgeous. Make yourself comfortable and I'll go and check on the food,' Elizabeth replied, bringing him into the drawing room and taking the flowers through to the kitchen.

Just then Anthony stirred. 'Sorry, I must have dropped off. It's the wretched medication I'm on,' he yawned, rubbing his eyes. 'Hello, Richard.'

'Elizabeth tells me you're on the mend, which is the most important thing.'

'So how *was* your little jaunt to Vienna?' Anthony said, a sly note in his voice.

'Actually, it was really productive,' Richard replied, not bothering to elaborate.

Anthony went on, a little sneer in his voice, 'Have to say, all that stuff about that so-called long-lost cousin of my wife's who'd conveniently just crawled out of the woodwork, sounded like a bit of a tall story to me.'

Richard was about to offer the response this deserved, but then thought better of it. Elizabeth had mentioned that her husband's medication made him unpredictably argumentative, which no doubt explained his contentious stance.

Just then, Elizabeth appeared carrying their first course.

'Right, let's eat,' she said. 'I've set the table outside on the patio. Hope you like Vichyssoise, Richard. Anthony, would you mind getting the wine from the fridge? We're having fish, if that's OK.'

'That's great, but you really shouldn't have gone to all this trouble on my account,' their guest replied, passing through to the pretty back garden.

'I'm dying to know how you got on with the Editor at the *Herald*,' Elizabeth said, now her husband had joined them at the table with a chilled bottle of Chablis.

'It wasn't quite what I'd expected,' the guest hedged, offering up his glass to be filled.

'Why, what happened?' Elizabeth asked, picking up a negative vibe.

'To start with, he came up with some feeble excuse that he didn't think another wartime story would sit well with the newspaper's owners. Most of them are risk adverse these days, especially when it comes to reminding their German masters in the EU of their past.'

Richard wasn't going to disclose that he hadn't even made the trip to Vienna in the first place! He was aware of the possibility that he might get found out but money or specifically the lack of it was the issue and, in any case, he had got everything he really needed from Elizabeth, so, in his mind, it had been a chance worth taking. This should have left him with a bad conscience, except that guilt had never been an issue as far as Richard Overton was concerned. The fabrication was merely a ploy to keep the momentum going and, importantly, for the McCrearys to keep their spirits up.

'You mean the paper won't run the story?' Elizabeth came straight back, fearing the worst.

'Not unless another paper were to get there first, then they'd soon change their mind,' Anthony interjected.

'That's exactly right,' Richard nodded, taking a spoonful of soup. 'Which is why I've a couple of others fighting over getting the exclusive, purely as a back stop' – which wasn't entirely untrue, if somewhat exaggerated.

'That sounds really encouraging,' Elizabeth said.

'Wait! It gets better.'

'I don't know what you're so pleased with yourselves about,' Anthony said nastily, feeling that he'd been left out of the conversation.

'I'll explain,' Richard Overton replied, turning to him. 'It's going to be nearly impossible for you to get the justice you deserve without first exposing the British Independent Party and their prime backers for what they really are – and even then, it could be an uphill task.'

'Richard, you should be broadcasting what those fascists stand for – and I should know, because my father's one of them!' Anthony exploded. 'But oh no, instead you've decided on an obscure roundabout route involving the testimony of some old dear. And that's all you've been able to come up with?'

Elizabeth gave her husband an angry look. She felt highly embarrassed. Had he no idea of how to behave?

'I'm sorry, Richard,' she mouthed.

'I realise that it may seem that way to you, Anthony,' the other man said evenly, 'but if my hunch is right, the article will at least draw attention to an injustice on a much larger scale. I don't know if you're aware of the Nuremberg trials?'

'Yes, of course. That's where prosecutions were brought against Nazi atrocities committed during the Second World War,' Anthony replied, still impatient.

'That happened to include the heads of a giant German pharmaceutical company complicit in carrying out all sorts of medical experiments on its victims, young and old,' Richard told him, repeating the information he had gleaned from his father, Raymond Overton.

Anthony pushed his plate away. 'Quite right, that those bastards should pay heavily for what they did,' he muttered.

'The fact is, that only touched the tip of the iceberg,' Richard revealed.

'You *have* been thorough with your research,' Elizabeth joined in, slightly aggrieved. Why hadn't the man been sharing this information with her up till now?

'Unfortunately, it was only the high-profile criminals, the ones who were directly involved who faced prosecution, enabling the lesser-known ones – those who were present and who collaborated by turning a blind eye to what was going on – to get away with it,' the reporter continued. 'Therefore, it may well have allowed those who provided Crediton with its seed capital, to slip through the net.'

There was a short pause, while his hosts thought about what had been said.

Directing his comments to Elizabeth, Richard said, 'I assume you filled Anthony in on our meeting with Jacob Holtz?'

'You mean that chappie who you'd hoped would provide you with an insight into Crediton's wartime activities?' Anthony responded, now fully alert.

'More specifically, when it was just a family concern,' Elizabeth added.

'A pity you weren't at least able to drag the name out of him,' Anthony said.

'Even assuming that our intuition about his involvement could be verified, he would never have told us the truth,' Richard defended himself, whilst inwardly acknowledging that it had been a glaring error on his part not to have at least tried. 'However, the records show that the company which changed its identity to the Crediton Trust was called Obermann – not much to go on except Holtz told us that it had come about through several mergers itself.'

'Surely what we really need to establish are the names

of the component parts that make up the whole?' Anthony said.

'I have a contact at the German Chamber of Commerce who is working on getting us that information,' Richard revealed. 'Also, I'm hoping the feature might encourage other survivors to name names.' He didn't admit that having only received circumstantial evidence so far, at the moment they were very much dependent on others coming forward.

'I think you've both underestimated the scale of what you're getting us involved in,' Anthony said heavily.

'What do you mean by that?' Elizabeth asked, startled.

'To begin with, how many concentration camps were involved?'

'Apart from Auschwitz, there were five others,' Richard replied.

'Assuming they were staffed by, say, two or three doctors, together with assistants . . . that would make thirty or more persons who were potentially liable,' Anthony calculated.

The table suddenly went quiet.

'Anthony's right,' Overton said, the first to break the silence. 'I hadn't adequately considered the wider implications. I suggest we just proceed, one step at a time, and see what reaction the article brings, and we'll take it from there.'

'If you're contemplating legal representation, that's going to cost!' Anthony warned him.

'Yes, I've already thought of that. We'll need a fighting fund. Have *you* got any suggestions?'

'How much are we talking about?' Elizabeth asked.

'A few hundred thousand at least, otherwise I very

much doubt any reputable firm would take it on,' her husband told her.

'We can get it together,' she affirmed.

'Are you absolutely insane?' Anthony cried, red in the face. 'Where are we going to get that type of money from when we've barely got enough for our own needs since I've been off work!'

'I'll explain the situation to my mother. Once she knows what's at stake, there's a good chance she'll be supportive.'

Anthony made a face. 'I find that a little hard to believe since she hasn't exactly been forthcoming when it came to talking about her own family, left behind to the mercy of the Nazis.'

'That's true,' Elizabeth agreed. 'The difference is that if she can help bring justice to others who suffered a similar fate as herself, knowing my mother, she'll react differently.'

'The shoemaker's children go barefoot – that syndrome. I know it well,' Richard said.

'I'm glad you do. With our kids it's the complete opposite – their parents go barefoot,' Anthony quipped, bringing a welcome respite of laughter to the table.

'On that subject, do you mind my asking whether either of you have had any contact with William McCreary?' Richard asked, changing tack.

'None whatsoever,' Elizabeth replied for them both. 'I doubt his father is even aware that Anthony has been unwell.'

'I can imagine that's most upsetting from a personal perspective but, taking into account that what we're working on is pretty explosive stuff, it's no bad thing for the time being to let him carry on thinking that he's got away with it,' Richard said thoughtfully.

With a general election almost certainly going to take place sometime next year, Overton was acutely aware of the extreme urgency of bringing a case that would hold up against Crediton *before* that happened – no easy task, considering that the Trust wasn't yet facing any charges. Nevertheless, being a staunch socialist, he had his own agenda in making absolutely sure that the British Independent Party, which he was convinced was inexorably linked with the Crediton Trust, was stopped firmly in its tracks before it was too late.

20

After hanging around for three weeks after the dinner party, Elizabeth had grown tired of waiting for Richard Overton to get in contact. She was convinced he was avoiding her but she didn't know why. Just as worrying, there was no sign of the article on Freda Hirschman in any of the papers. She began conjuring up different scenarios in her head as to what might have gone wrong, but it didn't help.

To add to her problems, Anthony was becoming more and more difficult. Richard Overton was now completely discredited in his eyes. His vitriolic attack on the reporter, whose far-flung plans had come to nothing, she interpreted as his way of getting back at her. The feelings of loneliness she had experienced just months before, had returned with a vengeance. In her private moments, she found herself fantasising about Gideon Halevi and regretting that she hadn't followed him to New York. Of course, she was aware that she wasn't thinking clearly and that running away wasn't going to solve anything, but the truth was she couldn't see a way out of her predicament. Money was running short and they hadn't received so much as a sniff on the house – not surprising when they'd gone against the estate agent's advice and put it for sale at too high a price. Something needed to happen shortly, otherwise she could see the four of them turning up on her mother's doorstep with their suitcases packed.

One morning at the beginning of September, she was getting ready to leave for the women's group session that she'd recently started attending again, when she was suddenly drawn to a headline that flashed across her morning television screen.

Elderly man found hanged at his home in the village of Rotherwick Hampshire identified as Jacob Holtz. Hampshire Police are eager to interview any persons who may have had contact recently with him.

It took a few moments for the name to register before Elizabeth realised it was the man calling himself Jacob Holtz whom she had met in the Coach and Horses pub with Richard Overton, a few weeks ago. All of a sudden, she had a flashback to being in the ambulance with Oscar Gruber. Gripped by same fear that she was going to be subjected to a police investigation, she tapped Richard's number into her mobile.

After a few seconds, she heard a familiar voice say, 'I suspected it might be you. Our first rendezvous in half an hour? It's not safe to speak on the phone.'

'Richard, can't you at least tell me what on earth is going on?' Elizabeth retorted but it was in vain, the line had gone dead.

Placing her previous plans on hold, she put on her tracksuit and left the house on foot. A brisk jog across Regent's Park was what she needed to try to clear her head. It all became obvious now: instead of them working closely together, as she'd assumed, she had been left in the dark whilst Richard followed his own agenda. Perhaps, as she'd always suspected, he was only out for himself. Anger filled her.

Twenty minutes later, she spotted a familiar figure on an iron footbridge, throwing bits of bread to the ducks in the canal below.

'I suppose I do owe you some sort of explanation,' Overton said with a smirk as Elizabeth approached. In contrast to the tension that had gripped her, his habitual relaxed demeanour had remained completely unchanged.

'Are we in trouble?' Elizabeth asked, trying to catch her breath.

'In what way?'

'Richard, don't be obtuse. You know exactly what I'm referring to!'

'I assume it's the snippet about Jacob Holtz?' The man idly threw more bread into the water. 'Anthony may have been right,' he said carelessly. 'Perhaps we have bitten off rather more than we reckoned with.'

'That's hardly a consolation, when we've come this far,' Elizabeth said crossly. 'Whatever possessed you to go and see Jacob Holtz again, that's what I can't understand. I assume that is what you did?'

'Very perceptive of you to have worked that out.'

'Don't patronise me, Richard. You seem to forget that I've got a lot more at stake than just having my career on the line!'

'It came out wrong. I'm sorry. Of course you're absolutely right. I did go down there again.'

'But after last time, what did you hope to achieve?'

Richard produced a tape from his anorak pocket.

'What's that?'

'That evening when I came to dinner? Some of the things Anthony said about the proof we needed to make these charges stick crystallised my thinking.'

'Well, it is *his* domain,' Elizabeth responded curtly.

'So I took a chance, that's all.'

'But how did you know that Jacob would talk to you again? If you recall, he suddenly went cold on saying anything further when we had lunch.'

'I simply suggested we get together again since there were a couple of things that we'd omitted to ask and he agreed that I could come to the house. He then explained that his wife died ten years ago; the poor fellow spent the first half an hour going through albums of their life together.'

'Was his wife also German?' Elizabeth enquired.

'No, her name was Pamela Robins. She was working at the local doctor's surgery when he first came to England. Probably helped to provide a front for a past he wanted to forget about.'

'Did they have children?'

'A son Peter, who died when he was very young of some rare blood disease.'

'In other words, he had nothing left to live for,' Elizabeth deduced.

'You could say we'd got him at the right time,' Richard added, 'which was just as well, really.'

Elizabeth produced a puzzled look

'You see, examining what we had – an account of a Holocaust survivor, Freda Hirschman, albeit in great detail but unsubstantiated, and the verbal testimony of Holtz, one of Crediton's former executives, that didn't exactly constitute an admission of guilt – those things on their own were not going to get us anywhere. However, if I could find a way of linking the two, we might have something.'

'And did you find a way?' Elizabeth demanded, wanting to be convinced that this wasn't just an attempt to pull a rabbit out of a top hat.

'The only possible connection, if I'm not mistaken, is that they both mentioned a man named Otto,' Richard answered, implying falsely that he had heard it from Freda Hirschman.

'Otto was the name of the man who Jacob first went to work for,' Elizabeth recalled.

'And the name of the doctor who Freda remembered,' Richard said, continuing with the deception. 'True, it's not much to go on but then I struck lucky.'

'What happened?' Elizabeth asked, eager for some positive news.

'Chas Blackstone at the German Chamber of Commerce came up trumps with the name of the original company Jacob Holtz had worked for.'

'So come on, don't keep me in suspense, who were they?'

'They were called K Pharma.'

Elizabeth shrugged. She had never heard of them.

'Anyway,' Overton went on, 'the next step was to convince our friend Jacob that his past was about to catch up with him. I told him that I had a contact who was ready to identify him as part of the team that carried out experiments in Auschwitz. In other words, Freda.'

'But you were bluffing,' Elizabeth blurted out, horrified.

'Jacob didn't know that.'

'So you led him on?'

'Listen, Elizabeth, I didn't feel that great about it at the time and there was no doubt that it was a high-risk strategy.'

'Are you saying he fell for it?'

'In a way that not even I could have expected,' Richard replied, glancing at the tape in the palm of his hand. 'He admitted to everything – his role as an assistant in the family enterprise, procuring and supplying many of the drugs right across the network of concentration camps; he even gave me details of the bank account into which their Nazi paymasters provided the funding for these experiments to take place. Elizabeth, it's all here.'

Elizabeth couldn't find the words to speak. She'd been completely blown away by what she just heard. Now, after what felt like a lifetime, encountering one obstacle after another, there was definite progress at last.

'So that's why Jacob Holtz took his life?' she said, slowly recovering her poise.

'Yes, but the police don't know that.'

'I presume he didn't leave a note?'

'Nor anything else that could trace his last breath back to us. From what I've managed to glean from my colleagues on the tabloids, in the absence of any motive, the police are merely attributing it to the suicide of a lonely widower who had nothing left to live for, which happens to coincide with the coroner's initial findings.'

'So what now?'

'Just wait for things to settle down and then we'll get out Freda Hirschman's testimony with a few added bits,' the reporter told her.

'Surely you're not suggesting doctoring her interview?'

'Only enough to attract the attention of some bright spark of an Editor. Then we'll carry on drip-feeding more stuff until that Editor makes a firm connection between the two.'

'But that's immoral!'

'I shouldn't worry. Things like that occur all the time. Anyway, it's not as if the old girl would mind, especially if it leads to correcting the injustice she suffered. Also, now the bloke's dead, there's nobody out there who can claim that Freda didn't know him.'

Elizabeth stared at him. 'Where's the proof that his recording is authentic?' she wanted to know.

'You're quite right to ask that – which is why it has to appear to have come from him.'

'Richard! You've lost me again.' It was hard to keep track of this man.

'Shouldn't be a problem. Once I've edited out my voice and made copies, the press will have a field day.'

'And how about the fact the tape just happens to turn up three weeks after he killed himself?' Elizabeth queried, her voice dubious.

'I've already thought of that,' Richard responded, grinning like a Cheshire cat.

'Then I don't suppose you'll object to filling me in?'

'We'll need to plant a copy in Holtz's house; that way, it'll be assumed the authorities will have missed it when they investigated the suicide.'

'And how will we gain entry?'

'Easy enough,' he shrugged. 'Holtz told me he always kept a key under the mat so that he didn't lock himself out.'

'And how about his dog, the German Shepherd called Erich?'

Richard grinned. 'Taken in by the neighbour next door if the barking I heard was anything to go by.'

'Sounds like you've thought of everything.'

'And the icing on the cake is that once it makes front-page news the police end up with egg on their face,' Overton said.

Elizabeth shuddered.

'Are you OK?' he enquired.

'It just seems so real,' she replied.

'Great! Then there's every chance those newspaper Editors will think so too.'

Elizabeth turned to him and said in a quiet voice, 'Do you really think Jacob was capable of doing those awful things?'

'I'd put that firmly out of your mind if I were you, otherwise you'll end up feeling sorry for him – and he doesn't deserve that,' Richard told her, throwing the last of the bread to the ducks. 'Now, I don't know about you but I'm starving. Do you know a decent place around here for lunch?'

21

Mayfair, Central London

It had finally stopped raining that mid-October morning as a smartly dressed woman, accompanied by two men in sombre suits, stepped out of Green Park tube station. Crossing the main Piccadilly thoroughfare, in lighter than usual rush-hour traffic, they entered the discreet offices of solicitors Purcell, Roby & Smethers.

'We have a ten-thirty appointment with Roderick Purcell,' the woman announced to the bespectacled male on reception.

'And you are?' his enquired from behind the glass division.

'Mr and Mrs McCreary and Mr Levinson,' Elizabeth responded.

'I'm afraid Mr Purcell is running late. Please take a seat and his PA Mary will come and fetch you when he's free,' the man told her before returning to his work on the computer.

Elizabeth produced a heavy sigh. She just wanted to get a move on. Once she'd reconciled herself to Anthony's insistence in coming along, she strangely felt more relaxed. Although what they were going through had developed into a much larger scenario, it had, as he reminded her, begun with him and therefore he had as much reason to want to carry it through to its conclusion as everyone else. What's more, his prediction of the Crediton Trust's reaction had proven correct in that the company had issued a writ within a matter of days of them being mentioned in the press.

Naturally, the initial response of the *Herald*, where the article on Freda Hirschman first appeared, was to retract the accusation – that was until Richard had assured them that it could be corroborated. Replica pieces following swiftly on in two of the main weekend supplements had the desired effect of emboldening the morning paper to continue running with the story. Preferring to keep a distance, Richard proposed that Barry Levinson should attend in his place. To his credit, Barry was now fully committed to seeing the case through, and they all agreed that his professional experience in negotiation could be put to good use, particularly in relation to costs, which had become pertinent since Elizabeth's mother Lillian, more than likely influenced by her husband Allen, had had second thoughts about giving them the funds.

After a few minutes, a plump woman with a kind face trundled across to meet them.

'Mr Purcell sends his apologies for keeping you waiting. He is free now, so please follow me,' she said, climbing the stairs with surprising agility. 'He's waiting for you in the boardroom on the first floor.'

Entering a large room with a high ceiling and three large sash windows which in some way resembled a doctor's waiting room, Elizabeth noticed a strong smell of furniture polish. An upright elderly man sitting at the end of a long oak table puffing furiously away on his pipe immediately stood up and greeted them.

'Please help yourselves to tea and coffee and biscuits on the sideboard and make yourselves comfortable. I'll be with you in a jiffy. It's this wretched couple's divorce I've been landed with,' he muttered out loud. 'Would you believe that an American billionaire wants a change of spouse after thirty-two years of marriage? Still, it takes all sorts.' He put his previous file to one side and waited until his visitors were sitting, ready to begin the meeting.

'Right, well, this is far more interesting,' he said. 'By the way, Mr McCreary, I hope you don't mind me mentioning that unfortunate business with our supervisory body. A lawyer of your undoubted calibre is a great loss to the profession.'

'Thank you,' Anthony replied softly.

'I assume you'll already have received offers of private work?' Mr Purcell asked him.

'None that I might have been able to take advantage of, since I became ill shortly after that business with the regulatory people – and then, lending a hand with this meant there hasn't been much time to think about it.'

'Of course, I understand,' Purcell said sympathetically. 'Good, so to the business in hand then! I'm compelled to say, at the outset, that taking on the likes of the Crediton Trust is going to be tricky.'

'In what way?' Elizabeth asked, picking up on the note of negativity in the lawyer's voice.

'Well, to begin with, a company of that size is going to have unlimited funds at its disposal.'

'Surely it should be more about the severity of the

crime than the financial clout that they can wield?' Elizabeth said, wondering whether they had chosen the right representation.

To counter Crediton's action against the *Herald*, Barry had tactically advised that they hit the company with a criminal lawsuit of their own, based on Freda Hirschman's testimony and with the aim of buying time until Jacob Holtz's admission was discovered and released. Then, with Crediton fearful of how much more incriminating evidence might be thrown at them, Barry and the McCrearys were banking on getting an admission of guilt and achieving a substantial settlement.

'My clients are fully aware of the size of the task they've undertaken, but there's far more at stake here than a mere defamation suit,' Barry Levinson interjected, glancing at Anthony as he spoke.

'Indeed. Well, let's proceed, shall we?' the lawyer replied, clearly uncomfortable at being challenged. 'I've reviewed the papers that were sent to me and on the face of it, Crediton do have a case to answer. It will, of course, involve Mrs Hirschman attending a court hearing.'

'Here, or in Germany?' Anthony asked, speaking for the first time.

'That's a good point,' Purcell nodded. 'If we're talking about war crimes, the jurisdiction is in The Hague, but remember that only pertains to crimes perpetrated by individuals. From what I understand, with the death of that man Holtz and in the absence of being able to identify any other such people, the case would have to be brought against the company in our national courts.'

'What do you assess our chances of success would be,

in that situation?' Elizabeth wanted to know.

'Quite high, actually,' Purcell told her. 'There are a few precedents where large companies have been successfully prosecuted for criminal wrongdoing. I have to say, however, that if there's a chance of other survivors coming forward, it would add considerable substance to our claim.'

'I agree a class action lawsuit would be preferable,' Barry said, giving his ten cents' worth.

'As far as we know, there hasn't been a further reaction by any of those who may have been similarly affected,' Elizabeth disclosed.

'But I'd be surprised if the situation remains the same once the press at large get their hands on the story,' Anthony interjected.

'Quite so,' Purcell remarked, glancing up from the notes he'd been scribbling on his pad.

'So are we to understand that you are prepared to take the case?' Anthony asked.

'Time to put me on the spot, eh?' Purcell said light-heartedly. 'I assume that you'll be requiring our firm to work on a success fee basis?'

'Yes, we would. As you're aware, it's not at all uncommon in cases of this nature,' Anthony said.

The older man thought for a moment and then said, 'I'll have to put it to the other partners. Don't be surprised if they require something up front – you know, just enough to keep the wolf from the door. Other than that, I think we can reach an accommodation.'

Elizabeth breathed a sigh of relief. To have a firm of the reputation of Purcell, Roby & Smethers on their side would give them more of a fighting chance.

'My own view, for what it's worth,' Purcell continued, 'is that if Crediton is indeed guilty of the charges levied against it, the company should get what it deserves. You see, I was a young corporal in His Majesty's Forces in a platoon that liberated Bergen-Belsen on the fifteenth of April, 1945. The images of what I saw will stay with me for the rest of my life.'

Roderick Purcell stood up and shook their hands in turn before escorting his new clients down the stairs and out of the front door, back into the noise and clamour of Piccadilly.

*

Ten days later in the Devon village of Crediton, 200 miles from London, an impromptu weekend meeting of the Crediton Trust had just commenced. The mood in the top-floor suite of offices of the former corn mill was tense. Several copies of the morning newspapers were splayed out on sofas, occupied by a group of poker-faced executives dressed in casual clothes and drinking neat whisky from heavy crystal tumblers.

'I can't believe what could have possessed old Holtz to do such a thing,' a cropped-haired man complained, 'unless he'd suffered a sudden attack of conscience after reading about that Austrian woman?'

'More like a mental aberration if you ask me,' grunted the man next to him, clearly put out at having his round of golf cut short.

'I'd wager the old hag was paid a tidy sum to talk about her wartime experiences,' the first one ranted.

'Do you think that his admission was authentic?' asked the fresh-faced youngest board member, whose untidy appearance resembled that of an overgrown schoolboy.

'Jacob obviously thought so – although claiming that he was directly involved in those experiments seems wide of the mark,' the bean-pole Head of HR replied in a high-pitched voice.

'What the hell difference does that make?' another whined. 'We've been implicated, that's the problem.'

'Sure – for something that occurred sixty years ago. The whole thing is completely absurd,' the golfer said pettishly.

'The most important thing we need to know is whether there is any truth in the claim that the original owners of K Pharma assisted the Nazis?' the Marketing Director Nigel Willan wanted to know.

The silver-haired chairman, Franz Werner, decided it was time to speak. 'You seem to be inferring that cooperating with the government in Germany at that time was an unusual occurrence,' he said stiffly. 'We were no different from any other decent-sized firm in those days.' He looked down his nose. 'The only reason why it's even an issue is because Germany was on the losing side. Nevertheless I assume we've refuted these allegations!'

'Oh absolutely,' confirmed Roland France, the Group Finance Director. 'Our brokers have already put out a circular to calm investor nerves, and it seems to have done the trick since the share price is holding firm.'

'Good. Because whatever happens, we cannot allow this to affect the Braniff takeover,' Werner stressed.

'That's already done and dusted,' Roland France assured his superior. 'In fact, as soon as we've signed off on the deal at the beginning of next week, we'll arrange for the boys from Chicago to come over so we can present the enlarged group to the City. Capitalised in excess of thirty billion pounds, according to my reckoning that would easily make us world leader in biotechnology!'

A short burst of cheering broke out.

'On to more mundane matters. Has there been any response to the writ issued against the *Herald*?' the chairman enquired once the din had died down.

'Not so far,' Roland replied.

'Probably reassessing their position,' the golfer speculated.

'Waiting to see if any other papers follow their lead, more likely,' another called out.

'In the meantime, why not get our PR people to come out with a campaign specifically tailored to raising our image?' suggested Nigel Willan. 'Instead of waiting for any further adverse press comments, we should be highlighting things like our substantial donations to charitable causes both here and abroad, not to mention the clean-water projects we sponsor for the under-privileged in Africa and our projects in other Third World countries, as well as our numerous awards for breakthroughs in medical research.'

'Hear, hear!' came the rousing response.

'Mr Chairman, one area that may need a rethink concerns certain of our political affiliations,' Willan said, clearing his throat delicately.

'It's on record that we support all the main parties,' Werner said gruffly. He suspected the comment was aimed specifically at William McCreary's British Independent Party. He knew they should have extricated themselves from that association a long time ago, but the thing went back many years and, with more important things on his agenda, he had just let it run. In the current circumstances, however, it was crucial that Crediton had at least to appear to be beyond reproach. Consequently, he thought grimly to himself, that particular funding might have run its course!

Just then, a hunched man wearing a worried expression entered the room. It was Derek Coulson, the in-house lawyer. 'Sorry to be late,' he said, and the room hushed. 'I've been on a conference call most of the morning. It's bad news, I'm afraid, gentlemen. Proceedings have been taken against us.'

'Oh really, by whom?' the Chairman drawled.

'On behalf of a Freda Hirschman.'

The statement brought about a shrug of shoulders and blank expressions around the room.

'Who's she when she's at home?' the golfer said rudely.

'She's the Jewish woman that we were talking about,' someone shouted out.

'And what's so special about her?' Werner sneered.

'I think I can answer that,' the in-house lawyer replied. 'New revelations are about to be released linking her to that interview with Jacob Holtz.'

'What? How's that possible?' several of the men were asking each other.

'I'm not privy to the exact details but my source at the *Herald* said we should brace ourselves for some pretty damning stuff,' Derek Coulson stated.

'Derek, is there any way out of this?' Roland asked.

'We could agree to settle,' the in-house lawyer replied. 'If we could get out of this with damage limitation, it must be worth considering.'

'Oh, you think so, do you?' Franz Werner snapped, clearly incensed that this couldn't have blown up at a worse time.

'I've taken the liberty to write a statement that we could put out, if you agree?' the lawyer said, completely misreading his superior's mood.

'Perhaps you'd care to read out loud exactly what we would be admitting to,' Werner said, his face like thunder.

'It's nothing incriminatory, I can assure you.' Then clearing his throat, Derek Coulson began:

'In its formative years in 1930s Germany, when it was a modest family concern, it's not inconceivable that in the normal course of business, the company may have had dealings with the ruling government of the time. But that in no way constitutes an acknowledgment of the charges levied against it in the recent articles in the press. However, in consideration of any individuals who may have suffered as a result of the company's aforementioned participation, it is, without prejudice, willing to make a goodwill gesture of two hundred and fifty thousand pounds in full and final settlement of such claims.'

'And that's it?' Werner demanded, appearing ready to explode.

'Yes, sir. Of course, it's only a draft. Do feel free to make any amendments,' the in-house lawyer said, handing across the typed script.

'There's only one thing this is good for,' the Chairman said as he began furiously tearing it up into small pieces.

'But Mr Chairman, think of the effect on our reputation if this goes any further,' the other man protested.

'Derek, my dear fellow, you seem to forget that a

company of our standing cannot be seen to cave in over some two-bit story that hasn't been substantiated. I appreciate your efforts but I'm prepared to see this through. In the meantime, my instructions are quite clear. Admit to nothing and there's every chance this whole thing will just evaporate.'

22

Dorset, south-west England

The sense of foreboding that had plagued William McCreary since leaving London resurfaced as his chauffeur-driven Mercedes came to a halt on the blustery quayside of Poole harbour. His biggest donor had suddenly gone cold, and he had no idea why. He had waited impatiently, but when there was still no sign of the £2 million pledge from the Crediton Trust, he had to find out what was going on. And that was easier said than done when Franz Werner hadn't returned any of his calls over the past week. Worse, the Party had entered into commitments that it wouldn't be able to honour, which would seriously jeopardise its election chances unless there was an immediate solution.

Escorted by a member of the crew, the BIP Treasurer boarded the 120-foot yacht moored just a few yards away. He found the Head of the Crediton Trust in jovial mood, showing a group of all-male business types around the state-of-the-art cruiser.

'Be with you shortly!' Werner called down from the bridge.

McCreary wondered if the high-profile takeover that

his company was involved in had taken all Werner's attention and might have been the cause for the slip-up – or whether that was just wishful thinking on his own part.

'So, my friend, I assume the journey down was good?' Werner said, seeing off the last of the previous gathering.

'Yes, it was absolutely fine,' McCreary replied, allowing his main benefactor to lead the way.

'I've taken the liberty of asking Chef to rustle up something for lunch. Alas, I've another meeting at two but that should still give us ample time to talk,' Werner explained, taking the stairs down to his private dining quarters.

'You're probably wondering about the hold-up of funds you were expecting,' he said, pouring out two tumblers of Scotch from a decanter.

'You could say I was a little surprised, especially since there was never an issue with previous contributions,' the visitor replied.

'I must apologise for the sudden change of plan but it couldn't be helped.'

'Is it a temporary delay or something more serious?' McCreary asked.

Before there was a chance of a reply a waiter arrived, balancing a tray of food on his shoulder and setting it down in the middle of the table.

'Ah good, lunch has arrived. Please – help yourself. I don't know about you but I'm starving. Must be the sea air – always gives me a hell of an appetite,' Werner beamed, helping himself to a large piece of lobster from the platter. Slightly bemused, William put some of the lunch on his plate, but he wasn't remotely hungry.

'Sorry, old boy, you were saying about the funds . . . yes, well, I'm afraid we're having to keep a low profile on things like that for the time being. You're aware from the financial press of what's going on with the company's activities – and we really can't afford to rock the boat, if you'll excuse the pun.'

'I appreciate you've got a lot going on, but that has put me in quite a difficult position,' McCreary answered, playing around with the food on his plate.

'Look, William, it's not as if you're just a here today and gone tomorrow bunch of fly-by-nights. We're talking about a serious political party, with how many members currently?'

'Ninety-five thousand.'

'See? That's what I'm saying! You'll have no trouble attracting other funds.'

'In due course maybe, but Crediton pulling out will leave us with a substantial hole in our finances, and this will impair our capability of fighting the election.'

'How is that possible? What about the three mill we've already given to you?'

'Spent on the new London premises, marketing and providing working capital for the three hundred and fifty candidates. I thought you knew that's how it works?'

'Well, I'm sorry, old boy, but there's no way I'm going to sanction any more funds. You'll just have to make do.'

William McCreary tried to keep his cool. If he wasn't careful, he could see all his hard work for the last ten years go up in smoke and, quite frankly, he wasn't prepared for that to happen.

'Listen, Franz, you and I go back a long way. I really

don't want us to fall out over this,' he tried.

'As do I, but believe me, if there were any other way . . .'

'You could always make up the shortfall personally.'

'What! You must be joking, William. I don't have that sort of money available.'

'That's not what I've heard.'

'I haven't the faintest idea what you're talking about,' Werner said, his voice harder now.

'No? The substantial trust funds for each of your three children that you've often bragged about?'

'You know they can't be broken.'

'And then there's the offshore bank account in Liechtenstein . . .'

'How do you know about that?' Werner asked, suddenly feeling less sure of himself.

'And that's relatively mild to other things I could put my finger on – if pushed.'

Werner laid down his knife and fork. 'You should know by now that I don't take kindly to threats, if indeed that's what this is.'

'In that case, I'm sure we can put this down to a mere misunderstanding between old friends,' William said steadily.

'Otherwise, you'll do what exactly?' Werner asked.

'Let's just say, what the press have printed about your former employee Jacob Holtz is just the tip of the iceberg compared to what could be uncovered if they suddenly took it upon themselves to dig further. However, I'm sure you'd agree that wouldn't serve either of our interests particularly well?'

William McCreary wiped his mouth on his linen

napkin, stood up and then with finality said, 'I'll give you till this time tomorrow to make good on your promise and then we can put this behind us. Now, if you would be so good as to arrange for your chap to drop me back at Bournemouth station . . .'

Franz Werner looked on impassively as the man he had come to regard as one of his closest friends disappeared from view. He knew very well what William had been alluding to – and although it wasn't unexpected, he should never have underestimated what the fellow was capable of. And now here it was, about to bite him on the arse!

Franz had been advised to use the clever young patent attorney William McCreary for a new generation of genetic products that had been developed shortly after the company, now named the Crediton Trust, had relocated to England. He had never expected that the inquisitive McCreary would do his own research and uncover the serial numbers relating to a whole different range of highly controversial drugs, manufactured in the past by the company at the behest of the Nazi government. Naturally, the two men agreed to keep it a secret between themselves: in return, discovering that they shared the same political vision, Werner and McCreary agreed to strive to make Britain a nation state of a single ethnicity. But all good things come to an end. That was a rule of life.

In any unexpected turn of events, the trick was to know how to make good use of the opportunity it presented. He hadn't been a decorated officer in the Abwehr German Military Intelligence without learning the skill of being one step ahead of his adversaries. William McCreary was misguided enough to think he had him, Franz Werner, over a barrel, not realising that the situation had, instead, left him exposed – a position which Werner had every intention of exploiting, starting with the meeting with the press reporter he had easily tracked down. Werner set about his lobster, accompanied by a glass of sparkling water and without a care in the world.

Fifteen minutes later, an unshaven Richard Overton, dressed in faded jeans and an oversized naval sweater and thereby indistinguishable from the rest of the crew, made his way unobtrusively onto the luxury yacht on time for two o'clock meeting.

23

Elizabeth glanced across at the empty seat that should have been occupied by Freda Hirschman. They had placed so much dependency on her testimony that Elizabeth knew she had allowed her disappointment to take precedence over consideration for the old lady's welfare. It had all been arranged. Freda would come to London for a few days and stay with Lillian – the perfect opportunity for the two women to get to know each other and for Lillian to hear, first-hand, about her sister Erica and her Uncle Theo. That hope was put paid to with the letter that had turned up two days ago, enclosing the return train ticket Freda had been sent together with a terse note expressing her regret that she wasn't up to making the strenuous trip, after all.

It did occur to Elizabeth that someone might have talked her out of it; but with Gideon Halevi no longer on the scene, she couldn't come up with another realistic possibility. Maybe, even if Freda had come, the experience of reliving the trauma of all those years ago, via the type of questions likely to be thrown at her by both sets of counsel, might have been more than she would have been able to endure.

Although it was unquestionably a major setback, she and Anthony had sought for a final meeting with Roderick

Purcell, on the off-chance that something could be salvaged.

'So where do we go from here?' Elizabeth asked, coming straight to the point. She knew there was no easy answer to the question. With the only witness unable or unwilling to leave Vienna, there was no more ammunition in their armoury.

'There is one bit of good news in that we haven't heard a dicky-bird from Crediton's lawyers about the writ,' the firm's partner disclosed.

'I expect they've got bigger fish to fry with their takeover talks,' Anthony said, 'but that doesn't mean they won't come back when they're good and ready.'

'I'm afraid your husband's right. That's what a corporation the size of Crediton can do. What's more, they could afford to drag this out indefinitely,' Roderick Purcell replied.

'You mean they're just stringing us along?' Elizabeth said, letting her frustration show. 'And how about the potential damage to their reputation?'

'With everything else they've got going on, as Anthony intimated, it's probably already been forgotten.'

'Well, that doesn't do us much good, does it!' Elizabeth was furious and dismayed.

'I'm sure you don't want to hear this, but it's my duty as your legal representation to advise you to cut your losses.'

'You're saying we should just give up?' Elizabeth demanded, raising her voice.

'Our witness's testimony hasn't been lodged with the court so there's no harm done and I'm confident the firm will be prepared to write off its costs to date,' the lawyer said.

'Elizabeth, he's right,' Anthony said. 'It was a good try but you need to accept there's no way we can win this. If we carry on, we'd only be throwing good money after bad.'

'So, we are just going to let them get away with it, as if nothing ever happened?' Elizabeth snapped. 'We can find a way of picking ourselves up off the floor and starting again. But how about Freda Hirschman? Don't we owe it to her and others like her who *didn't* survive, to find the justice that has hitherto been denied to them?'

The two men just looked at each other sheepishly.

'Very well, that means we should be working on a new plan of action,' Purcell said, staging a swift recovery.

Elizabeth began wracking her brains for anything they could pin their hopes upon. Impulsively, she checked her mobile phone and saw a message from Richard Overton that simply said, *Pages 2 and 7 in today's paper*

'Can we get hold of a morning newspaper?' she asked urgently.

'We get them all. Which one in particular?' Purcell enquired, picking up the phone to his secretary.

'The *Herald*, probably, but I'm not entirely sure,' Elizabeth called across, guessing that was the one to which Richard was referring.

The legal secretary soon appeared at the door, carrying a selection of the morning dailies under her arm. The lawyer took them from her with thanks.

'What is it that you're looking for, exactly?' Anthony asked his wife, who had begun frantically going through the pile that was handed to her.

'Here it is!' Elizabeth announced, having successfully scanned the paper for the article in question. 'Crediton have issued a rebuttal on the articles in the press that have implicated them in any wrongdoing.'

'That's not much of a surprise,' Anthony quipped.

'Wait, there's more. It goes on to say that they have every reason to believe they are the victims of blackmail, which is likely where the rumours originated. To that end, they are undertaking strenuous efforts to determine the persons behind it and cooperating fully with the authorities to clear their name.'

'That doesn't make any sense,' Anthony frowned. 'We all know where the stories came from. What do you think they're playing at?'

'Seems a bit of a mystery,' Purcell agreed, puffing on his pipe.

Elizabeth turned to the second piece Richard had mentioned. Its headline read *British Independent Party in Talks with the Conservatives*.

She thought for a moment before passing it to the others. Reading between the lines, Richard had obviously picked up a connection between the two.

'It's probably just a shrewd move to gain more credibility by linking up with an established Party,' Purcell surmised.

'There has to be more to it than that,' Anthony disagreed. 'My father wouldn't compromise his principles for anyone.'

'Unless, of course, he had no choice,' Elizabeth pointed out.

'What are you inferring?'

'We know that Crediton was his paymaster. What if it suddenly stopped for some reason?' Elizabeth continued.

'You mean as in they've suddenly gone cold? That's possible, except it's a bit late in the day.'

'The BIP held their inaugural conference last week at the Norfolk home of the Duke of Carrow – quite an elaborate affair by all accounts,' Purcell said, adding his weight to the conversation. 'What some of the speakers on the podium were saying was apparently disgraceful and the audience was lapping it up. From what I've been able to find out, it was like listening to one of Oswald Mosley's Fascist speeches.'

'I didn't realise they had so much support,' Elizabeth said, wondering how it was that the other man was so well informed.

'Don't be under any misapprehension, these people are extremely dangerous and might easily snatch power,' the lawyer warned.

'That's probably why they were in such a hurry to seek an alternative,' Anthony said. 'But that still doesn't mean there's anything else linking the two. It might just be a coincidence that both pieces came out at the same time.'

'There's one way of finding out,' Elizabeth said, texting the reporter. She'd be surprised if he didn't know more about it.

A flurry of texts passed back and forth until she announced, 'Richard Overton is on his way over.'

*

'So let's get this straight. You're saying that *you* were behind those articles?' Anthony said to the man who'd walked into the meeting just a few moments before.

'A bit of luck really,' Overton replied, seeming perfectly relaxed.

'I think you owe us an explanation,' Elizabeth said, sharing her husband's dismay for what appeared like a treacherous approach to the other side.

'It simply shows what a good bollocking can do. You see, I'd been summoned by the Editor because of the writ he'd been served.'

'But I thought the paper had agreed to print the articles!' Elizabeth exclaimed.

'I know they did, but someone had to carry the can – that's how it works in our industry. It's the only time things are sure to be delegated. Anyway, they insisted I issue a retraction, which I had no intention of agreeing to and so I resigned.'

'Then what happened?' Elizabeth asked. Perhaps she had been premature in judging the fellow now taking centre-stage.

'I got a phone call yesterday morning from the Editor saying that Crediton had been in contact wanting a parley, and that I should get down there double quick as it was my one chance to save my arse. Of course, I knew there had to be more to it than wanting a personal apology.'

'And you were obviously proven right,' Anthony said, not holding back on his admiration for the reporter.

'What I'm about to tell you came as a real surprise. At first, I didn't believe a word of it because it sounds so incredible. Basically, the bloke wanted to do a deal.'

'Who – Franz Werner?' Purcell asked.

'Yup! What gave him the impression I had the authority to negotiate on the paper's behalf, I haven't the faintest idea.'

'So what was he proposing?' Elizabeth questioned, completely spellbound by the change of events.

'He wanted me to present their side of the story, clearly showing that Crediton was being blackmailed. In return, the company would withdraw the writ against my paper. Naturally, my Editor jumped at the chance of safe-guarding his job and the *Herald*'s reputation and told me to go ahead. As he said, it wasn't any of the paper's business to question the man's motive.'

'Yes, but was there any truth in it?' Elizabeth asked, hardly able to contain herself.

'Possibly. Although it did seem a bit odd that he didn't appear too bothered about tracking down the culprit.'

'That's because he knew who it was,' Anthony interrupted.

'Meaning?' Purcell asked, having trouble following.

'Our friend knows very well the only person it could be,' Anthony said. 'I'm referring to my father William – which is why the piece on the BIP happens to appear at the same time. Isn't that so, Richard?'

'Anthony, your train of thought, though impressive, isn't entirely correct,' the journalist responded.

'In that case, hadn't you better fill us in?'

'Actually, it was purely the paper's idea,' Richard explained.

'You mean they made the whole thing up?' Elizabeth said, bewildered by the complexity of it all.

'I agree it's a little unorthodox but it was effective in terms of diverting attention away from Crediton. Remember, at the end of the day, we're a left-wing paper, and if it can help prevent the BIP getting into power, we'll have done a good job.'

'But in that case, aren't you leaving yourself open to more potential lawsuits?' Elizabeth wondered.

'What, for spreading false rumours? That's hardly likely. Taking into account that it wasn't exactly a transparent arrangement in the first place, neither of the parties mentioned could claim they've been harmed.'

'Richard's correct on this one. It's not a method I'd approve of, but I fear it's all too common these days,' Purcell lamented.

'The Conservatives have already denied there's any truth in the piece,' the journalist confirmed.

'Absolutely brilliant!' Anthony boomed. 'What you've done is to pre-empt them seeking support from the only place they were likely to get it.'

'That was the general idea and it seems to have paid off.'

'So now they've been seriously weakened, with luck they won't be able to find their way back,' Elizabeth said with renewed optimism.

'It's a bit soon to be sure of that, although there are other steps that might end up putting the final nail in their coffin,' Richard smiled.

'I'm dying to hear what you've got up your sleeve,' Elizabeth said.

'OK, but it would mean having to strike quickly while the momentum is still with us.'

'Go ahead, Richard, we're eager to know what you're thinking,' Anthony encouraged him.

'It would entail Crediton coming clean about their dealings with the BIP,' the journalist began.

'Do you think they'd do that?' Roderick Purcell interrupted.

'Let me finish!'

'Sorry,' the solicitor muttered.

'But wouldn't that be tantamount to an admission of guilt?' Elizabeth then interrupted.

'Hardly, when as far as they're concerned, they probably don't think they've done anything wrong,' Anthony replied.

'So what's their incentive?' Elizabeth came again.

Richard took charge. 'If I'm correct in my assumption that there's been an acrimonious parting of the ways with William McCreary, there's only likely to be one winner,' he stated. 'Don't forget, getting the City to approve that billion-dollar deal is always going to be Crediton's main priority.'

'Which in turn means they must appear whiter than white,' Anthony stressed. 'If they need an out, all they need say is that they didn't sign up to the policies currently being expounded by the BIP.'

'Exactly right,' Richard nodded.

'And you're confident that you'll get them to agree to it?' Anthony pressed.

'No, but you will,' the journalist countered.

'Me? You c-can't be serious,' Anthony stammered.

There was no immediate response from the other two, just expressions of disbelief at what sounded like a bizarre suggestion.

'Anthony, don't forget you are the one who has been wronged in this whole episode,' Richard emphasised.

'That's true, but I still don't see what part I'd have to play?'

'All we need to do is to convince Franz Werner that his company is not the only victim here. He's probably unaware that you were denied the opportunity to defend yourself.'

'How did you know about that?' Anthony replied, startled for the second time in the last few minutes.

'It's my job,' Richard said dismissively. 'But now's the time for you to put things right.'

'It all sounds rather ambitious to me, I must say,' Purcell remarked.

'Though it just might be worth considering,' Anthony said, gradually warming to the idea.

Then Elizabeth, who had remained pensive, suddenly said, 'I think I know how your devious mind is working.'

'It would be a surprise if you didn't,' the reporter replied with a flirtatious smile.

'The reason why you want to involve Anthony,' she continued, 'is so that once the BIP is properly discredited, your paper will get the exclusive – and you, Richard Overton – will come out smelling of roses.'

'There is that, of course,' Richard admitted unabashedly, 'but there's something else equally important, which is that Anthony will be building a case to bring against his father.'

'Good gracious, he's absolutely right!' Purcell enthused.

'I hadn't thought of that,' Anthony said, immediately attracted to the proposition.

'Assuming, of course, that is still on your agenda?' the reporter asked.

'What do you think? I've just been waiting for the day when that bastard would get his comeuppance! All it would take is for Crediton to confirm that I had absolutely no part in any of its dealings with my father.'

'The difference now is that William McCreary has lost the patronage of his biggest supporter: that means you may be faced with little resistance,' Richard Overton divulged.

'So, what can we do to get the ball moving?' Anthony asked, now fully committed to the idea.

'A meeting has already been arranged,' the reporter smiled, 'for tomorrow at their offices in The Strand. I'll pick you up at nine a.m.'

*

Vienna

A tall man wearing a baseball cap and thick-rimmed glasses passed unnoticed into the 2nd District apartment block. With no caretaker present to account to, Oscar Gruber proceeded directly to the home of its oldest female resident: Freda Hirschman, the only one of the names in Theo Frankl's letter of fellow Jews who was still alive, and whose deportation to Auschwitz Theo had been unable to prevent.

Although Oscar had been influenced initially by the intimidating tactics to discredit him because of his Jewish heritage, Freda's interview with the British press that he'd come across by accident shortly before they met, had caused him to dig deep into his conscience about the role that his own family might have played in facilitating that evil decree against the Jewish community.

All of a sudden, he became obsessed with getting hold of even the smallest details that might enable him to gain a better insight into his father, Theo Frankl.

Now he was fully able to substantiate the wild claims he'd received from Elizabeth McCreary about his childhood and his birth father, Oscar also understood why he had never received an entirely satisfactory response to questions about Theo Frankl while his mother was alive. It must have been her intention that his Jewish identity should remain hidden for ever. Whether that was purely for his benefit or just to allay her own sense of guilt, he'd never know.

Freda Hirschman recognised the discreet knock at the door as that of the leader of the Austrian Freedom Party, who had befriended her six months previously. In the beginning, suspicious of his motives, she had failed to understand why Elizabeth hadn't mentioned anything about him being Theo Frankl's son, her recently discovered second-cousin. It was only by obtaining Gideon Halevi's confirmation that the elderly woman was able to accept that what Herr Gruber had learned about himself was indeed authentic.

More difficult to absorb was the discovery that she had seriously misjudged his father, Theo. The latter had not been the selfish character she had thought him to be, only out for himself. Now she owed it to Theo's son and his great-niece to help them in any way she could.

'You'll have to excuse the fact that I'm not quite finished dressing,' she explained, ushering in her early-morning visitor. 'Please, sit down and help yourself to coffee and some cake.'

'I am pleased you heeded my advice about going to London,' he said, removing the disguise that he'd resorted to assuming in public ever since the attack on his life, six months earlier.

'I appreciate it was out of concern for my well-being,

but Elizabeth had gone to such trouble – and I was so looking forward to becoming acquainted with your Cousin Lillian,' Freda lamented, not revealing that it was Gideon Halevi, rather than her visitor, who had been the one responsible for her cancelling the trip.

The old lady fell silent as a new thought entered her mind. Then she spoke again while Oscar sat and listened.

'There were other things about Auschwitz that I couldn't recall before but I can see them quite clearly now,' she rambled on as painful memories filled her mind.

'My dear Freda, I'm sure that Elizabeth will have understood,' Oscar said soothingly. Although he couldn't allow it to just slip by, the chance that it might have presented an opportunity to find out more about the British pharmaceuticals conglomerate with purported Nazi roots which the British press were crudely linking to Freda's article. Not that it would come as any great surprise. The British Establishment's on-going love affair with the fascism of the 1930s was well known; quite ironic when it spent six bloody years trying to defeat it! That was the difference between the two nations. Austria and Germany had moved on, which was why they were deservedly the powerhouse of Europe.

24

Elizabeth had a spring in her step as she and Anthony left the City offices of the OSS, the Office for the Supervision of Solicitors.

'I don't think that could have gone any better,' she said, holding on to her husband's arm as they proceeded down towards Bank tube station.

'I suppose we should thank your friend Richard for that,' Anthony replied.

'Don't do yourself down, *you* were the one putting up a very good argument to the panel that they had acted too hastily without knowing all the facts.'

'This helped,' he said, glancing at the formal declaration stating unequivocally that he, Anthony McCreary, was not known to nor had ever had any dealings with the Crediton Trust. 'I still find it hard to believe they were so ready to dump my father after all this time. When it comes to loyalty, it seems there is none. Except, it still seems slightly worrying that Franz Werner was so keen to strike a deal . . .'

'What are you getting at?'

'Suppose my father had stumbled on something substantial that they thought would never come to light?'

'We already know about K Pharma and Jacob Holtz,' Elizabeth reminded him.

'I'm referring to something on a far larger scale,' Anthony said, frowning.

'If you're right, are you implying that your father would threaten to use it against the company?'

'No, he's far too canny for that. Knowing him, he'll be more occupied at present in trying to salvage his beloved Party than wreaking vengeance on Crediton. But make no mistake, he'll be saving that up for a more opportune moment.'

'How do you propose we approach him about coming clean to your regulative body so you can obtain complete vindication?' Elizabeth asked.

'I'll drive up to see him. He's probably keeping a low profile with everything else going on.'

'Don't you want me to come with you?'

'I think it's best I go alone.'

'But he'll intimidate you, Anthony, you know what he's like.'

'Elizabeth darling, I've learned the hard way how to deal with him. Anyway, you've more important issues to cope with at home. You know I only blame myself about Freddie,' Anthony said in a low voice.

'Let's not go over that again. What's done is done. Hopefully now our son is home, we can keep an eye on him.'

'But that whole drugs scene he was involved in! I just can't get my head round why I never saw what was going on right under our noses.'

'And how about the lying,' Elizabeth sighed. 'He was so convincing. All those times when we thought he'd gone over to Gus's house in Camden Town to study, he was out

God knows where, getting high.' She winced, remembering her own stormy adolescence at public school, and the near-fatal trouble she'd got into with drugs.

'Where did he get the money from, that's what I want to know,' Anthony said.

'Probably from some of the kids he mixed with at school. I know a few of them are from extremely wealthy homes; parents away a lot, leaving them up to their own devices. Believe me, it happens. And as you are aware, our son has got low self-esteem, which obviously made him more susceptible.'

'I shouldn't have expected so much of him,' Anthony said – but without any conviction.

'Perhaps you just shouldn't have made it so obvious in front of Emily?'

'Moving him to that crammer in Belsize Park for his GCSEs is probably what the boy needs to get him back on track,' Anthony said, reverting to type. He just wouldn't stop pushing Freddie into a direction the boy wasn't suited to.

'Not as much as spending quality time with him will,' Elizabeth responded, looking directly at her husband. She'd long accepted that her son wasn't of an academic bent, even if Anthony hadn't – but with things so much better between them recently, it wasn't the right time to labour the point. 'Let's just say we all need to start afresh,' was all she said.

'No time like the present,' Anthony smiled.

'Actually, he's going to be staying with my mother for a few days,' Elizabeth told her husband.

'Really? I didn't know.'

'With everything he's been through, a change of environment might prove beneficial, and remember, Lillian did have a similar experience with her own child in the past.'

'I remember you telling me,' Anthony said softly. 'Look, on reflection, perhaps we should go to the Cotswolds together. I'll book us into the hotel there overnight. We'll just need to tell Francesca to make sure that Emily is ready for school in the morning.'

'Sounds a bit romantic,' Elizabeth said, surprised.

'And not well before time,' Anthony responded, determined to have the final word.

*

It was early evening by the time they reached the Wiltshire Cotswolds. Spotting William's Rolls-Royce Silver Wraith on the forecourt of the magnificent property, Anthony went up to the house and rang the bell.

A strained-looking Margaret McCreary appeared at the door. 'You didn't say you were coming, Anthony. And you have brought Elizabeth? How nice!'

'Hello, Mother,' Anthony replied, entering the childhood home that he'd come to detest.

'If you're here to see your father, I should wait if I were you. He has been acting very strangely of late,' Margaret said quickly. 'He has hardly moved out of his office for the last two days.'

But it was too late to stop Anthony from striding resolutely ahead. Elizabeth followed closely behind in order to catch her husband up so he wouldn't have to be alone to face what was bound to be an unpleasant confrontation. Until recently, she would have dreaded this encounter because of the adverse effect it might have on his health, but he had become far more emboldened as a result of his recent experiences and maybe he saw this showdown as something that had to happen in order to prove that he could stand up to his father.

Suddenly, there was the deafening sound of a gunshot. Calculating that it came from William's study at the end of the hall, they desperately tried to open the door, but found it locked from the inside.

Elizabeth recoiled in shock as memories of that night at Oscar Gruber's penthouse came flooding back; the difference, this time, was the eerie silence now in evidence. This was no terrorist attack. As Margaret McCreary came hurrying along the corridor, her face a deathly white, Elizabeth sat her down in the drawing room then ran around to the rear of the house, where Anthony had managed to prise open a pair of French doors leading into the study. William McCreary, dressed in his silk dressing gown, lay on the carpet, his hand still clutching the Luger pistol. A large pool of blood had formed around him.

The only clue as to what drove the man to take his own life was the newspaper open on an otherwise cleared desk with a headline that read: *Crediton Trust Blackmail Link to British Independent Party's Founder.*

*

In the absence of any other evidence to the contrary, the coroner had no alternative but to record a verdict of suicide.

On a cold November morning, in a private family service, William McCreary was buried in the village cemetery less than a mile from his home. The obituary that followed, a few days later, highlighted his achievements as an accomplished City lawyer but made no reference to the controversy that had caused his untimely demise.

*

Vienna
Oscar Gruber sat broodily at the Editor's weekly meeting of his newspaper group in the Central District. In normal circumstances, the implosion of the British Independent Party would have hardly attracted his interest, and yet recent events in London that he'd been following closely had left him with the distinct feeling of unfinished business. Even a man as despicable as William McCreary, the leader of that extremist party, didn't take his life just because his political aspirations happened to have gone up in smoke. And the fact that his death had hardly received any coverage in the press smelled to Oscar like a cover-up! He was now convinced something of a sinister nature was going on in England, something which his media group was perfectly placed to take advantage of.

*

Crediton Head Office, Devon
Derek Coulson, the in-house lawyer to the Crediton Trust, cut a lonely figure at six o'clock that morning. He'd spent another sleepless night consumed with worry of how to break the latest batch of disastrous news to his Chairman. But there was no getting away from the 150 communications from WIPO, the World Intellectual Property Organisation, that had landed on his desk in the space of seventy-two hours, effectively cancelling the patents on all but a handful of the drugs that were the

company's lifeblood. His first reaction was that it had to be a hoax, except for the official letter that had accompanied the forms, making it clear that the decision had been made after a lengthy investigation.

Twenty years' service and just eighteen months off retirement, if any of this were to see the light of day, he could kiss goodbye to his pension and peaceful retirement at the cottage in Cornwall. Just as well his wife was still in work. Whether they could manage on her legal secretary's salary was another matter.

Removing a pill-holder from the breast pocket of his tweed jacket, he popped two statins into his mouth, hoping this would ward off the flurry of palpitations that had got gradually worse, while he waited for his colleagues to arrive.

25

Christmas Eve, 2000

Elizabeth stood next to her husband admiring the Christmas tree that had taken prime position in the corner of the living room.

'What a bloody awful year! Thank God it's at an end,' Anthony said, taking a gulp from his champagne glass.

'Looking on the bright side, you're well again, you've got back the firm and we don't have to sell the house,' Elizabeth countered.

'Actually, I was thinking of Freddie. You do think he's going to be all right, don't you?'

'Of course. It'll just take some time. How did it go when he came to the office the other day?'

'Really well, actually. We put him to work going through some contracts. With the right encouragement, I think he may have an aptitude for the law.'

'A new McCreary generation of solicitors – that really would be something,' Elizabeth teased, sipping her drink.

'Hold on! I'm not done quite yet and, remember, Jess is taking her Bar exams.'

'I'm so glad she's returning to London. It'll be like old times,' Elizabeth said happily.

'I'm staggered she turned up at the funeral, taking account of what our old man subjected her to,' Anthony said. 'But after all, we're the only family she's got and she wants to be closer to Mother. It wouldn't surprise me if the old girl ups sticks and moves to London.' He made a face. 'The Cotswolds never did that much for her.'

'What's going to happen to the house?'

'Probably go to auction. It's the only thing of any value. The stuff she's been left with doesn't add up to much.'

'I thought you told me your father was loaded?'

'He should have been, but it transpired he used most of his spare cash to prop up the Party. He may have been deluded but no one can say that he wasn't committed to the cause.'

'You're not still feeling guilty?' Elizabeth said, alerted to her husband's resigned expression.

'I can't help thinking that I was partly to blame. If I hadn't sold him out to save my own skin . . .'

'Anthony, you did what you had to do. Don't forget what he'd put you through.'

'I realise that, but if we'd got to him earlier, there was a good chance he'd have come up trumps with the Disciplinary body.'

'That's the difference between you two – which makes me wonder who you inherited your strong sense of morals from?'

'Probably a distant relative somewhere,' Anthony said flippantly. 'But seriously, if you look at what's happened to Crediton, their takeover cancelled and their share price down by twenty-five per cent, you'd have to suspect there was something far bigger going on.'

'And you think your father knew something?'

'It's possible.' For a moment Anthony looked stricken, the horror of his father's violent suicide still vivid in his mind. More quietly he added, 'We have no idea what he was doing in his study before he died.'

'We went over all of that extensively with the police and they found nothing suspicious.'

'All I'm saying is that his death, coinciding with Crediton's sudden troubles, appears too much of a coincidence.'

'Even assuming you're right, isn't it best to leave things well alone so we can get on with our lives?' Elizabeth said softly.

'Darling, if I've learned anything from the events over the last twelve months, it is not to stand by if you can correct an injustice.'

'I can't quite believe what I'm hearing,' Elizabeth replied. 'For some bizarre reason, you seem to be implying that your father is the victim in all of this?'

'In a way, he was. After all, he did pay with his life. What I'm getting at is that although Crediton is on the skids because of those patents, they haven't got their full comeuppance . . . yet.'

'What have you got in mind?' Elizabeth asked, taken aback by her husband's show of boldness.

'Just to get to the bottom of what they've been involved in before it's swept under the carpet. And we know just the fellow to help us, don't we?' he added with a mischievous smile.

'Richard Overton?' Elizabeth replied.

'He's on a roll at the moment so it wouldn't surprise me

if he were already on the case.'

'There's only one way of finding out,' Elizabeth said, taking the initiative and reaching for her mobile.

'Darling, have a little consideration,' her husband chided her. 'Remember it is Christmas.'

'With anyone else, you'd have a point,' she conceded, before going ahead with the call. Then: 'It's gone straight to voicemail.'

'He's probably already immersed in the festivities,' Anthony shrugged.

As he spoke, Elizabeth's phone pinged with a text message that simply said, *Up north with the folks. Returning day after Boxing Day. Speak then. Happy Xmas.*

'We'll just have to be patient,' Anthony said. 'You should know by now that's not one of my better qualities.' Then, drawing his wife to him, he said, 'I don't suppose I can interest you in an early night?'

'That all depends on what you've got in mind,' Elizabeth responded seductively.

*

Claridge's Hotel, Mayfair
A black cab pulled up at the main hotel entrance in Brook Street. Elizabeth got out and went on ahead while her husband paid the driver. Entering the five-star establishment, she was in better spirits than she could ever have imagined just a few weeks ago.

Christmas lunch at her mother's, which she normally dreaded, had passed without incident; even Allen seemed to have made a remarkable recovery from his recent health setback. The more settled atmosphere that she and Anthony were now enjoying at home had obviously permeated through to the rest of the guests at the table. Asking Margaret McCreary was a thoughtful gesture, in the circumstances, but the fact that the invitation had been extended to Jess and her partner Aisha was, Elizabeth knew, a sincere effort on Lillian's part to bring the family closer together. As she said, it sometimes takes a tragedy for the ones left behind to bury the hatchet.

Most importantly, Freddie had turned a corner; his stay with his grand-mother appeared to have achieved the desired result in that it had instilled in him a new sense of self-worth.

Just then, lost in thought, Elizabeth caught sight of the reporter sitting in the foyer. Richard Overton was looking far from his usual buoyant self.

'This is a bit extravagant, isn't it, Richard?' Elizabeth said, joining him at his table.

'You've come on your own?' he asked distractedly.

'Anthony's here too. He's probably popped to the loo.'

Elizabeth thought she saw a flash of disappointment on the journalist's handsome face. Perhaps he was having difficulties with his female partner, Amanda. He'd mentioned once before that their relationship was under strain. Elizabeth had noticed the signs from the first time they met, that he wouldn't have been averse to something more between them. But that was then and she certainly wasn't going to put her marriage at risk, not with everything that it had taken to get it back on an even footing.

'Now tell me what could possibly be so important that it needed to interfere with my Christmas celebrations?' Richard enquired only half-seriously.

'It was Anthony's idea. You can ask him yourself,'

Elizabeth replied, waving her husband over.

'Richard, it's good to see you again,' Anthony said, taking a seat. 'Has Elizabeth mentioned why we wanted to get together?'

'Actually, she was going to leave it to you.'

'Right, let's eat first,' Anthony said, summoning over a waiter. 'I don't know about you but I'm famished. Must be that early-morning run that did it.' He picked up the brunch menu.

'I have to say you do look remarkably well on it,' Richard congratulated him.

'Had the all-clear from the doctor. I've no noticeable after-effects from the palsy to speak of, except that I'm on an aspirin, daily, which is supposed to prevent a recurrence.'

'That's good news. Now, I've got a pretty good idea what this is about,' Richard said, being the last to order. 'But if I might offer you a piece of advice, it would be: don't try to exact vengeance, if that is your intention.'

Elizabeth threw her husband a sideways look. His response to Overton was defiant.

'Look here, Richard, you've got it completely wrong. That's the last thing we're trying to achieve.'

'Well, if it's got nothing to do with Crediton, I'd be more than happy for you to put me right,' the journalist replied, with none of his usual self-assurance.

There was no immediate response from the other two, so he carried on.

'Look, Anthony, let me speak plainly. You got what you wanted, which was to clear your good name, so why don't you just get on with your lives?'

'Is injustice a good enough reason?' Anthony asked.

'It's the way of the world. The fact that we were able to win against a global multinational with a huge amount of resources at its disposal, just defies the odds.' Richard appealed to Elizabeth. 'Tell your husband that he's being naïve.'

There was a brief interlude as two waiters appeared with their food. In one simultaneous movement, the table was swiftly laid by one, whilst the other placed the dishes correctly in front of each diner before they both disappeared as noiselessly as they had come.

'I'm surprised by your reaction,' Elizabeth said, taking up the conversation. 'I would have thought you'd be deeply immersed in following through with another piece. After all, it's public knowledge that Crediton has been severely rattled by the so-called withdrawal of a number of its most important patents. So much so that the company felt obliged to issue a substantial profits warning, did it not?'

Overton tried to shrug it off. 'That's not so unusual with pharmaceutical companies except, perhaps, for the scale involved.'

'I suspect that, having the best legal brains on the case, they'll find a way of wriggling out of it again,' Anthony said pessimistically.

'Possibly, unless we can come up with something to precipitate their downfall,' Richard said, beginning to perk up and sensing a potential new angle.

'You mean like the fact that when this blew open, it just happened to coincide with my father's suicide?' Anthony said flatly.

'You reckon there's a possible connection between the two?'

'I'm speculating that my father had something on the

company which he'd agreed to keep under wraps, perhaps going back years. Then, when he had the rug pulled out from under him, he had nothing to lose by going public.'

'So Richard, in one sense it *is* about revenge – but not ours,' Elizabeth clarified.

'An interesting theory and certainly very imaginative, but I think you might have underestimated what would be involved in terms of money and effort to prove it,' the journalist said.

'So nothing's changed then. Situation normal,' Anthony quipped, bringing a lighthearted moment to the meal.

'It's a pity because we thought that looking into those patents would be right up your street. I've obviously misjudged you,' Elizabeth said.

The journalist, beginning to realise that he had underestimated the McCrearys' resolve and was in danger of doing himself out of what might be the biggest assignment of his career, then said, 'Meticulous research is going to be the key,' not disclosing that his father, Raymond, had been on the case since before Christmas.

'So I suggest we take things one step at a time and wait to see what emerges. Agreed?' Anthony said.

But Overton failed to respond.

'Richard, is there a problem? You don't seem that keen,' Elizabeth noted.

'To tell you the truth, after last time I can't afford to put my job on the line again. Don't get me wrong, I'm pleased you got your livelihood back, but my own position is a lot more precarious.'

'Please make yourself clear,' Elizabeth said, becoming irritated by the apparent lack of transparency.

'Basically, my paper won't take kindly to revisiting the Crediton case.'

'Are you trying to say that they've come to an agreement to leave it be?'

'I'd put it as more of an understanding.'

'But that's absurd!' Elizabeth protested.

'So in return for withdrawing their writ against the *Herald*, the paper agreed to go easy on them in future, is that it?' Anthony surmised.

'Something along those lines,' the journalist admitted sheepishly.

'Richard, I thought you'd be the last person to sell yourself out,' Elizabeth said, not holding back.

'I can understand you drawing that conclusion,' he answered, 'but unfortunately, it's the way things work in the business world. Also, Anthony, I'm sure you don't need reminding that you yourself were ready to take advantage of a not too dissimilar arrangement to get back your position as senior partner.'

'He's not wrong,' Anthony replied, directing his comments to his wife.

They finished their lunch in awkward silence, refusing coffee afterwards.

'So that's that,' Elizabeth said begrudgingly and began gathering up her things. 'Frankly, Richard, I fail to understand why you agreed to meet us in the first place.'

'I didn't say I wasn't willing to help you. It just can't be done under the auspices of the *Herald*, that's all.'

'Unless I missed something, isn't that the same thing?' Anthony asked.

'Elizabeth, hear me out first before you get up and go,'

the journalist said.

'All right, go ahead,' she said, reluctantly sitting down again.

'Apparently, one of the European papers has picked up on the bust-up between Crediton and the British Independent Party,' Richard revealed. 'Making a point of emphasising how the British, the so-called bastion of democracy, was ready to allow political extremists to operate with complete impunity.'

'Anything else?' Anthony asked.

'Just how, in contrast, the Viennese government is doing its bit to protect the same ethnic minorities from feeling under threat, as they are in the UK.'

'You didn't mention that it was an Austrian newspaper,' Elizabeth said.

'Didn't I? Sorry, but you're right.'

'So I assume it's printed in German?'

'Which is probably why it didn't come to our attention until recently,' Overton hedged.

'All interesting stuff, I'm sure, but where do we fit in?' Anthony wanted to know.

'The paper is part of G Medien International, if that rings a bell?'

There was no response apart from a bemused expression from the other two.

'Oscar Gruber?' Richard tried again.

Elizabeth nearly fell off her chair at the mention of her high-profile relation. It had been months since there had been any contact between them. She wondered what had suddenly drawn Oscar's attention to their case, when he'd proven reluctant to follow up on what he had discovered about his Jewish past – and especially, as Gideon had mentioned, as he was running for President. Something didn't make sense.

'And the reason you've come up with this is, I assume, that you think that Gruber wouldn't be intimidated by the likes of Crediton?' Anthony speculated.

'Plus the fact that he's got the financial muscle to see it to its conclusion,' the journalist nodded.

'What you're suggesting is that we should be looking to him to force the pharmaceutical company to come clean on everything?' Elizabeth concluded.

'Correct. And you, Elizabeth, are in a prime position to make it happen.'

'When do you think we should approach him?' she asked.

'Probably when Richard here has had a chance to investigate the dark history surrounding those patents,' Anthony interjected.

'I should have something tangible in a few weeks,' Richard said. 'Why don't we reconvene in, say, the last week of January?'

'That's fine for us,' Elizabeth replied on her husband's behalf.

'Right. I'll get the tab because I have to be somewhere,' Richard said, attracting the waiter's attention.

'You really don't have to,' Anthony told him, producing a gold Amex card from his jacket pocket. But he was too late. The journalist was already on his way over to the cashier to pay the bill.

Elizabeth looked at her husband and said, 'Why does it feel as if we've been duped?'

'I know what you mean but I think set up might be a more accurate assessment.'

'What the point was of that charade, I've no idea. Why didn't he just come out with it in the first place?' Elizabeth questioned.

'You can be pretty certain he's got something carved out for himself somewhere along the line, and it wouldn't surprise me if it's with Herr Gruber's outfit,' Anthony speculated.

'Forever the cynic,' Elizabeth said wryly. 'Of course, it could simply be that, like us, he wants to see justice done.'

'If that's so, it's a bloody funny way of going about it,' Anthony answered back.

26

Islington, North London, three weeks later

Richard drained the last of the bottle of Spanish Rioja he'd opened a few hours before, and slumped back on the sofa. The prospect of a quiet night at home with a pizza and a DVD of Sergio Leone's classic film *Once Upon a Time in America* had been put paid to with the Special Delivery package that was waiting on his door-mat when he got home from work. At least his girlfriend Amanda was no longer around giving him grief. The split, when it came, had been amicable enough. The relationship wasn't going anywhere and knocking on thirty, the children's TV presenter had considered, quite reasonably, that since she wanted to start a family, she'd be better off seeking pastures new than waiting indefinitely for Richard to commit himself.

But now he had far more important things on his mind. Despite the flippancy he had displayed in front of the McCrearys, it had been far from straightforward getting his hands on the highly sensitive documents. Even trying to take advantage of the slightly unorthodox relationship between Crediton and the *Herald*, and using the pretext of obtaining an exclusive into the story, he had been unable to glean anything useful. When the response from the World Patent Office had predictably proven just as elusive, Richard felt as if he was beginning to run out of options. Fortunately, the conclusion drawn by his father, Raymond, that the intellectual properties relating to those rediscovered patents had been stolen from Jewish families during the early years of the war, was unequivocal. Then, with the assistance of a trusted childhood friend, a retired patent attorney from whom Richard was able to determine that the documents had been skilfully doctored to avoid any possible association with their previous owners, he could see why he'd been fobbed off with the official company line stating that the Crediton Trust had fallen victim to an unsuccessful attempt at industrial sabotage and that the patents in question had, in any event, long expired.

Since all this had remained hidden for more than fifty years, the ruling powers of the Crediton Trust must have felt safe, believing that the truth was unlikely ever to be uncovered. They were wrong, and now the question of what to do was causing them to panic. One thing was for sure, if any of this were to appear in the press, Richard knew he could kiss his career with the *Herald* goodbye, since it wouldn't take a genius at the paper to work out who was behind it. Even then, there was no guarantee that the findings wouldn't be discredited again.

On the other hand, his conscience wouldn't allow him to sit on the truth and pretend it didn't exist. He frowned and pondered the matter for the fiftieth time. Perhaps there was a middle road? He then had another thought.

What if he were to release some of the findings to Oscar Gruber's media group? With its clear agenda of exposing the English as unsuitable European partners, the Austrian billionaire could well jump on the chance to embarrass them further by exploiting the woes of one of its major corporate institutions.

That would be Step One. Step Two would be for Elizabeth McCreary to approach Oscar concerning her own and Anthony's involvement and their attempt to pursue justice. How far Gruber's organisation would take it after that would depend on how successful she was in convincing him that the claims were authentic. Richard sighed deeply. The plan wasn't foolproof but it was the best he could come up with. As far as his own position was concerned, he was prepared to see the whole thing through to its natural conclusion and worry about the rest later.

*

Oscar Gruber normally made a point of *not* sitting in on the weekly Editor's meeting. The secret of success, he had realised long ago, was delegation, which was why he had a first-rate management team in place. That had all changed with the events of earlier that morning. Now he was compelled to take a hands-on approach.

First had come the phone call from a British journalist called Richard Overton, claiming to have information concerning a wide-scale deception which, at first, seemed pure sensationalism until the throwaway comment that Overton was closely associated with the McCrearys. The transcript that followed, providing details of the drug patents purported to have been plundered from

Jewish-owned businesses during the war, immediately alerted Gruber to the controversy surrounding a major pharmaceutical company based in south-west England – about its origins in Nazi Germany and the sinister use to which its drugs had been put – that he'd been tracking for the last couple of months. His instinct told him that the Crediton Trust was the one of which the journalist spoke.

The prospect that Elizabeth McCreary was somehow involved in the matter should have come as no surprise, when he had witnessed her ingenuity at first hand except that, for his second cousin to be embroiled in something of such sinister proportions, he knew there had to be more to it. It was then it struck him.

The key was the death of her husband's father, William McCreary.

*

February, 2001
The Austrian Airways Boeing 737 touched down at Vienna International Airport, on time, at three minutes past nine in the morning. Elizabeth smiled at her husband in the seat next to her, secure in the knowledge they were as one. It had taken the death of his father, she thought, for him to emerge as the independent-minded individual who had been suppressed for so long. And the fact was, she now felt able to take a back seat after the gruelling events of the last year. Elizabeth knew that, had it been left to her, she would have been inclined to let things lie with regard to the damning evidence Richard Overton had established, implicating Crediton over those stolen patents, but Anthony was determined to pursue a case against the giant drugs concern.

When the couple disembarked from the aircraft, a stretch Mercedes limousine was waiting on the tarmac to take them to a meeting with Oscar Gruber. How different from her original 'three days in Vienna' that had begun as an innocuous journey of self-discovery, Elizabeth mused.

As they approached the Ringstrasse, she noticed that her husband had a curious look on his face.

'Is anything wrong?' she asked.

'So this is where the two of you got to meet, I assume,' Anthony said without warning.

Elizabeth's heart sank, sure that for some unknown reason it was a sudden reference to Gideon Halevi.

'Nothing happened, I assure you,' she said impulsively.

'That's odd. I was under the impression you got quite close to one another.'

'You mean to Oscar? Yes, yes, of course!' Elizabeth replied, breathing a great sigh of relief that she'd got her wires crossed.

'Who else did you think I was talking about?' Anthony jested, taking her hand.

Less than an hour later, they had reached the home of Austria's President-in-waiting. Elizabeth looked up at the fine stone building that had been completely refurbished following the terrorist attack twelve months earlier.

Passing through a number of security checks, the two visitors were escorted to the same lift in which Elizabeth had travelled on the night of the bombing, the one that went solely to the penthouse apartment. Then, after one final frisk, they were permitted entry to the palatial rooftop abode.

'Crikey! I've been in some beautiful homes in the

past, but nothing compared to this. It goes on for ever!' Anthony whistled, looking around in amazement at his opulent surroundings.

'It is rather impressive,' Elizabeth concurred, wondering how long they would be kept waiting and strangely, feeling none of the angst she'd anticipated in returning to the scene of her traumatic experience. However, it had come as a surprise that Oscar had bothered to get in contact, since she felt that, even with the efforts Richard had made, there was no logical reason why he'd be prepared to do anything about the case against the Crediton Trust. The more she'd thought about it, the couple of times they'd met seemed very much a cut and dried occurrence.

As she was thinking this, she noticed a familiar-looking man in gym shorts and trainers striding down the marble corridor towards them.

'Elizabeth! It's so good to see you again.' Oscar Gruber greeted her with a kiss on each cheek. 'I see you've brought reinforcements this time,' he joked, shaking his hand and giving Anthony a once-over inspection. 'Right, do follow me. We've got a lot to catch up on. How's your mother, my Cousin Lillian? Well, I hope?' he said, proceeding at a fast pace back the way he had come.

'A little older but she's fine,' Elizabeth answered casually, having conditioned herself to accepting that Lillian and Oscar would probably never meet.

'Coffee is on its way,' Oscar announced, entering the vast room where that fateful gathering had taken place the previous year. 'So . . . I'm intrigued by what you've been up to since you were last here,' he said, relaxing back on a deep-seated leather sofa.

'Actually, it's quite difficult knowing where to start,' Elizabeth began.

'If you don't mind I'll try and explain,' Anthony interjected. 'Oscar, I take it you're familiar with the changing political landscape in Britain?'

'In terms of your EU membership or the forthcoming general election?' Oscar replied.

'I'm referring to the growing disenchantment with the former amongst large sections of our people,' Anthony clarified.

'We have extremist elements here in Europe, as well you know, but not to the extent you have in Britain,' Oscar said, trying to get the measure of the younger man.

'My father was one of those proponents of change to whom you are referring,' Anthony said without emotion.

'Yes, I remember hearing about his sudden death. I'm sorry for your loss,' Oscar said politely, thinking to himself that even a man as controversial as William McCreary would not have taken his life just because his political aspirations happened to have gone up in smoke. However, the fact that the death had received hardly any coverage in the press made him smell a rat.

'Thank you. The thing is, we believe my father's death wasn't quite as clear cut as was reported,' Anthony said.

'You mean he didn't take his own life?' Oscar probed.

'Oh yes, that part is true. In fact, it was Elizabeth and I who discovered his body together. What I'm saying is that he was more than likely driven to it.'

'My dear fellow,' Oscar said firmly, 'whilst I have sympathy for you on a personal level, I'm not sure how any of this is relevant to me. It's no secret that my Party doesn't share the same ethos as the British Independent Party, and I've gone on record saying that the extreme elements in your country which may only have been an undercurrent in the past, are in no way compatible with my vision for a new Europe.'

An uncomfortable silence fell upon the room.

Elizabeth sensed that it was time for her to take over, even if it meant taking advantage of their closer relationship. She wanted to get Oscar on their side.

'Oscar, those patents that were brought to your attention had been altered to avoid detection,' she said, coming straight to the point.

'By whom, may I ask?'

'William McCreary,' Elizabeth replied.

'Go on,' their host said, showing more interest.

'My father started his legal career as a patent attorney,' Anthony said, taking up his cue. 'That was when a Germany company – K Pharma, as it was called then – moved to England and reinvented itself as the Crediton Trust. To complete its transformation into a blemish-free concern of the highest repute, it needed to extricate itself from any wartime connections and, for that, they required the services of someone like my father. It so happened that he also shared the same xenophobic views of its senior management, who were happy to extend their influence into politics. So you can see that, as far as my father was concerned, it was a marriage made in heaven.'

Oscar nodded. After a moment, he asked, 'What changed?' He knew full well why the relationship had gone sour, but wanted to hear it directly from the son.

'The company had ambitious expansion plans and

quickly came to realise that its association with the British Independent Party was causing damage to the image it wanted to portray,' Anthony said, not giving too much away.

'Very well, but I suspect there must have been something else – a catalyst, I think you'd call it, to precipitate the sudden change of course?' Gruber prompted.

Elizabeth exchanged looks with her husband. They hadn't expected to have to divulge the full details of the deception that had threatened to tear their family apart, but that's what they were being asked to reveal. Not receiving any definitive signals one way or the other from her husband, she made the decision to tell all.

The older man listened intently for the next hour, offering the occasional nod of approval or look of dismay at the unravelling of the series of events.

Finally he concluded, 'Although it's certainly a story that captures the imagination, I'm not at all sure that our interests are aligned. You, Anthony, seem to be motivated by revenge, curiously not so much against your father for what he put you through – and which is in no way a criticism – but more because you consider he was wronged by Crediton. Am I correct?'

'Yes, I suppose so,' Anthony replied hesitantly.

'What I'm unclear about, unless I have missed something, is how you managed to get reinstated as a lawyer?'

'Basically, I managed to convince the profession's regulatory authority that I was largely blameless,' Anthony said, avoiding mentioning the deal he was party to with Crediton.

'Really? How resourceful of you,' the Austrian leader quipped, his expression indicating that he suspected there was a lot more to it.

'However, the main thrust should be an action against the company for what amounts to war crimes,' Elizabeth said, firmly grasping the initiative.

'You're probably right, if what you say about the patents can be substantiated,' Oscar agreed.

'We have experts who are willing to testify to that effect,' Anthony confirmed.

'And I take it that no one else has had sight of these findings?' the older man asked.

'Absolutely not! The journalist Richard Overton who released those details to you is completely trustworthy,' Anthony assured him.

'Really? In my experience, that breed of journalists would normally prostitute themselves to the highest bidder,' Gruber said. Then: 'So, for your various reasons, you're looking to us to bring this out into the open?' He knew full well that his media group was the only ball-game in town.

'As a first step, yes,' Elizabeth replied, relieved that they had managed to get this far.

'And then what?' Gruber asked. 'Because I imagine the company would immediately issue a retraction, followed by a counter claim.'

Elizabeth and Anthony stayed silent, allowing the other man to think things through.

'There's no question it would make a great story,' Oscar mused, 'but the prospect of my Group being at the centre of a protracted legal battle is not something we'd relish when all our efforts should be focused on our own forthcoming elections. I'm sorry, Elizabeth, not to be able to offer you better news.' And then he stood, making it clear that the meeting was at an end.

Elizabeth was stunned. This wasn't the outcome she'd anticipated. She looked up at her husband, who was already on his feet, resigned to the fact that their mission had ended in failure, and knew that she had to come up with something quickly to salvage the situation. Suddenly it came to her. It was time for her cousin to fulfil the obligation to his father, Theo Frankl.

'There is, of course, an even greater cause at stake,' she said, resolute in holding her ground.

'And what might that be?' Oscar said impatiently.

'Justice for the Jewish families who were victims of the theft.'

'I assume you'd be able to establish those concerned?'

'They're actually listed on this transcript,' Elizabeth informed him, removing a folder from her attaché case and passing it across to an embarrassed Oscar Gruber.

'You've obviously done your research,' he remarked, examining the contents properly for the first time. 'There certainly appears to be a case that requires answering.'

'And you are the one best placed to make it happen. Isn't that so, darling?' she said, springing it on her husband, who appeared completely bemused by what was going on.

'I thought I'd already explained that this is not going to be possible,' Gruber told her, just as obdurately.

'Oscar, do you recall when I came to see you at the hotel, still badly shaken from the previous night?'

'Yes, of course. It showed a lot of courage.'

'And do you happen to recall the purpose of the visit?'

'You'd delved into some old records that revealed things about my past that I hadn't previously known.'

'About your Jewish father, my Great-uncle Theo, to be precise. And you remember the correspondence in that dusty envelope, pertaining to Jewish property in the old ghetto that particularly attracted your attention?'

The leader of Austria's Freedom Party remained silent. Reminded of what he had done at the time to suppress this news was bad enough, but shying away from meeting his cousin again, he realised now, had exacerbated it. Even when he had started to come to terms with his Jewish heritage, he still wasn't ready to fully comply with what had been asked of him – not if it meant jeopardising his political career. Now, with Elizabeth's reappearance, his conscience would no longer permit him to abrogate his responsibility.

Turning to her, he said: 'All right. What exactly do you want me to do?'

Unsure that she had heard correctly, Elizabeth needed a few moments to catch her breath before proceeding.

'I suppose I should prep the editorial boys to start releasing a few details of that transcript,' Gruber said, answering his own question, 'just enough to create a bit of a stir. In the meantime, we'll need to establish whether any of those Jewish families are alive to give evidence.' He was thinking specifically of Freda Hirschman and accepted that he was no longer at liberty to protect her from reliving the horrors she'd experienced.

'Taking into account their ages, that might not be so easy,' Anthony stepped in, trying to regain some authority.

'We'll get Richard on to it straight away,' Elizabeth affirmed, undeterred by her husband's note of pessimism.

'He's the journalist chap you've been working with on this?' Gruber asked.

'Yes. He's been really supportive of us throughout,' Anthony confirmed.

'Makes one wonder why he wouldn't want to have the story himself, though?' Gruber probed.

'Probably because he thinks he'd be more effective operating behind the scenes?' Anthony suggested, giving nothing away.

Oscar Gruber took charge again, saying, 'Right, I think we've gone as far as we can at the moment. How long do you intend on staying in Vienna?'

'We've booked on the eight p.m. flight,' Elizabeth replied, taking the hint that the meeting was over by gathering up her things.

'That's a shame. I thought we could at least have dinner.' Gruber smiled. 'Still, there will be other opportunities, now that fate has brought us back together.'

'I'm sure there will,' Elizabeth said, smiling warmly. 'Actually, there's someone else I'd like to see, if there's time. She was extremely kind when I stayed at her apartment in the Leopoldstadt.'

'A Holocaust survivor?' Oscar quizzed, accompanying his two visitors to the door.

'Both she and her husband were survivors, but unfortunately he passed away shortly after we met,' Elizabeth explained, seeing no reason to disclose the Hirschmans' identities.

*

Elizabeth tried Freda Hirschman's phone number a second time but there was no answer. Without having any other means of getting in contact with the very special old lady, she couldn't help but think the worst.

27

Elizabeth stood in Victoria station and gazed up at the arrivals board for the umpteenth time. She needn't have worried, for the overnight train from Vienna via Brussels was just pulling into the station. It was hard to guess what was going through her mother's mind. Despite recovering from a heavy cold, Lillian had insisted on accompanying her, saying it would show bad manners if she wasn't there in person to greet her house-guest. Elizabeth thought of the painting her son Freddie had uncovered of the Vienna railway station and wondered if it now brought back Lillian's memory of sixty years ago at Liverpool Street station, when she had met her foster-parents for the first time.

It still hadn't completely registered that it was Oscar Gruber who had facilitated Freda Hirschman's visit, even more so the unlikely friendship the two had appeared to strike up. But it now all made sense. In his quest to come to terms with his past, Oscar had managed to connect with the one person, still alive, who had known his father and was, therefore, able to help him on *his* journey of self-discovery.

What a difference six weeks can make. The helter-skelter range of emotions she and especially Anthony had experienced since the positive meeting in Vienna had, subsequently, threatened to send them back to square one. First, making use of Oscar's contacts on the ground in Berlin had unfortunately failed to turn up anything on any of the Jewish families who had been stripped of their businesses. The subterfuge had been so successful that it was as if these people had never existed! Then, when Crediton convinced the World Patent Office that they had acted too hastily and were successful in having the patents reinstated, all seemed lost. Elizabeth had learned since, that that was just the impression Austria's next President wanted to convey. As he explained afterwards in a series of conference calls with Anthony and herself, in which Freda Hirschman was the main topic, he had the ace up his sleeve in their pursuit for justice. Although he wasn't prepared to divulge precisely what he had in mind, he did say that it would involve the old lady coming to London to give evidence against the Crediton Trust Corporation.

Seeing most of the passengers already off the train and no sign of Freda Hirschman, Elizabeth had resigned herself to yet another setback when, all of a sudden, she caught sight of two solitary figures together with a porter's trolley making their way slowly to the ticket barrier.

Expecting Freda to have travelled alone, it took several moments for Elizabeth to make out that the person in a long trench-coat and Trilby hat accompanying her, was her second-cousin, Oscar Gruber. So stunned was she that Elizabeth was initially too flabbergasted to speculate on the reasons for his unexpected presence.

'Ladies, good of you to meet us,' Gruber said courteously, doffing his hat, oblivious to the surprise he'd created. 'May I present Frau Hirschman,' he said, addressing Elizabeth's mother Lillian.

'I'm very pleased to meet you at last,' Lillian replied, taking hold of Freda's gloved hand. 'I think you already know my daughter Elizabeth?'

'Yes, I've had the pleasure of making her acquaintance. How have you been, my dear?' Freda asked softly.

'I'm very well, thank you. How was the journey?' Elizabeth replied, struggling to regain her equilibrium.

'With the presence of my esteemed companion here, the time passed really quite quickly,' Freda answered.

'Freda, I'm sure you're in need of rest,' Oscar put in at this point. 'I know I certainly am, so I suggest we get together tomorrow. Lillian, I believe you've kindly agreed to accommodate Freda during her stay?'

'Yes, everything's been organised. We do have the space for you as well, Oscar.'

'That's very thoughtful but I've made separate arrangements,' Gruber replied.

'A girl in every port, I'd expect!' Freda said naughtily, which brought a round of laughter. And when he looked embarrassed, she went on, 'Oscar, you seem to forget that I knew your father, Theo, and I dare say that you may take after him in that respect?'

'Right! So where can we find a taxi?' Gruber enquired, diverting attention away from himself.

'There's no point all of us going together,' Elizabeth intervened. 'Mother, why not let Freda go with you and I'll drop Oscar off and then take the taxi home?'

'That sounds like a sensible plan,' the Austrian said, bidding the older ladies good night and heading to the taxi exit with Elizabeth at his side.

'Where to, guv?' the driver asked, keeping a safe distance between himself and the other black cab in front.

'Browns Hotel, Mayfair,' Gruber answered.

'And then on to Primrose Hill, please,' Elizabeth said.

'I'd hoped we'd have some time to become reacquainted?' Oscar told her, sounding genuinely disappointed.

'You said you were tired and I shouldn't want to take undue advantage, but of course I'll spend time with you.'

Gruber laughed. 'I'd almost forgotten about the cool character to whom I'm related. It does seem like such a long time ago since our paths first crossed.'

'A lot has happened since then,' Elizabeth countered sombrely. She could never have anticipated the way things had turned out after her first, semi-clandestine trip to Vienna. Was this the end of the journey, or just another twist in an extraordinary sequence of events? she wondered.

When the taxi pulled up at the five-star establishment in Albemarle Street, Oscar helped Elizabeth out, saying, 'Give me a few moments to check in and I'll join you in the bar,' as he paid the driver.

*

'So what brings you to London?' Elizabeth enquired, sipping on her glass of champagne.

'I couldn't very well allow Freda to make the trip alone,' Gruber answered, munching on a handful of peanuts. 'Also, I've got some business to attend to in London, so you could say it all worked out rather well.'

'Really? I thought you detested the place,' Elizabeth said, thinking it was the last place he'd choose.

'I do, but I've had to learn in life to put personal

preferences aside. Actually, I'm closing on a deal tomorrow that your journalist friend put my way.'

'You mean Richard Overton?' Elizabeth knew about the initial approach but had no idea that the two had remained in close contact. Though, having experienced the reporter's opportunistic nature, it would have been foolish to put anything past him.

'He certainly proved his worth with his insight into Crediton,' Oscar Gruber nodded.

'I don't understand. I thought those articles were purely generated by *you*, in-house?'

'And I can understand you drawing that conclusion, especially taking into account his newspaper's unholy alliance with that pharmaceutical company.'

Elizabeth frowned in puzzlement. 'I just didn't think . . .'

'What – that he'd take the chance of ruining his career? Suffice to say, he's going to be far better off in future with the backing of our media group behind him.'

'You're saying that you've offered him a position in Vienna?'

'No, he'll be running the show in London.'

'I think you've lost me,' Elizabeth conceded.

'I'm just being flippant, forgive me.' Gruber looked at her. 'We're purchasing the *Herald*, that's all.'

'You're not serious!' Elizabeth gasped. Although it was now obvious that Richard had blown any prospects he might have had with his employers, surely there had to be more to it?

'Absolutely. Whatever I may have thought about that incompetent bunch of shits, they do have an influential voice in Fleet Street and a healthy readership in terms of numbers.'

'And that readership can be swayed to your way of thinking?' Elizabeth muttered.

'Naturally,' Oscar said, grinning. 'However, the most important consideration is that there's nothing now to prevent us from going in heavy against Crediton. Believe me, with what we've got planned they'll not find it so easy to wriggle out of it this time.'

'Now I'm beginning to understand.' Elizabeth couldn't help feeling that she was in the presence of a master tactician.

'That's the easy part,' Oscar carried on. 'More delicate is how the threat of Frau Hirschman's appearance in the witness box will get you what *you* want from those bastards.'

'You're making it sound like some sort of quid pro quo,' Elizabeth said suspiciously.

'I didn't mean it to be. Naturally, I realise that our interests are aligned, but an awful lot is going to be dependent on the evidence our frail ninety year-old lady can present.'

'Surely you must have thought it was significant? Otherwise, it makes what you've just said about having a go at the company inconsequential.' Elizabeth was somewhat irritated by the lack of transparency.

'Do I detect a note of sarcasm in your tone?' Oscar Gruber asked.

'It's just I find it hard to comprehend what could have suddenly come to light that we weren't already aware of months ago. Remember, Freda gave everything she knew to Richard when she agreed to that interview.'

Gruber pondered a few moments before sighing heavily

and responding, 'Elizabeth, I have to inform you that the interview you're referring to never took place.'

'But that's impossible!' she cried. 'I made the arrangements myself. Richard reported back to us as such, when he returned from Vienna.'

'I'm afraid you were simply taken in by a very resourceful individual.'

Elizabeth thought back to the dinner party she and Anthony had hosted the previous summer. On reflection, Richard had appeared a little too glib when she had asked about his visit, but she'd put this down to the negative reaction he said he'd received from his Editor on the *Herald*. Now she knew the truth, it explained why Freda hadn't seen fit to make the previous visit; she must have felt she'd been badly let down, which was pale in comparison with the deceit of having the article printed without Freda's permission; assuming, of course, that she'd even been aware of it in the first place.

'I can predict what's going through your mind. Let me just say you shouldn't let it detract from the efforts the fellow has made on your behalf. It's just his way of doing things.'

'You mean by lying through his teeth,' Elizabeth retorted.

'Yes, sometimes – but as long as it achieves the right results.' Oscar patted her hand. 'I'm sure I don't have to continue.'

'In the same way as there's no need for me to ask how it was that Freda divulged everything so freely to you?'

'I'm not sure I get what you're driving at,' Gruber said warily.

'It was hard enough of a mental adjustment to think of you two getting together in the first place. Then, there's this one piece of firm evidence linking Crediton directly to the Holocaust that has conveniently just come to light – and, most pertinently, I ask myself what lies behind your sudden desire to drive this forward?' Elizabeth glared at him, awaiting his reply.

Oscar Gruber took his time in formulating a response. Put in a corner by a highly intelligent woman whom he'd clearly underestimated, was a novel experience and, if he were honest, he quite enjoyed it. It just made him wonder why on earth he had wasted so many years going for looks rather than brains?

'I admit it was a process that took time but I got there in the end, that's all that matters,' he said tersely, waving a hand in the air in dismissal. 'Far more important is the assistance I can offer to you and your husband in the time I have available before returning to Austria.'

28

McCreary's Solicitors, late spring 2001

The bright morning sunshine blazed through the first-floor room of the recently refurbished building in a street near Waterloo Bridge. Elizabeth gazed at her husband, sat behind the relative safety of his senior partner's desk.

With the worries of the world on his shoulders, it wasn't surprising they'd hardly had a word to say to each other over the last ten days. She guessed that the winding up of his father's estate had thrown up some unforeseen issues, which was the reason why Anthony had asked that they meet away from the house so they could speak without any distractions. The great sense of expectation of just a few weeks earlier had evaporated: first, when Oscar Gruber, who had assumed the prime position in their camp, returned to Vienna earlier than expected, and secondly, when the running of Anthony's legal practice had to take precedence over everything else, once more at the expense of his family. It was as if everything they'd been through over the past year had become completely insignificant, Elizabeth thought.

'We're in a hell of a mess,' Anthony announced flatly.

Elizabeth was startled. 'Do you mean us or the firm?'

she asked, bracing herself.

'I'm afraid it's much the same thing. Unfortunately, the estate isn't in a position to repay the huge debts my father ran up in a last-ditch attempt to save his beloved British Independent Party.'

'You mean after Crediton pulled the plug?'

The lawyer nodded, and went on heavily, 'Which means, as joint executors with my mother, the banks will look to us for repayment. To *us*, Elizabeth!'

'I presume you've included the house in the Cotswolds in your calculations?' Elizabeth asked.

'Oh yes – as well as the London flat in Sussex Gardens. And even after they've been sold, there will still be a shortfall of a couple of million,' Anthony revealed.

'So, if the worst comes to the worst, we'll just have to sell Primrose Hill. It was on the market at that price before,' Elizabeth said pragmatically.

'That's out of the question. I'm not going to put our family through all that again!' Anthony protested.

'Have you got a better alternative?'

'Don't you think I've been wracking my brains trying to come up with one?' he snapped.

An uncomfortable air of despondency filled the stuffy room. All of a sudden, Elizabeth came to life and said, 'The only way out of this is for McCreary's to initiate an action against Crediton.'

'Have you lost all sense of reality?' Anthony muttered.

'Why? It's just the high-profile case your firm needs to get back on track, not to mention that it would prove extremely lucrative,' Elizabeth told him, standing her ground.

'To counsel, perhaps, but it wouldn't begin to scratch the surface with the amount we need to conjure up – and in any event, there's the agreement I came to with Franz Werner that needs to be considered.'

'That was then – and if I remember correctly, it worked both ways,' Elizabeth replied.

'That's as maybe – but how would it look if I were instrumental in bringing an action against his company?'

'Quite frankly, they wouldn't think twice if the boot were on the other foot, and you know that's true,' his wife stressed.

'All right, I give up. Obviously you've got a fairy godmother tucked away somewhere.'

'It's a lot simpler than that,' Elizabeth said, not allowing herself to rise to her husband's sulky words. 'All you have to do is to negotiate a deal with counsel based on results.'

Anthony frowned, then he said, thinking aloud, 'You'd have to be talking about a sizeable settlement if we won the case, which is a big *if* since, at the last count we don't have substantive proof that Crediton were involved in those patents.'

'Freda apparently has something or other that might prove useful,' Elizabeth said.

'Well, if that is the case, why hasn't she or anyone else come forward with it before now?'

'Even if they had, you've been so preoccupied on other matters, it would have fallen on deaf ears.'

'I admit that it wasn't foremost on my mind of late with everything else going on,' Anthony said, sounding more conciliatory. 'There is, of course, the other matter of who is going to fund the case, assuming there's a chance of it ending up in the courts,' he added.

'That's unlikely to be a stumbling block,' Elizabeth said, smiling for the first time that morning.

'Don't tell me you've thought of that as well?' her husband replied.

'I haven't – but surely it's not hard, even for you, to come up with the right person.'

'You're not referring to Herr Gruber, by any chance?' Anthony said.

There was no need for Elizabeth to respond. They'd made progress, albeit through a tortuous route, and they had something concrete to aim towards. In the meantime, hopefully, they could resume being a normal family again.

'I dare say we should try to get to see Freda Hirschman as soon as we can – if you really think she could make the difference?' Anthony said.

'I just hope that Freda still has the energy to pursue it,' Elizabeth said. 'You must appreciate it's a tall order to keep asking her to revisit such a painful episode from her past.'

'I can imagine it is,' Anthony muttered. 'She is still staying with your mother, isn't she?'

'Yes, but there's no saying when she'll decide to return to Vienna.'

Elizabeth didn't disclose that Lillian had persuaded Freda to stay on in London indefinitely. The two had hit it off immediately. As her mother had mentioned, she felt that in Freda she had discovered the aunt she never knew she had. Strangely, Lillian didn't have the same empathy towards her real first cousin, Oscar, whom she regarded as exuding arrogance. Elizabeth avoided asking whether he resembled his father, Theo, in that respect.

*

Later that afternoon, Elizabeth replaced the house phone on its base, unaware that she had broken out in a cold sweat. She had detected from her mother's tone that something was amiss but assumed that it concerned Allen's recurrence of his heart trouble. Informed, instead, that Freda had suffered a serious fall and was in an ambulance on the way to hospital, had thrown her completely. Snatching up her car keys, she rushed out of the house and drove to the nearby St John and St Elizabeth Hospital, a mile away in St John's Wood, praying that she wasn't too late.

Hurrying to the Outpatients department – a place she knew well from the times she had taken Freddie with his injuries incurred on the sports field – Elizabeth found her mother in the waiting area, sat at the end of a packed row filled with fractious young children with their parents. Lillian was looking ominously glum.

'Do we know how she is?' Elizabeth asked anxiously.

'Not really – except that I overheard the ambulance crew who brought her in, saying between themselves that because of her advanced age they would be surprised if she made it.'

'Look, she might still pull through. Freda's had to face stern tests before, so let's try and look on the bright side,' Elizabeth said, putting an arm around her mother.

'The poor soul hasn't even got anyone for us to contact,' Lillian said sadly.

'Only Oscar,' Elizabeth replied impulsively. 'He'd definitely want to know.'

'I didn't have much of a chance to get to know him before he went back to Vienna, although from first impressions, he seemed like a real character, somewhat pleased with himself,' Lillian sniffed.

'That's a pretty accurate assessment,' Elizabeth smiled. 'The thing about Oscar Gruber is that he's always working in so many different directions, it's hard to keep up with him.'

'You mean he's a wheeler dealer, a bit like his father, my Uncle Theo, by all accounts,' Lillian said perceptively.

'Is that what Freda told you?'

'Not exactly, but she did say that there was an uncanny similarity between them; strange, when you consider he didn't know a thing about his real father and his Jewish heritage until you discovered it and revealed it to him. Makes me wonder about his reaction when he found out.'

'It's a long story that you couldn't have made up if you wanted to,' Elizabeth replied, recalling the tense unravelling that had reached a climax with the wonderful Bishop Hoffman, who had provided her with the proof she was seeking. But that was then and this was now: and here she was, facing another testing situation; one no less closer to home. Her heart sank as it suddenly dawned on her that so much of her family's future depended on Freda Hirschman's survival.

'I'm going to get a cup of tea – do you want something, Mum?' she asked.

'Black coffee might be a good idea. I think we'll be here for a good while yet,' Lillian replied.

When her daughter came back, Lillian told her, 'This reminds me of the time *you* were rushed into the Brompton Hospital and Aunt Charlotte had the job of calming me down. She must have taught you well.'

that your relentless campaign to discredit our company is completely without foundation and has to stop as of right now!'

'We have sufficient reason to believe that the claims you are referring to in the *Herald* are not only true, but can be substantiated,' Anthony said, speaking for the first time.

'Ah, the turncoat does have a voice,' Werner retorted angrily, the smile gone from his face. 'You obviously need reminding of the agreement you entered into with your journalist friend next to you.'

'That was on a different matter entirely and was specifically limited to the fall-out between you and my father, in which I was an innocent victim,' Anthony stressed.

'Though I wouldn't expect your Regulatory Authority would be too happy, learning the lengths to which you were prepared to go, to clear your name,' Werner responded, not disguising his threat.

'The extensive coverage of William McCreary's untimely death and your company's close connection with his British Independent Party has, I have on good authority, superseded any interest the Law Society might have had in Anthony,' Barry Levinson said calmly, and his words brought nods of appreciation from the others in his team.

'I suppose your newspaper can come up with a similar excuse?' Werner said condescendingly to Richard Overton.

'Now the *Herald* is under new ownership, I shouldn't imagine any prior agreements there may have been are going to be valid, since they are excluded in the warranties given by the previous management,' the journalist replied in his usual laid-back way.

'That was a long time ago,' Elizabeth said, handing the plastic cup to her mother, adding, 'Careful, it's very hot.'

'It's odd but I've been thinking a lot about Charlotte recently,' Lillian divulged. 'Perhaps because I had visions of Freda staying for a longer period of time, in which case I was going to ask you what you thought of her moving into the flat along the corridor? We've really become quite close.'

'Mother, that's a wonderful idea,' Elizabeth said warmly.

'Do you honestly think so? I wasn't sure you'd be in favour.'

'It would be beneficial for both of you – and just think, Charlotte would definitely have approved.'

'That's settled then. The place will need some sprucing up but I'm sure the porters can recommend a reputable firm of decorators,' Lillian said cheerfully.

Just then, a fresh-faced young doctor in a spotless white coat and carrying a clipboard made his way over to them.

'Mrs Paul, hello, I'm Dr Josephs,' he said, addressing Lillian. 'I take it you're a relation of the patient, Freda Hirschman?'

'I'm just a close friend,' Lillian said. 'She is going to be all right, isn't she?'

'I should really be notifying the next of kin,' the doctor said apologetically.

'Freda has no one else,' Elizabeth intervened, fearing the worst.

'In that case I'm sorry to tell you that she passed away, peacefully, fifteen minutes ago.'

*

A week later, Freda Hirschman was buried in the adjoining plot to her husband Ernst in Vienna's main Jewish cemetery.

*

It was an unseasonably cool June morning, when Elizabeth set off from Primrose Hill, on foot, relieved to escape the atmosphere at home and exchange it for the relative calm of her mother's flat. Perhaps she had expected too much, asking Anthony if he would accompany her to Vienna when Freda's funeral took place. He'd never met the woman, was his brusque response, so why should he attend her funeral? Elizabeth knew that he inevitably felt let down since with Freda's death, he'd seen his main hope of salvaging his firm dissipate. Oscar had lived up to his commitment, with the newly acquired *Herald* going in all guns blazing against Crediton's dubious origins, but in the absence of a killer punch, the Company was able to get away with a number of well-timed rebuttals that appeared to satisfy its critics.

Fortunately, Oscar was also able to help make the arrangements with the Jewish Burial Society in Vienna to have the body flown back to Austria, once all the relevant paperwork was completed.

Elizabeth arrived at her mother's apartment just after nine-thirty, and she found Lillian in the airy guest bedroom, already making a start on the deceased woman's personal effects.

'I thought you wanted me to give you a hand?' Elizabeth said, going up and kissing her mother.

'Allen spent another restless night in his chair,' Lillian lamented. 'To be truthful, I was glad of the distraction.'

'I know exactly how you feel,' Elizabeth said, helping her mother to fold the clothes that she had taken out of a handsome armoire.

'I know you've not had an easy time of it recently,' Lillian empathised. 'It's all credit to you that you've stuck by Anthony with everything he's put you through.'

'That's the last thing I would have expected to come from you,' Elizabeth said, genuinely surprised. 'I thought you held the McCrearys in high esteem.'

'That, I have to admit, was a serious error of judgment on my part. My belief that you'd just blend in with an established traditional English family, ignoring your completely different backgrounds, was naïve to say the least.'

'Perhaps I'd also convinced myself,' Elizabeth replied, wondering what had caused the change in her mother's outlook.

'The important thing is that you managed to discover about your real family for yourself.'

'Only because I felt you'd kept so many things from me.'

'That's true – but then there was that moment when it really seemed to matter.'

'You know, it wasn't just the painting or Charlotte's letters,' Elizabeth told her.

'Of course, but they were the catalyst, the wake-up call you needed,' Lillian replied. 'Then you came back from your journey to Vienna a changed person.'

'Was it really that noticeable?'

'More to your husband than it was to me.'

'Why, what did he say?' Elizabeth asked, by this time less fearful of the anticipated response than she might have been previously.

'Anthony thought he'd lost you to "some sort of change of life thing" as he so delicately put it.'

'And you went along with it too?'

'I did, when he talked to me about it, just to put his mind at rest. I thought that, with all the difficulties he had with his father, the poor chap had more than enough to cope with.'

'I assume you thought there was more to it though?' Elizabeth probed.

'Let's just say I had my suspicions,' Lillian said, distracted by something she had found amongst Freda's possessions.

'And who or what made you see things differently?' Elizabeth asked. But her mother was no longer listening.

'This looks like it could be something interesting,' Lillian said, preoccupied, examining a small and battered round wooden case 'See? It's embossed with a family crest of *Danziger* and dated 1880. There's nothing inside apart from empty compartments that probably held medication of some sort.'

'Why do you suppose Freda hung on to it?' Elizabeth asked

'I'm not sure, but if it's got anything to do with the war, we owe it to Freda and possibly many others as well, to find out, don't you think?' her mother said.

'Yes, I agree,' Elizabeth nodded. 'And I've got a fair idea who might be able to throw some light on this . . .'

29

Elizabeth glanced nervously again at the clock above the ornate fireplace in the Royal Automobile Club in Pall Mall. Midday had come and gone and with still no sign of the Devon contingent, she began to worry. The Committee Room on the first floor had been settled on as a compromise location by the two sides.

Forming a crescent around one end of an extraordinarily large table with Richard Overton and, surprisingly, Barry Levinson, was her husband Anthony with his young female assistant, representing Austrian victims of the Holocaust. Had it been down to her, Elizabeth would have gladly stayed away. For some unknown reason, Anthony had insisted that she attend, saying that she had done more than anyone in enabling the action to be brought.

It had taken less than twenty-four hours to identify Asher Danziger from his concentration camp number as one of the names on the transcript, since his family's patents had been plundered by the Nazis. It now seemed certain that Freda had befriended Asher himself, the records obtained from the Jewish building on Seitenstettengasse indicating that they would have been of a similar age. The small wooden box that held his asthma medication, left with Freda, was undisputed proof of his presence in Auschwitz.

Suddenly, there was the sound of voices approaching, and six smartly dressed individuals from the Crediton Trust entered the room. They were led by a craggy-faced man, markedly older than the rest, whose only other distinguishing characteristic was the white rose he wore in his lapel.

'Good afternoon, gentlemen and ladies! Should I assume by you placing yourselves tactically at one end that we should take our places at the other?' Franz Werner said smugly. 'In which case, the only person missing is the referee, no?' This brought the expected laughter from his colleagues. 'I do hope that we will be offered refreshments at half time and then we can change ends?' the Chairman continued to bellow for the benefit of his audience.

'Coffee and drinks are on the sideboard for you to help yourself,' Elizabeth said, taking an immediate dislike to the man. Her husband had described him perfectly.

'And who might you be?' Werner quizzed, his eyebrows raised.

'Elizabeth McCreary,' she announced tersely.

'Of course, I should have guessed. I had the pleasure of your father-in-law's acquaintance for many years. A real tragedy that he's no longer with us.'

Elizabeth couldn't believe the gall of the man. Looking over at Anthony, she could see that his face had become flushed with anger and that he was just about to offer a retort until a firm hand from Barry Levinson restrained him.

'So, since we're all busy people, I think we should get down to business,' Werner said, taking charge of the meeting. 'The only reason we are here is to inform you

'Ah, yes.' Werner looked down his nose at him. 'You should be aware that I know Herr Gruber quite well. Perhaps we should be meeting with him rather than his junior legal team that we've been palmed off with?'

'If you know him so well, in that case you would also be aware that, being in the running for President of Austria is higher on Oscar's list of priorities at the present time,' Elizabeth answered.

'Yes, of course, that's quite understandable. I obviously didn't realise your relationship entitled you to be on first-name terms,' Werner said, wrong-footed and disconcerted at being shown up.

A heavy silence fell on the room, which Elizabeth sensed provided a welcome break for Franz Werner and his deflated colleagues as they tried to recover from the hammering they'd encountered. The relaxed mood at her end of the table couldn't have contrasted more. Confident that Crediton had nothing left in their armoury to defend their position, and as she had been designated as the spokesperson, Elizabeth couldn't wait to get restarted. She stood up.

'The evidence we're about to present will prove conclusively that those patents which the original Crediton Company claimed as its own property, were in fact plundered from one Jewish family for certain and, therefore, more likely from others as well,' she said, holding nothing back. She then held up the wooden case.

'Not being an expert on products of this type, and certainly for those in existence sixty or so years ago, at first glance this didn't look like anything special. It had no redeeming features except for the name *Danziger* engraved on the exterior. There was no indication as to whom it might have belonged, just the faded number 165204: not really much to go on, you would think.'

There were blank expressions on all the faces of the Crediton delegation including Franz Werner's.

'The truth is that it was left in the safekeeping of a fellow concentration camp internee, and it only came to light when she died a few weeks ago,' Elizabeth explained.

'And who was this female?' enquired one of the young executives with a long, beaky nose and thick-rimmed glasses.

'Her name was Freda Hirschman,' Elizabeth said, and sat down.

The name hung in the air. It brought little recognition, until Derek Coulson spoke up for Crediton.

'We know of that particular lady,' their in-house lawyer disclosed. 'She was the same person, if you recall, that the *Herald* had attempted to link us to through Jacob Holtz.' His statement led to mutterings of 'disgraceful, pernicious and libellous' from the rest of the Crediton board.

'The same person whose claims of mistreatment you summarily dismissed at the time as fantasy,' Richard Overton replied steadily.

Elizabeth certainly had not expected that from the journalist, now she knew that he had faked the interview with Freda and lied to her and Anthony. On the other hand, if a settlement had been agreed, they wouldn't be sitting around the table now.

'Presumably you are going to reveal to us exactly what you consider is so damning about that medication-holder and the owner thereof?' Coulson demanded.

'I don't recall anyone mentioning that it had anything to do with medication?' Anthony came in, quick as a flash.

'I just assumed that's what it must have been. That *is* why we are here, is it not?' the lawyer stumbled, trying to make up for his error.

'Quite so, and to obtain justice on behalf of all the families like Otto Danziger's. He was the victim in question, whose personal asthma medication was taken away from him before he perished, in the same way as you stole the intellectual property rights to his family's pharmaceutical patents,' Anthony said passionately, followed by the words: 'Oh, and by the way, in case you *gentlemen* are wondering, that was the number tattooed on his arm in Auschwitz, as these records will confirm.' He slid up a document from the Jewish Archives in Vienna which had been stamped by the Austrian authorities.

'So you can see that now everything ties up, we have all we need to bring a class action in the British Courts,' Anthony continued.

There was a complete silence before Franz Werner cleared his throat and said, respectful for the first time, 'If that is the route you wish to take, of course it is your prerogative, but I assume it's not your preferred choice?'

He was perceptive, Anthony thought.

'Obviously,' Werner went on, 'a case of this nature would involve a lengthy process and be costly for both sides, although I have to say that we have sufficiently deep pockets to fund such a case, if it comes to it.'

'I'm sure it doesn't need mentioning what the effects of all that publicity would do for Crediton's rating in the City,' Barry Levinson said, going on the offensive.

'That sounds very much like a threat, which I don't take at all kindly to,' Werner hissed.

'Maybe, but from our point of view, it'll make a hell of a good story,' Richard intervened.

Werner needed time to think. 'Would you allow us a short time for a discussion?' he requested, at which point the meeting was adjourned for twenty minutes.

*

'What do you think they'll come back with?' Elizabeth asked of the others on her side, who had remained in their original positions at the table.

'It's going to be a question of whether they've got the stomach for a fight,' Richard said, yawning and stretching.

'There's always a modicum of bluff in these situations,' Barry advised.

'Looks like they're ready for us,' Anthony said, detecting the gathering making its way back to the meeting room.

'We've come to our decision,' Derek Coulson began once everyone was re-seated. 'Whereas we are quite confident of our legal position, it is not, we consider, in the interests of either party to let this drag on any longer. Having said that, if we can come to a modest settlement that is agreeable to both sides, then we should be able to conclude matters.'

'That surely depends on what your idea of modest is,' Anthony replied, unimpressed.

'We're prepared to put a number forward, should you wish, but I have to warn you it's likely to fall well short of your expectations.'

'We're prepared to take that chance,' Anthony said.

'We're thinking in terms of five million pounds in full

and final settlement of any future claims.'

Elizabeth tried to gauge the interest of her side, which seemed to be positive.

'And there's one other condition,' the lawyer said, 'which is that you have twenty-four hours to agree or the offer will be withdrawn and we'll see you in court.'

'I'm afraid it's likely to be the latter,' Anthony said unemotionally.

Elizabeth was taken aback by her husband's response. Impetuosity was normally so against the grain as far as he was concerned, she just hoped he knew what he was doing.

The meeting broke up shortly afterwards, without reaching agreement but with the offer still on the table.

*

Anthony glanced again at the fax that had just come through and smiled to himself. He dialled his home number and waited for a response.

'Hello, Elizabeth, it's me,' he said.

'Well, have we heard anything?' she asked, unaware that she was raising her voice.

'It's just come through. They are prepared to increase the offer slightly.'

'To what? Come on, tell me!' Elizabeth demanded, hardly able to contain herself.

'Ten million!'

'But,' she stammered, 'that's double the original offer. Surely you're going to accept it now?'

'I probably would have done,' her husband said gaily, 'except that it doesn't take into account our firm's fee.'

'So you're saying you want more?'

'Only a couple of mill. That will allow us to pay our costs and get us off the hook with Barclays Bank, who said they'd be prepared to write off a chunk of the debt so we could keep our business, along with sufficient working capital to run the firm.'

'As long as you're confident you won't lose the deal?'

'Don't worry, they'll agree. It's only small change as far as they're concerned. They'll think they got off lightly!'

'Will you let me know when it's done?' she requested, now seeing her husband in a completely new light.

'Of course, darling! Drafting the agreement is going to take a bit of time and I want it all put to bed before I leave, so tell the children I might be late home.'

30

Presidential Palace, Vienna, three months later

The late-evening sun bore down on the historic building, lighting up the reception area into a wide sea of red and gold. The dulcet tones of Mozart from a string quartet pervaded the room, which was packed with dignitaries from around the world who had descended on Vienna for the elaborate event, hosted by Austria's retiring President.

Elizabeth passed a glass of champagne to her mother. Lillian was looking far from relaxed in the stifling August heat. She obviously had the same aversion to such stuffy events as she did, Elizabeth thought. She had tried to refuse, but Anthony had told her that they must attend. Perhaps now the case against Crediton was finally over, he'd felt they should make the effort to come from London, although it was a close-run thing. Oscar's desire to have the final word and to publish a full exposé very nearly scuppered the deal. Fortunately, Richard Overton persuaded Gruber otherwise, saying that the company's reputation had been sufficiently damaged and, having gained the moral high ground, they shouldn't jeopardise their position by going any further.

Why this event needed to be spread over two days, Elizabeth couldn't fathom, except that someone in her second-cousin's office had let slip that it involved some sort of special ceremony, and letting her know that her mother Lillian must be sure to be included in the invitation.

Just then, out of the corner of her eye, Elizabeth saw Anthony making his way towards her, accompanied by the man with whom he'd been in close conversation. From a distance, and only seeing his back view, Elizabeth had thought that the fellow's casual stance seemed familiar.

'I believe you two know each other,' Anthony said, not bothering to introduce the Israeli by name.

'Hello, Gideon, what a surprise. I thought you said you were going to take up a new position in New York?' Elizabeth replied, flustered and saying the first thing that came into her head.

'I wasn't aware you were on first-name terms?' Anthony said light-heartedly.

'Our paths crossed when Elizabeth was in Vienna last year,' the Israeli replied smoothly.

'Ah yes, that's when she uncovered all that stuff on our man Herr Gruber over there.'

'Elizabeth came to find out things for herself about members of my family,' Lillian said, choosing that moment to join in the conversation.

'And the rest, as they say, is history,' Anthony remarked vaguely, his attention now elsewhere. He had spotted someone he knew – an obese man in a cummerbund. 'There's a chap from the Foreign Office I should say hello to. I assume you don't mind if I leave Elizabeth in your capable hands, Gideon?' he said, before sauntering off in the opposite direction.

'So this is your mother you told me so much about. I don't think we've been introduced,' Gideon said, going over to Lillian.

'Yes, this is my mother Lillian Paul,' Elizabeth told him, beginning to recover from her first discomfort.

Gideon took Lillian's hand, saying, 'I am delighted to meet you, Mrs Paul.'

'As I didn't know anyone in Vienna, Gideon's help was invaluable,' Elizabeth explained, hoping to keep the conversation from becoming personal.

'But I take it you're not Austrian?' Lillian probed.

'No, I'm Israeli but I was here on business at the time,' he replied glibly.

'Business, eh? That sounds to me like the blanket excuse for something enticingly more dangerous,' Lillian smiled, 'not that I should expect you to divulge your real mission.'

'Mother, you've watched too many spy films,' Elizabeth said, blushing. Once again she had underestimated Lillian's capability of seeking out the truth.

'Look, Elizabeth darling, Anthony seems to be getting on like a house on fire with that chap over there. Perhaps I'll gatecrash the conversation and see what they're up to,' Lillian said, sloping away.

'She's certainly nobody's fool, ' Gideon observed.

'I forgot that you have a thing for older women,' Elizabeth said, flirting unashamedly.

'Careful, Elizabeth, remember you don't want to get involved with something you can't finish.'

Elizabeth felt her heart racing. Hopefully, it was just the three glasses of champagne because she didn't want to admit it was the effect the handsome Israeli still had on her. Was she really ready to risk everything in a mad moment like this? she wondered.

Gaining control of herself, she asked, 'So what are you really doing back in Vienna?'

'After Freda's funeral, let's just say I found a reason to stay.'

'I'm curious. How did you manage to find out that she had died?' Elizabeth asked.

'Look, I should tell you that the whole New York thing was a façade,' Gideon admitted.

'What do you mean?' Elizabeth replied, unsure that she had heard correctly.

'The truth is that I never left Vienna.' He shrugged.

'So why did you come to London that time?'

'Elizabeth, you'd achieved everything that was asked of you. It was time for us to take over.'

'By us, I assume you mean Mossad?'

The Israeli nodded.

'I think you should explain,' Elizabeth said. She had a strong feeling that she'd been used in some underhand way.

'You remember that your cousin never showed up at my flat after you arranged for us to meet?'

'Yes. He'd had a lot to digest and I presumed he was just taking time to come to terms with everything I'd told him about his past.'

'That wasn't just a coincidence,' Gideon told her.

'You're implying that he was told to stay away?'

'Let's just say that it would only have complicated the situation.'

'So all that crap about you being replaced by that female

operative was merely a lie?'

'I just had to make sure that you weren't going to come back to Vienna any time soon.'

'Wait a minute! Surely you're not suggesting that I was going to come looking for *you*?'

'I couldn't take the chance that you might want to carry on where you had left off with the family thing,' Gideon said evasively.

Elizabeth didn't expect this. Although her coming to Vienna had clearly created the opportunity Mossad had been searching for to get to Oscar Gruber, she naively hadn't expected their involvement to continue after she went home. It now seemed certain that they had got to Oscar, which explained Gideon's presence.

The more she thought about it, it now made sense that the reason why the lines of communication with Oscar and probably with Freda too had gone dead, was at the behest of the Israeli, who was pulling their strings in the background in order to ensure she kept well away. However could she have been so gullible, Elizabeth thought – foolishly kidding herself that she had had even the slightest influence over any of the events of the last year?

Another thought suddenly occurred to her.

'I don't understand *why* you wanted me out of the way,' she blurted out. 'Didn't you trust me?'

'The truth is, yes, in the beginning we had our doubts.'

'What the hell is that supposed to mean?' Elizabeth hissed, suddenly furious.

'Your connection with the British Independent Party was a potential problem.'

'That was my husband's father and nothing to do with me!' she protested.

'Then there was your mother's friendship with that German woman for over forty years.'

'You mean Charlotte Brown?'

'Eva Schlessinger, to be more precise. Born Berlin 1926, the daughter of a Luftwaffe officer, lover of a Nazi doctor in the Medical Corps who settled in England after the war. Shall I carry on?'

'I'm aware of all that, but Charlotte denounced her past. Ask my mother!' Elizabeth replied defensively, unable to hide her astonishment at how far Mossad's intelligence reached.

'It's our business to know at all times what we're up against,' Gideon said by way of an explanation, recalling how thorough their European operative David Goldstein had been in his research.

'I was extremely close to Charlotte. Please believe me, she really wasn't sympathetic to the Nazis,' Elizabeth confirmed. But thinking of her aunt's personal letters to her German lover, she realised that they gave the contrary impression. She wished now that she had destroyed them.

'She did make some amends before she died,' Gideon revealed.

'In what way?' Elizabeth enquired, wondering what she was about to hear for the first time.

'She donated a large amount of money to a charity working on behalf of victims of the Holocaust, whose property had been plundered by the Nazis.'

Elizabeth thought for a few moments. There had to be some mistake. Surely Lillian would have known if her closest friend was wealthy, rather than the near-destitute woman she had taken under her wing. And it didn't make sense, did it, that after selling her own modest flat in West Hampstead, Charlotte should be so grateful for the offer of the vastly superior apartment next door to Lillian's, with an affordable rent tailored to her means – something that Lillian had generously arranged for her dear friend and to which she, Elizabeth, as the owner and landlady, had given her unequivocal consent.

Nevertheless, none of this altered the facts. Elizabeth deeply resented having been under suspicion.

'You obviously don't think very highly of me,' Gideon said, sensing the sudden change in mood.

'There's really nothing else to say,' she stated, turning away.

'Wait! It's not quite as straightforward as you may think.'

'Straightforward? That's the last way I'd describe it,' Elizabeth said, determined to keep her distance.

'We need people on the ground, especially in Europe – people we can depend upon,' Gideon told her, coming straight to the point.

'So what's that got to do with me?'

'Elizabeth, you're perfectly placed to assist us.'

'Gideon, I haven't the faintest idea what you're talking about.'

'After the Second World War, my government was able to call on a handful of Holocaust survivors living in Europe, who were willing to provide us with valuable information on their authorities' sentiments towards their Jewish communities.'

'So you've already told me that's why you were in Vienna.'

'Actually, it was in response to an urgent plea from one of our contacts here, whose identity you can probably guess.'

'Freda?'

'Exactly. Together with Ernst, the couple were able to keep us abreast of developments, particularly with the rise of the far right.'

Elizabeth pondered for a few moments. 'Let me get this straight. You're suggesting that I take Freda's place?'

'Yes – but not in Vienna.'

'Then where?'

'London.'

'That's completely insane!'

'We've designated the UK as a place of high risk. I can't imagine you'd be prepared to relinquish all responsibility to the Jewish community there?'

Elizabeth was initially too stupefied to offer a response. Could it be that, in addition to being used to do Mossad's dirty work and having come through the test successfully, she was now being recruited by them?

'You also need to know that none of this changes the fact that I've not been able to forget what we had together and what we could have again,' Gideon said unashamedly. It had been a long time since a woman like the beautiful Elizabeth McCreary had got to him, so much so that he had to remind himself again that he had a job to do.

'I'm afraid it's a bit too late for that,' Elizabeth said quietly, and with as much dignity as she could muster, she went to find her husband.

*

Elizabeth had mixed emotions, looking down from her hotel terrace high above the Karmelitermkt Square. A heavy police presence was already in place, hours before the ceremony was due to begin. Less obvious were the twenty or so highly trained individuals from the specialist terrorist unit brought in as additional protection for Austria's newly appointed President-in-waiting.

After the episode with Gideon Halevi the previous evening, she had wanted to get as far away from Vienna as possible. Fortunately, Anthony had drunk far too much champagne to detect that there was anything wrong. In any case, she had to remind herself that she'd accepted the invitation more for her mother's sake than her own since she hadn't wanted Lillian to make what was bound to be an emotional return to Vienna on her own.

Her thoughts were interrupted by the arrival of a lorry with a load under a tarpaulin, slowly making its way through the crowds to the centre of the square.

With a great sense of expectation from the crowd that had gathered, the hoist was activated, picking up its special cargo, before carefully lowering what appeared to be a bronze statue into its designated place.

A few minutes later, right on cue, an open motorcade appeared carrying a waving Oscar Gruber, flanked by more security. It came to a halt in a space that had been cleared for his arrival. Within minutes, he had begun speaking from the makeshift stage.

'I certainly didn't expect such a large turnout,' were his opening words. 'Many of you are no doubt intrigued why I chose to appear here in the Second District?'

Elizabeth exchanged looks with her husband and

mother, both equally perplexed and neither with the least inkling of what he was about to say. Unlike them, however, she couldn't help wondering whether it had been his own decision to appear here or whether, as was more likely to judge from his diffident body language, he'd been cajoled into it and the whole thing was just a façade.

'The explanation,' Gruber went on, 'for those who are unaware of its significance, is that this is the site of the former Jewish Ghetto. It is a shameful episode in our country's history that we Austrians stood by while the community here, one which had contributed richly to our heritage for centuries, was brutally victimised. Of the near eighteen thousand souls who lived here before the war, only eight thousand survived – but that number would have been fewer still, had it not been for this gentleman,' he said, pointing to the statue. 'This is Theo Frankl, the man who I only recently found out was my father.' He cleared his throat before going on.

'Apart from saving countless families whose passage he facilitated out of Vienna to the safer havens of England and America – and at great risk to himself – he left me with a valuable heritage, which I am proud to continue. To demonstrate my new-found commitment, I'm prepared to match the settlement, a sum in excess of twenty million Euro that was achieved in a recent out-of-court settlement in England, in favour of our Jewish community.'

The statement brought only muted applause from the largely bemused gathering. Elizabeth instinctively searched out Gideon Halevi. She just wanted to share that special moment but he was nowhere to be seen.

'I shouldn't take it personally. I dare say something

else cropped up which the chap had to deal with,' Lillian murmured, as if she were able to read her daughter's thoughts.

Elizabeth forced a smile. She began to question what she really wanted. The prospect of returning to her former life that had merely been postponed by all the turbulence of the last fifteen months had suddenly become an unwelcome reality. Perhaps her mother was right, she was a changed woman and needed to move on. One thing was certain: Elizabeth knew she hadn't got over the Israeli, however much she tried convincing herself.

Epilogue

Early January, 2002

There was an icy chill in the air that Monday morning, when Elizabeth, well insulated in her woollen bobble hat and thick country jacket, joined the rush hour of backpack-carrying commuters and committed joggers negotiating the gentle slopes of Primrose Hill. From there, the stunning view of the City of London skyline was clearly visible in the distance.

By the time she had covered the two-mile trek up to Hampstead Village's parade of cafés and chic boutiques, already open for the first trade of the day, she had worked up a healthy sweat. And this was just the easy part of the strict exercise regime she'd imposed on herself to get back into shape. The discipline of a personal trainer twice a week had made the main difference, even though the sessions with Jess, the sister of her estranged husband Anthony, had led to a few uncomfortable moments.

Elizabeth knew what most people were saying about her attempts to get fit: they believed it was an attempt to 'showcase herself' in preparation for a new romantic relationship.

There was no denying that her marriage was on the rocks, but that didn't mean that it was unsalvageable –

and in any case, she wasn't ready to hear that, even if that was what her therapist believed. It had actually caused Elizabeth to reconsider whether she was prepared to continue with the twice-monthly appointments that she'd stuck to religiously since the previous summer.

The situation wasn't made any easier by her husband Anthony's steadfast refusal to accompany her to couples' counselling.

For a brief period, when their problems seemed to be behind them and their lives were back on an even keel, it was tempting to believe that they could resume where they had left off – except it was clear to nearly everyone but Elizabeth herself that it was just a futile attempt on her part to cover up the cracks.

Passing down a narrow lane of former artisan dwellings, she caught sight of a small grey-haired woman in a bright yellow caftan, balancing precariously on a stepladder outside her home, pruning her roses, whilst Ruben, her café-au-lait Siamese cat, kept his eyes peeled for intruders.

'Howzit, Elizabeth?' Marlene called in the South African accent she'd been unable to lose. 'I'll be with you in a jiff,' she said, trying to make herself heard above the distinctive rhythms of Paul Simon's *Graceland* album that was playing in the background.

Elizabeth entered the small two-bedroom abode and made her way to a space off the kitchen that served as a consulting room. It was furnished with a heavy wooden desk, two matching chairs, and emitted a strong aroma of jasmine from the collection of plants strategically placed along the terracotta tiled floor.

She made herself comfortable and waited for Marlene,

who soon appeared with her notes and two mugs of steaming Earl Grey tea, one of which she passed to her patient. A brief glance at a small clock on her desk indicated the start of the forty-five-minute session.

'So how have things been?' Marlene asked, taking up her usual relaxed pose.

'Not much change, I'm afraid. Anthony is still staying later and later at the office. Makes any excuse to avoid coming home. It wouldn't be so bad if we only had ourselves to worry about, but there's Freddie and Emily's welfare to think of.'

'I meant since you moved out?' the therapist interjected.

Elizabeth was taken aback. It was as if the words had penetrated her whole being. But it was a fair question. Perhaps because she still took Emily to school, whenever the thirteen-year-old permitted it, the reality that the family unit was no longer intact hadn't fully registered.

When it became clear that continuing living under the same roof was untenable and a trial separation was agreed upon, the opportunity presented itself for Elizabeth to go and look after her recently widowed mother.

Fortunately, Lillian's shrewd management had made sure that her daughter would have just enough money to live on without having to look to Anthony for financial support, and that the bulk of her substantial inheritance remained intact in order to prevent Anthony from being able to lay his hands on it.

That was three months ago. Now that Lillian's 'forgetfulness' had been diagnosed as early-onset dementia, it was a blessing in a way, since it made her husband Allen's loss slightly easier to bear.

Thank goodness, Elizabeth thought, that she had her music degree at Goldsmith's College to keep her sane. Of course, being by far the oldest student in the class, the situation seemed a little surreal at times, but her role as their class spokesperson, taking on the arrogant Head of Course, Tom Wilkie, had given her a new raison d'etre.

'And the children, are they taking sides?' Marlene asked, not beating around the bush.

'Anthony has always been closer to our daughter. As far as he's concerned, Emily can't do anything wrong,' Elizabeth replied, regaining her equilibrium. Taking a sip of her tea, she went on, 'The trouble is, he makes it so obvious that she's his favourite. Freddie doesn't stand a chance. So I try to compensate and overdo it, even though our son has got some serious issues.'

'And you were never able to seek help for the boy? I remember you once telling me the school had a counsellor but that Freddie never took to him.'

'And now he's reached eighteen, neither Anthony nor I have any jurisdiction,' Elizabeth disclosed.

'In what way do you mean?'

'Freddie just does his own thing,' Elizabeth said, forcing a weak smile that did little to disguise her concerns about her son.

'I assume that his relationship with the rest of you is not what you'd call ideal?'

Elizabeth was near to tears. 'If anything it's got worse, I'm afraid to say.'

'Perhaps he is more sensitive than you realised and troubles at home really affected him?'

'Come to think about it, you're probably right. He was

always the one who got most upset when Anthony and I argued, whereas Emily just laughed it off.'

'And didn't you tell me how he took it upon himself to organise and look after the family while you were delayed in Vienna, the first time?'

'And last summer as well. He seemed to thrive on the responsibility when he was thrown into the deep end, especially when it came to keeping his sister in check; Emily can be quite headstrong at times.'

'Bright children often can be – but it sounds as if she looks up to Freddie?'

'True, but unfortunately that has done little to improve his standing with his father.' Elizabeth sounded emotional.

'Go on.'

'Anthony had our son's future all mapped out for him and just couldn't accept the fact that Freddie isn't lawyer material and won't be carrying on the McCreary dynasty.'

'And the upshot of that has been?'

'His father has effectively washed his hands of anything to do with him! After that last lambasting, our son had had enough and left home to share a flat with a friend. It's only in Highgate, which is quite convenient for the job he's found for himself at a local secondary school.'

'That's interesting. Good for him. What is he doing, might I ask?'

'He's a sports assistant,' Elizabeth said proudly. 'Freddie has always excelled at most sports, particularly football. In fact, when he was eleven, I managed to get him a trial at Chelsea.' She beamed, momentarily.

Marlen Katz nodded. 'What an outstanding achievement, to have been invited. After all, the competition must have been fierce.'

'Actually, they were going to offer him a junior contract at the time, but that would have meant disrupting his schooling, which his father wouldn't sanction.'

'That seems a little unfair,' the therapist replied. 'Didn't you mention how much your husband *enjoys his golf at weekends?*'

'As well as tennis and the occasional charity cricket match,' Elizabeth added. 'The fact is, I reckon he couldn't stomach the possibility that Freddie could excel at something that he couldn't.'

'But that's disgraceful!'

'Yes, I know. I simply had to inform the club that we had changed our minds. It wasn't true.'

'Freddie must have been devastated at having his dreams dashed.'

'The one condition I imposed to go along with the deceit was that Freddie should never know the truth.'

'So how did the boy take it?'

'Quite philosophically really. He didn't let his disappointment affect his support for the club he has followed since childhood.'

'And the Mossad agent, is he still on the horizon?' the therapist asked, suddenly changing tack.

'There's been no contact with Gideon since Vienna,' Elizabeth replied.

'But it must be almost two years ago now that you went to trace your maternal family?'

'There were a couple of trips to Vienna since then. I'm sure I've mentioned them,' Elizabeth said tiredly.

'I remember you saying that you met up in London, a

few months later. There was another occasion as well.'

Elizabeth nodded.

'Do you want to talk about it?'

Elizabeth pondered on the matter for a few moments. She then began to explain. 'Last summer, Anthony and I were invited to attend a reception at the President's palace in Vienna.'

'This is the man to whom you discovered you were related?'

'That's correct, Oscar Gruber. I had no idea that he and Gideon knew each other, which was why I was so surprised to see Gideon at the reception.'

'And presumably you were able to find out what the connection was?'

'Only because Gideon decided to divulge it – for a reason that became clear later.'

'What went through your mind when you were suddenly thrown together again?' the therapist asked.

'Surprise, initially, but then I realised that it wasn't purely a coincidence.'

'Please go on,' Marlene urged, leaning forward, intent on catching every word.

'Gideon, I found out, always has an agenda, to which he alone is privy.'

'Does that equate solely to his interest in you?' Marlene asked.

'I'd hoped that was the case,' Elizabeth said honestly, 'but it didn't work out that way.'

'Why, what happened? I assume there *is* more?'

Elizabeth thought before answering. She had to be careful. Even if the session were completely confidential, she had probably said too much already.

'Suffice to say, Gideon seemed to be more interested in what I could do for his organisation, but I had absolutely no intention of getting involved with them.'

'And so, as far as you were concerned, that was the end of it?'

'Yes, so I thought at the time. I should have learned from experience that he doesn't give up that easily.'

'But as I understand it, you were only in Vienna for a couple of days so it didn't give him much time to get you to change your mind,' Marlene quizzed.

'He'd done enough harm just by being there,' Elizabeth replied, recalling the dismay she'd felt when Anthony suddenly put two and two together, and worked out that there was more to Gideon's presence at the function than he'd initially assumed. 'Needless to say,' she told Marlene Katz, 'that gave Anthony all the proof he required that our relationship wasn't purely platonic. He could tell that something had gone on between us.'

'And didn't you at least try to cover yourself, to protest your innocence?

'What was the point? I'd gone astray with Gideon before and would have willingly done so again, had the opportunity presented itself. Hardly the recipe for a trusting marriage, wouldn't you agree?'

'It happens quite often in my experience. Sometimes it can actually result in making the relationship stronger.'

'I couldn't live with the deceit. So I owned up and was prepared to take the consequences.'

'And didn't Anthony put up any kind of a fight?'

'That's an interesting question. I wish he had, rather

than just accept the situation lying down. You see, he finds it impossible to express emotion. Tht trait runs through the McCrearys. It's not really his fault.'

'But that trait didn't seem to bother you that much before all this blew up?' the therapist remarked.

'No, you're right, it didn't.'

'So to what do you attribute the change?'

'I'm not entirely sure.'

'Elizabeth, it appears to me that the first trip opened your eyes in more ways than one: first meeting Gideon and then finding out all that information about your mother's Uncle Theo and his paternal connection to Oscar Gruber. It was a huge amount for anyone to get their head around!'

'Yes, that's true. The thing was, it all fell into insignificance compared to the problems Anthony was facing at home, and they became my only priority at the time. I effectively put everything that had happened in Vienna out of my mind as if it had never taken place.'

'Not anticipating that these events had created an awakening in you that needed to be addressed,' Marlene nodded.

'I can see that now,' Elizabeth replied. 'The question is, what to do about it?'

'We've only talked about Gideon. But did what you discovered in Vienna affect you in any other ways as well? For example, receiving confirmation about the demise of your mother's immediate family in the Holocaust?'

Not for the first time, Elizabeth pondered on the guilt she felt for depriving her own children of their heritage. If they had been made more aware of being Jewish, at least they could have made up their own minds whether that was the path they'd continue to follow. As for Marlene's question, right at the moment, Elizabeth knew there was no way of answering.

'Well, I'm afraid we're out of time,' Marlene said. 'Perhaps we can take up where we left off at the next session?'

Elizabeth just smiled. Gathering up her things, she paid the hundred pounds fee and briskly made her way back to her two-bedroom flat in Regent's Park, to await delivery of the new piano she had treated herself to from Harrods. She had missed the feelings of serenity that playing provided when, like now, she needed an escape from an uncertain future.

Her mind turned to her Aunt Charlotte and the music lessons the woman used to give from the same premises, and couldn't help wondering whether it was a case of history repeating itself?

*

Twenty-four hours earlier, a few miles away in a nondescript office block opposite Finchley Central tube station, Gideon Halevi had just attended a confidential meeting with Michael Behrens, Director of the Community Guardians, the body responsible for the security of the United Kingdom's Jewish community.

'So Gideon, as you can see our situation is particularly precarious,' the older man said, handing across the latest monthly report on anti-semitic incidents that had occurred across the country.

'I suppose we were naïve in thinking that the demise of the British Independent Party would make our lives any easier,' he went on. 'The reality is that it had already attracted enough support, especially in the north-west, as the National Front proved in last June's general election – not that they faced much resistance with all the recent unrest up there.'

'You're referring to the race riots in Oldham the month before?' the Israeli replied.

'Yes. Ostensibly they were aimed at the Asian and black communities but, as Blair's government is fully aware, they were stoked up by white supremacists.'

'Then it's only a question of time before the Jews will be targeted,' Gideon stated.

'It seems inevitable, which is why it would have been so useful to have had a woman like Elizabeth McCreary on board to provide us with a possible insight into the newly formed English National Party.'

'The BIP in just another guise,' Gideon posed.

'And from what we've been able to find out, even better funded than before. In fact, Mossad might be interested to know we've been keeping tabs on one City institution in particular, which has a history of providing an endless line of finance to groups of racists.'

'And you'd be prepared to share that information?' Gideon asked, showing more interest.

'Naturally, since we're on the same side. Meredith's is an old-established bank run by a man called Rupert Meredith: the bank has been in his family for the last hundred years.'

'And how about the authorities?' Gideon queried, making a mental note to open a file on Meredith's Bank.

'Just turn a blind eye. This *is* England, don't forget,' the director stressed.

'There are other options to get what you need,' Gideon said, 'reverting to the immediate threat.'

'I don't suppose there's any point in asking what you have in mind?' Michael Behrens said, not expecting an answer.

Gideon gave a sly look in response. He certainly wasn't going to disclose that he hadn't given up on obtaining Eizabeth's allegiance to the cause, which was why, when he'd failed to make any headway with her in Vienna, he had been compelled to resort to more drastic measures. Not that the note he'd put under her door before she'd left for London had proven necessary now the split from her husband Anthony McCreary was practically a foregone conclusion and he was nearer to achieving his objective. Of course, none of it would have been possible without the cooperation of Elizabeth's mother, Lillian. So keen had she been to make amends for the past neglect of her daughter, that those amends included ridding her family of the McCreary name.

Lillian it was who had cunningly prised Gideon's mobile number from Oscar Gruber just as the last guests were leaving the function at the Presidential Palace. It was a pity that she wasn't younger, Gideon thought. Lillian would have been the ideal replacement for Freda Hirschman, the courageous woman and friend with whom they had both established such a strong affinity.

Lightning Source UK Ltd.
Milton Keynes UK
UKHW020914051221
395094UK00007B/230